MICRONAUTS®

THE TIME
TRAVELLE[R]
T[RILOG]Y

Book 3

STEVE LYONS

ibooks
new york
www.ibooks.net

DISTRIBUTED BY SIMON & SCHUSTER, INC.

PROLOGUE

I first saw the Time Traveler on the darkest day of my life—a day on which I didn't want to look at anything, didn't want to care. A day I might have wished to forget, but it is seared now into my memory, the deepest scar in my psyche. A day that began in utter despair, but ended with new hope.

I was shackled, but it was not only the weight of the slave collar that stooped my shoulders and lowered my gaze. *He* stood at my side: The Emperor, in his black armor and flowing cloak. The red visor of his helmet, opaque from without, burnt into my back like a malevolent eye, and I wanted to avoid its glare. I refused to hear my captor's words, didn't want to believe his promises of a new home, a new life. I just wanted my father.

I had been brought to the observation deck of the Emperor's glass-sided zeppelin. I shuffled across the transparent floor, with a sick feeling of floating. Or falling. My down-turned eyes now showed me a cloud of crimson smog, and, below this, a brooding shadow, gaining definition as we descended toward it. My first glimpse of Throne-World. He wanted me to see this. He wanted me to be impressed, as the sprawling city—*his* city—emerged at last from the miasma. I think he must have been proud. But the city was a monstrosity—grim towers and chimneys, reaching up to welcome us into their soot-blackened maws. Throne-World was as dark and ugly as its ruler, and I didn't want to look at it, didn't want to face my future, but I had nowhere else left to turn. The tendrils of fate were tightening around me.

And that's when I saw him.

A trick of the smoke, I thought at first. An indistinct silhouette above the jagged skyline. Then, like a sign from the heavens, a narrow shaft of sunlight pierced the clouds, just for a moment. And it glinted off a silver chest plate.

I stared at him, tried to bring him into focus, my light in the darkness. I wanted to know what he was doing here, hovering above the factories, apparently oblivious to the air traffic around him. I questioned the purpose of his golden attire, and the triangular control panel on his chest. And my stomach tightened, as I realized that his head was thrown back, his fists clenched in anguish. The Emperor was still talking to me, promising that I would be happy. But I knew his lies for what they were. He didn't understand what I was feeling—or, more likely, it didn't matter to him. Only one man could understand: a kindred spirit. A man who, I sensed even then, belonged no more to this drab world than I did...

I open my eyes, and sigh heavily. I no longer sleep as such, but my brain still needs the release of dreams. They creep up on me in idle moments, and snatch me away from the present. I am always disappointed to return to this room, to take in my surroundings anew, to see that nothing has changed. My private chamber at the heart of the Astro Station—how I have come to detest it. I long to wrench myself from this wretched seat, to tear out the wires and tubes that plug into my exo-suit, and into the wasted body beneath it. But I will not die until I have to. I cling to what little hope I have left.

Increasingly, of late, the dreams have taken me to that day, to my first sighting of the Time Traveler. I can no longer count the years, the decades, that separate me from that young boy, lost and alone in the hands of a tyrant. I look back on the memory as if it is not mine. I hear my words, as if they were spoken by somebody else.

"Who is that man?" I asked the Emperor, timidly, still trying not to look into that fiery eye. Beneath his black, finned helmet, a wide mouth with a hundred razor teeth split open a gray face. His smile was like that of a Sharkos.

"He is the reason that Throne-World exists," he said in a voice like cracking parchment, "or at least that it was built upon this spot. He has been here, unmoving, for a hundred years or more, and he will be here for a thousand yet. He is a symbol of constancy, a testament to the ever-lasting order that my fathers created. He reminds us of our past, and gives us hope for a future that is already written."

I have learned much about the Time Traveler since that day. I have heard many tales about him, some entirely fanciful, some holding precious grains of truth. Thanks to the efforts of lesser scientists than I, we know that his journey began in our future. The Time Traveler is moving backwards through time, his origin point unknown, the details of his fate already lost to antiquity. When first I had the privilege of analyzing him, I confirmed this fact. And, whereas the Emperor chose to view him as a symbol of time's immutability, I saw the truth.

By his very presence here, in the years before his

genesis, the Time Traveler has altered history. He has rewritten his own story. He gives me hope that I can rewrite mine.

But that hope is fading, along with my strength. Nutrients are pumped into my system from a glass vat behind my seat—the gurgling of the liquid is a constant background noise in my head—but I fear they will be unable to stave off death much longer. Sometimes, I feel that only my willpower sustains me—that, and my flux armor, this suit of semi-liquid metal in which I am entombed.

In the exo-suit, I feel like less of a person. My eyes are hidden behind triangular red lenses, which make me think of the Emperor and shudder each time I glimpse a reflection of myself. A line of red nodules stretches across my chest, each housing a jack plug. A recharging socket sits over my stomach, and into this are wired a jumble of multicolored cables. Not even my voice is my own, now, modulated by a mouthpiece in my sealed helmet and forever underscored by the sucking sound of labored breathing through my air tubes. I have worn this white shell for over sixty years, but it still doesn't feel like me.

I could have been an Emperor. I could have turned chaos into order—but it was not enough. Why stop at bringing order to the present, I thought, when I could bring it to all times? I could spare my father, and my people.

A bank of monitors relays to me the sights and sounds collected by my Biotron units, my eyes and ears upon the world beyond my door. A third of the screens are blank, representing units that are on downtime. Most of the rest show empty rooms and corridors. The Astro Station is shrouded in the gloom of artificial night, an unfortunate necessity for the health and sanity of my staff. Up on the bridge, our resident Galactic Defender watches over silent instruments, waiting for the forces that are grouped around my home to make their next move. In the laboratory outside this chamber, a single light pulses on a control panel, as a computer with the processing power of a billion intelligent minds chews over mile-long equations in five dimensions.

Inevitably, my eyes are drawn to the containment suit, hanging in its dark alcove, seeming to mock me. I designed it, of course, after the suit worn by the Time Traveler. One day, I swore, I would wear it. I, too, would become a Traveler, the suit protecting my flesh from the ravages of the time stream as I made my own fateful journey into history. I fuelled myself with dreams of what my younger self could achieve, armed with the knowledge that, through a lifetime of sacrifice, I would accumulate them for him.

But the Time Traveler's secret still eludes me. I aimed for everything, and have wound up with nothing. Worse, I have realized a darker truth. I have pinpointed the cause of my failure, and it threatens far more than my personal ambitions. I have come to believe that this universe is dying, and I don't think I can save it. I don't have enough time.

I feel my eyes closing, heavy with the threat of tears that I can no longer shed. My mind takes refuge in the past again, wallowing in the regret of what might have been.

My name is Karza. And my story, I fear, is almost at an end.

CHAPTER
ONE

They came out of the sky, spitting bolts of fire. One moment, my world was enveloped in a sleeping hush; the next, it was ablaze.

The Emperor's armada descended upon his enemies. To this day, I don't know how he found us. A minute later, and my father and I would have been sealed in the cryocrypts, awaiting reincarnation. We would have died without the pain of awareness, still dreaming of the time when our priesthood would wake to a new age.

Every day of my short life, Father had spoken to me of the future. My boyhood fantasies were of lines of Pharoids marching across the sands, an invincible army poised to take back the galaxy from a tyrant about whom I knew little. I never imagined we could lose. Victory was assured because we would wait for the time to be right.

That future died along with my father, shot from behind before he could grant me the mercy of a broken neck. I expected to follow him soon, anyway. I hadn't yet been taught to fight, didn't know how to harness my anger; it would be another man who inculcated that instinct in me. I fell to my knees, lost myself in Father's blank, staring eyes, and hoped that, when my own time came, it would end quickly.

It was in this way that I came to survive the massacre—a child alone amid the carnage, sand and smoke scratching at my throat. Black-masked troops surrounded me, but no one thought to put me out of my misery. And then I drew the attention of their leader; from that moment on, I was protected.

"What about you, little one?" His first words to me, still clear in my mind, still invoking a deep feeling of dread, after all these years. I can still see the reflection of my face as I looked up into that evil eye for the first time, distorted and washed in a bloody shade of red. "Are you a threat to me as well…?"

The sword was heavy in my hands. It glowed with an inner fire, flaring at the edges of its blade. It would cut through the Emperor's black armor. It could have pierced his heart.

He stood before me, unafraid. He was toying with me. I knew I shouldn't play his game, but a part of me was forever trapped in the depths of that red eye. A reflection of my anger, of the need for justice that was all I lived for. The image screamed at me, urged me to seize this chance, and I gave in to it. I let my instincts take over.

I struck, faster and with more force than he could have expected. Blood rushed to my head; I was giddy with the exultation of vengeance satisfied.

At the last possible instant, as the sword point cut into his chest plate, he twisted aside. I scored a line in his armor, but did not mark the flesh beneath. Tears rushed to my eyes. My momentary elation punctured, I howled and brought the weapon down again, but this second blow was mistimed and clumsy.

A gauntleted hand struck out, clawed fingers closing about my wrist until I felt bones grinding. The sword fell out of my numbed hand. As the Emperor released me, I followed it to the ground.

I was on my knees, expecting him to call for his guards, expecting to be punished again. But, when I dared look up, it was to find him smiling down at me. That familiar predator's smile. "You have the makings of a warrior, after all. I am proud of you, my son."

"I am not your son," I growled, automatically. It never made a difference.

"I am the only father you have, young Karza. The only father you need."

"You *killed* the only one I needed!"

"Forget that old man! He couldn't have given you all I can give. I can make you into the man you were meant to become."

"My father would have raised me in the priesthood."

"I offer you the future, Karza. *He* would have destroyed it! I know it's difficult for you to accept, but the old man was dangerous—to himself and to the galaxy."

"He would have trained me to kill you!"

"And what, then, of the billions who rely on me to keep them safe and warm and fed? The Pharoid cult would have brought down our civilization."

"They would have brought us peace!"

"They would have fomented chaos! Their backward idealism was a cancer, eating at our institutions, our ordered way of life. It had to be excised!"

I glowered at him, but said nothing. I had already learned the futility of argument. Let my enemy believe he was winning, that I was turning toward him. I had been trained to resist his brainwashing. All I had to do was cling to the things most important to me.

I knew what Father had wanted for my future. He thought I could make the universe a better place. A more peaceful place. I would honor his wish.

Biotron was dead. I killed him.

I felt a lurching sensation in my stomach, even as I denied myself such sentiment. What was he, after all, but a mere automaton? I could rebuild him a hundred times better. And yet, he had been the most constant, the most trusted companion of my teenage years. I had spliced DNA into his circuitry, granting him a capacity for abstract thought and a personality, or at least a semblance of one. I had to remind myself that his emotions had been programmed, his computerized brain detecting hormones and nerve-endings where there had been none. He had felt nothing. He hadn't suffered.

The light had gone out of one of Biotron's eyes. The other still shone, but the memory wafers behind it had disintegrated and poured out through a hole in his silver head. A maze of cracks had splintered across his red chest unit. I stared at him, speechless, watching the dancing reflection of the Rift's green light in his face until it died. And then Biotron's final light flickered, too, and was extinguished.

Later, when I regained my objectivity, I would be fascinated by his fate, by the variety of conflicting forces that had acted upon him. One of his clamp-like hands had rusted shut, flaking as I tried to pry its two clumsy digits apart. The other hand had devolved into the semi-liquid state from which it had been cast, oozing its way toward the ground. It had hardened again, in the sterile atmosphere of the laboratory, a silver stalactite still clinging obdurately to the white stump of a wrist.

Slowly, I realized that I had lost far more this day than just a childhood confidant.

The experiment had failed. Everything I had worked for lay in ruins. I had become accustomed to success—my designs were propagating across Throne-World, making life better for everyone—and I didn't know how to deal with this feeling, this almost physical blow that had left me shaking.

I had been so confident. I had almost leapt into the Rift myself, sure that there was no danger. I had mastered time, or at least taken the first step toward so doing. I had torn a ragged hole into it. Just a small one, enough for me to gain access: about two minutes in length, but five feet in height. Three days earlier, I had sent a probe through a similar, smaller tear. I had beamed with pride as it had reappeared, its chronometer showing a loss of some 38.54 seconds.

Was it Biotron's greater mass that had pulled the ravaging forces to him? Had the increased time displacement lessened the integrity of my makeshift tunnel? Most worrying of all, could it have been his organic components that were incompatible with the hostile environment of the time stream, attracting destructive eddies like antibodies?

I stood, wrestling with my feelings, for an hour or more. I stared at the shapeless, twisted sculpture that had tumbled out of the Rift into my arms. And, ablaze with angry denial, I came up with a fourth theory. A theory that, to my sorrow, I would ultimately prove.

A less driven man might not have entertained the notion. I confess, with the hindsight of years, that it took a certain amount of arrogance on my part to pursue it. But I refused to accept that I could have been so wrong. My calculations had been perfect.

The problem, I concluded, lay with time itself.

"Yes, yes, I think I see it." Professor Fzzzpa's eyes were wide beneath his bushy gray eyebrows as he beetled around the hologram to examine it from all angles. "Remarkable. This is quite remarkable!"

"The data is not one hundred percent accurate, of course," I said. "One cannot represent five-dimensional coordinates in three without accepting some compromise."

"Yes, yes, yes, of course." The short, bald scientist leaned forward, until his head was almost disrupting the graph's light patterns. His thick gray moustache twitched anxiously. "Of course, but these distortions in the wave effects..." He straightened suddenly, and fixed me with a watery stare. "You're quite sure of your figures?" He didn't wait for an answer. He was pacing pensively, his hands behind his back. "Of course you're sure, of course you are. The work you have done this past year...you have quite outshone the rest of us. I have never seen a mind like...like..." Fzzzpa ran out of energy at last, and fell onto a stool. He pulled a tissue from his lab smock, and dabbed at his reddened forehead.

"You concur, then," I said quietly, "with my analysis?"

"I...I...well, quite, yes...I don't see how there could be another...it's just...it's rather difficult to accept...our entire reality, everything we know, being eaten away..."

"A better analogy," I suggested, "would be that it is unraveling."

"Quite, quite, yes...and you believe the Time Traveler is the cause of this?"

I nodded, and indicated the graph, at the point

where the lines twisted away from a spiraling void. "His path through time lies at the center of the disturbance. When he left his present—our future—the Time Traveler punched a hole through causality. The tendrils of cause and effect around that hole are flapping, feeling for something to latch onto. In the absence of such an anchor, they begin to fray. They coil back upon themselves—and, inexorably, they begin to pull the rest of the fabric of time into the hole." I smiled at my diminutive colleague. "Don't worry, Fzzzpa, the universe has a few years left yet."

"Quite, quite," he panted. "Even so, something must be done about this. Something must be done at once. Yes, yes, at once!"

"My feelings exactly."

He was up and pacing again, muttering agitatedly. "If only the Emperor would…maybe, this time, he will listen. He will *have* to listen. If we could just make him see…" His round face crumpled, and he slapped a fist into an open palm. "But what if it is too late already? We should have known about this decades ago! If we had been free to pursue all avenues of research, if the Emperor hadn't kept our findings for himself…" He started, guiltily, and his eyes darted toward me. "I…I…no offence meant, my friend, I…"

"None taken," I smiled. "It's refreshing to hear the truth spoken. The Emperor has no interest in the advancement of science, only in the expansion of his own power. While his elite enjoy the benefits of your work, the masses are kept in superstitious ignorance!"

"I…I…" stammered Fzzzpa. "Yes, yes, quite." He hid his embarrassment by pretending to be engrossed in the graph again. "Can you locate the Time Traveler's point of origin? If he is from the future, if he has not entered the time stream yet, then perhaps we could find him. We could prevent this whole...this..."

"No, Fzzzpa. The Time Traveler has altered his own past by his very presence in it. He has sent us along new strands, knitted history into a new pattern. His present lies on a part of the fabric that we can no longer reach."

"Then your project is doomed. We can never travel in time, after all."

"I refuse to believe that!"

"But..." Fzzzpa's hands fluttered about him as he struggled to extend my metaphor. "But if we can't visit the past without tying these strands into a...a knot of paradox..."

I shook my head. "The Time Traveler's equipment was primitive. It should have eased him along the strands of time; instead, it sliced through them. The past can be altered, Fzzzpa, but only with precise, surgical cuts. We can change the pattern of history, but it must be done one strand at a time."

"And the damage already done? Can we repair that?"

I didn't answer him. He turned pale and swallowed. Then, gripped by determination, he lurched into motion again. "We have to try. The Emperor won't listen to us, but if he was no longer...if we had access to his resources, if we could...yes, yes, we must..."

Fzzzpa halted and turned back to me, his expression grave. "It is time you learned what we have been keeping from you, Karza. We knew you had been close to the Emperor, and we feared...well, no matter, now. You have shown that you share our beliefs, our concerns. We had you believe that our little community was loyal, devoted to the Emperor's service. But, these past few years, we have been pursuing a different agenda. Quite different indeed."

I raised an eyebrow. I kept my expression neutral. And I listened as my colleague told me everything I had been sent here to find out. Everything that I already knew.

His timing, I considered, was unfortunate. My sojourn on this world had been fruitful. Rarely before had I been allowed to pursue my goals without distraction. Even Fzzzpa had been useful to me. Intelligent and driven, he would have made an able assistant.

I didn't want to leave, but the words had been said now. I had no choice.

Footsteps approached my cell. I almost welcomed them. I had not seen another person, nor heard a voice, in days. But, more than that, the Emperor's continuing visits displayed his weakness. He could deny me my present, but he couldn't let go of his future. He should have had me killed, or abandoned me to rot.

I didn't know how long I'd been here; in my windowless prison, night and day had become one. I could measure time's passage only by the growth of my black hair, which reached to my chest and blanketed my chin. The cell's single feature was a two-tiered, circular indentation, its inner lip forming an uncomfortable stone bench. Sometimes, I didn't move from that seat for hours. I sat rigid, lost in contemplation, tuning out my gray surroundings to swim in a sea of equations. My equipment was impounded, my body caged, but I retained the most important tool of all. My mind was free.

"They are asking for you again," said the Emperor. He had removed his helmet to display his inner self. So, today he was here to cajole and reassure, not threaten and beat. Deep folds and cracks gave texture to his lumpen head. The Emperor looked old and tired, an impression not helped by the fact that his short, wide nose terminated almost between his round eyes. He looked as if somebody had taken his scalp and pulled, tightening his gray skin as they yanked back his face. I didn't know what race had birthed him, nor had I encountered another of his kind. He didn't speak of his past.

"They are impatient for the new world you promised," he continued. "They ask what became of your ideas for bridges and transportation tubes. You have threatened our order, Karza. My subjects were content with their lot, but you showed them more."

I didn't answer him. A part of me wondered if I still could, after all this time, and how my words would sound.

He walked around my circular pit, placing himself in my line of vision. I looked through him. "They are restless, eager for the accession. That is how it should be. My time is ending. The future will be yours, son, if you can only abandon this futile obsession!"

He scowled at my continued silence, his nostrils widening. "I was proud of you," he sighed. "The greatest scientist and the fiercest warrior in my service. You fulfilled the potential I sensed in you, and more. You may not be of my blood, but I have come to think of you as mine. Have I not treated you as such? Have I not been a good father to you?"

He must have seen the fire that flared within me at those words. He stepped into the pit and stooped in front of me, his eyes wide with sincerity. He spoke to me in a soft, persuasive tone. "The past is done. It can't be rewritten, else what would result? Everything would be possible, nothing certain. There would be no achievement that could not be snatched away by a jealous rival. War and peace, life and death, would become meaningless!"

He straightened, disappointed, seeing that his argument had not moved me. He turned away, clasping his hands behind him to keep them still. Despairingly, he made a final plea. "I thought I had reached you, boy. I sent you to live among my enemies, exposed you to their heresies, and yet you proved your fealty." He couldn't have seen my warning glare, he couldn't have known that he had brought the scent of blood and fire to my nostrils again. In my mind, I saw Fzzzpa's uncomprehending stare as he bled onto a dirty floor.

"You ended the scientists' rebellion before it began." They had welcomed me as a colleague, trusted me as a friend. "You acted quickly and decisively, to end their threat." Part of me was afraid that it might happen again. Another part welcomed it, contending that, even in the throes of my wild-eyed savagery, I had maintained control. "You fought instinctively and well, to preserve my order."

The objection rasped in my throat, my tongue heavy and clumsy. The Emperor turned, surprised and hopeful. "Not your order," I restated, more clearly. "Mine!"

The next time I saw him, I had a sword to his heart again.

There was no hesitation this time. No words. I saw no need for either. He didn't try to resist, as I drove the blade upward beneath his breastbone. I understood now. I knew what the Emperor had seen, those many years before: this moment, reflected in the tearful eyes of a lost child. He had seen immortality, the continuance of a line that stretched through generations. He had seen the act that would turn me into him. The new order, the same as the old, and the people baying for this. They had raised an army to overthrow a tyrant, to elevate the poor, abused heir to the throne, and the tragedy of it was that they truly believed this was what they wanted. They thought they were changing things.

When they offered me the crown, I would not take it. I rejected his future.

He lay at my feet, that red eye dulled forever, but I felt nothing. No pride, no joy. It was not over yet. I stared up through the throne room's glass dome at my inspiration, the Time Traveler, unmoved even by the passing of an empire. I renewed my vow to myself that I would know his secrets. I would have my reckoning with the Emperor, not in the present or the future, the battlegrounds that he'd chosen. I would face him on a field that he thought long conquered. I would claim the past, and the rest would fall to me like dominoes.

Only then would I have my vengeance. Only then would I establish peace, through order.

I knew what they said about me, in the streets of the city that was now called Micropolis. They called me a fool, hiding in my lonely tower, oblivious to everything but my work. They believed I didn't notice as the buildings burned around me, as the new rulers fell without understanding why. They were wrong. I noticed. I just did not care.

I took one final look at the city, laid out beneath me, before it disappeared into crimson clouds again. Flames glimmered in its concrete alleyways. In the twisting smoke patterns, I saw the world that could have been: a world of gleaming spires and clear skies.

An ordered world. I had licensed my designs for clean reactors and labor-saving machinery across the galaxy, such sidelines funding my primary project, but rarely had my innovations been adopted here, on my home world. Weak leaders had declared that resources were better directed toward so-called "relief efforts." They fought to prolong the lives of those for whom death would have been a mercy. In return, the demands of the needy grew along with their numbers. And, in time, they grew to expect more than their rulers could give them. They rewarded kindness with crime, disobedience and, ultimately, rebellion.

Next time, I swore, it would be different.

I allowed myself one tiny indulgence before I left that place forever. I brought my shuttle pod around, its proud nose dropping to the horizontal, cutting smog to ribbons. I knew exactly where I was going. He appeared in front of me: The Time Traveler, my old friend. I maneuvered as close to him as I dared; I had more respect for him than to fly through his incorporeal form. I drank in every detail of his posture, his coloring, the control panel on his chest. I knew them intimately, of course, could call them to mind whenever I wished or just examine any of the thousand images I had captured. But this was the last time I would see him like this. The last time I would be close to him.

Three days later, I saw my new home for the first time.

The Astro Station had been built by the Galactic Defenders, but it had long since fallen into the hands of an enemy, from whom I had purchased it. It was a clunky, boxy construction, old and decrepit. Transparent sections of hull were held precariously between two hexagonal frames. There were turrets for missile launchers, but they yawned open, the weapons themselves having been pried loose. The station was a heap of junk hanging in space, but I had expected this. It was all I could afford. Anyway, everything I needed for my work I had brought with me. I required only life support, relative seclusion and, when circumstances dictated it, limited mobility.

I sent out an encoded high-frequency signal, and a landing ramp extended obligingly, if a little shakily, from the station's side. I guided my pod down onto it, and it carried me into a dingy hangar. A hatchway creaked and clanged shut behind me, and I waited until the hissing of air jets had stopped and my instruments showed normal pressure outside.

There were no other vehicles here. A scan of the station had detected no life signs. Still, I sent a Biotron unit out into the hangar ahead of me—the only one I had been able to bring, due to space considerations; I would have to build more—and kept my sword at my hip.

My footsteps rang on the metal floor, and reverberated down dark, empty corridors. Dust tickled my nose. When I paused and held my breath, the silence was absolute.

The door to the bridge slid back as my escort and I approached it. I saw a shape in the darkness beyond. This is where I would learn if my contacts had betrayed me. I had taken every precaution during our dealings, but I was also prepared for the worst.

A pair of yellow eyes shone at me. »GOOD MORN-ING, SIR. MAY I WELCOME YOU TO THE ASTRO STATION, AND PLACE MYSELF AT YOUR SERVICE. I WILL NOW CALIBRATE LIFE SUPPORT AND LIGHTING SYSTEMS TO THE OPTIMAL LEVEL FOR YOUR SPECIES.«

I couldn't help but smile. The voice was a little flatter, more mechanical, than I was used to, but it was familiar to me. In fact, it was the most familiar voice in my life.

I knew that the station's previous owners had left a mech behind to maintain vital systems. I had not expected it to be one of my own design. I had been forced to sell the Biotron blueprints many years before, to a "businessman" named Ordaal, although I had kept back some secrets. Ordaal had marketed his "Cosmobots" across the galaxy, but this was the first time I had seen one. I found its gaudy yellow and purple coloring distasteful, and I noted the clumsy, two-fingered hands, which I had improved on more recent models. Otherwise, though, the unit was a reasonable replica of my own Biotrons—outwardly, at least.

»I AWAIT YOUR INSTRUCTIONS,« said the Cosmobot, falling still.

I stepped onto the bridge's main platform; reacting to my weight, the centermost of five curved seats spun to face me. I dropped into it, and it swiveled to show me the main control panel. I checked, cursorily, that everything was in order. Then I let my gaze drift out through the huge, transparent screen in front of me. I was tired after my long journey, and I lost my mind in the depths of space, between the flaring points of distant stars. I tried not to look at the numbers in my mind, tried to avoid calculating how far I was from another living being.

I must have let out a sigh, because suddenly my Biotron was at my shoulder. His shoulder flashes identified him as Unit #23. "DOES SOMETHING TROUBLE YOU, KARZA? WOULD IT HELP TO TALK ABOUT IT?" I grimaced. I was proud of my creations. They represented a great leap forward in science. But sometimes I wished I had made them a little *more* mechanical, less responsive to emotional stimuli. I wished that, like the Cosmobot, they would stand still and silent when they were not wanted. I would correct that flaw in the next update.

"THE FACILITIES HERE ARE LESS COMFORTABLE THAN YOU ARE USED TO," said the Biotron.

My gaze drifted past him, to two raised weapons stations. Both had been gutted. "It's not important," I said. "They are adequate."

"I COULD PREPARE QUARTERS FOR YOU, IF YOU WISH."

"No. Our priority is to unload my equipment and set up a laboratory."

He cocked his head. "I RECOMMEND YOU TAKE A FEW DAYS TO ACQUAINT YOURSELF WITH YOUR SURROUNDINGS FIRST. YOUR BLOOD PRESSURE—"

I tore at my hair, frustrated. "You will obey my instructions, Unit #23! There will be plenty of time to enjoy the fruits of my labor when it is completed. All the time in the universe! I have lost enough days already to this forced relocation. I will not become mired in the here and now. There is a wider picture here, Biotron, and we must never lose sight of it!"

The yellow light in the unit's eyes dimmed, and he bowed stiffly. "AS YOU WISH, KARZA. I WILL COLLECT THE EQUIPMENT FROM THE SHUTTLE POD."

I couldn't feel my legs. To my disgust, I was forced to lean on two Biotron units. I shouldn't have been surprised. It had been a year or more since I had left my seat. My flux armor kept me upright, with minimal support from my atrophied muscles. I should have received my guests in my chamber, let one of my assistants bring them to me. Had Persephone still been here, I would have delegated the task to her; she would have made a good diplomat. In the circumstances, though, I felt it wise to show a little courtesy. These new arrivals were important to me.

This, too, irked me—that I should be in need of help, from anybody.

I wondered if I should remove my helmet—but my true face, scarred and weathered with the passage of years, would not have made a good impression. Anyway, I needed its air tubes.

As the hangar door rumbled open, I stiffened my resolve, and my legs. I pushed the Biotrons away, determined that I could at least stand unaided.

I almost sagged again when I saw the lone figure awaiting me. My hopeful gaze flicked past her, to her ship—a Rhodium Orbiter, capable of carrying six people, but I saw nobody beneath its plastic canopy. I'd petitioned the Galactic Defenders to send a battalion. They had spared me a single soldier—and a female at that, young and lithe. Even the familiar gray-and-purple battlesuit didn't make her look like a fighter, although her stance was confident. The liquid metal of her orange-tinted, bowl-shaped helmet flowed down into her collar, to reveal dark skin and stringy black hair, and yellow eyes with no pupils.

She extended a hand toward me, and grinned. "You must be Karza. My name is Koriah."

I was trembling now, but not through weakness. My disbelief had turned to anger, and this gave me strength—but I had nowhere to direct either. My bile would have been wasted against this powerless child. I turned my back on her, and marched away.

To my surprise and disapproval, she followed me. She crashed unheralded into my chamber as a Biotron unit was still reconnecting my nutrient tank. Feeling exposed, almost violated, I screamed, "You don't enter this room without my permission!"

She squared up to me. "Now you listen to me, pal. I may not be everything you expected, but I've come a long way to help you!"

"Help me? You're no more than a girl!"

"I'm a fully trained Galactic Defender!"

"And I'm facing an army! I trust your superiors briefed you on our situation?"

"You've received a series of explicit threats from the Centauri."

"Petty gangsters!" I spat. "They don't know what they're meddling in, they're just out for what they can get. They're no better than Reptos!"

"If we could spare more troops," said Koriah apologetically, "we would—but you know the galactic situation. We're spread too thinly already."

"Everything falls to chaos," I muttered under my breath.

"And," she continued carefully, "this is only one space station."

"Don't you realize how crucial my work here is? Do you have the slightest inkling of what I'm trying to achieve?"

"As I understand it, you're experimenting with time travel."

I glared at her for a long moment, tempted to tell her the whole truth—a truth that would probably drive her insane. Instead, I calmed myself, and said, "You are fighting a losing battle against the symptoms of the problem. I will tackle the cause. The key to reestablishing order is to go back to the start, to excise the cancer before it can take hold."

Koriah smiled tightly. "I prefer to face my problems in the present."

Angrily, I brought my fist down on the arm of my chair. "At present, my enemies are massing around this station, preparing to take everything I have ever worked for. Only superior strength will keep them at bay. The Centauri knew I'd summoned assistance. They were biding their time; they don't pick fights with forces stronger than their own. But now...now, they'll have scanned your ship as it approached. They'll know the full extent of the reinforcements that your so-called Galactic Defenders have deigned to send me."

Koriah nodded, conceding my point. "We don't have much time. I could try talking to the Centauri. My organization does still carry some weight." I snorted derisively. "But my recommendation," she continued, unfazed, "is that we evacuate as soon as possible. How many people do you have aboard this station?"

"I will not leave my work to those criminals!"

"We'll take as much as we can carry."

"That is not acceptable!" I yelled. The girl blinked, taken aback by the sudden force of my protest. "I am an old man, Koriah," I sighed. "Science has extended my span beyond its natural years, but I must succumb to the inevitable soon. Before that happens, I will see my life's work completed. Nothing else matters. I don't have time to start again on a new station or a new world, even if I could find one that would take me."

"You...you still think you can do it, then?" she asked hesitantly, not wishing to upset me again. "You can build a time machine?"

I let out a burst of ironic laughter. "That, my girl, is the easy part. If only you knew..." A black cloud of fear swelled in my chest again, threatening to overwhelm me. Fear that my life would mean nothing. Fear that chaos would win. I closed my eyes, and tried to breathe through it.

"I have one last hope," I said. "One final chance of

claiming time before it claims me. I have picked a safe course along its tangled strands. I can almost reach my goal. I am close, so close!" I indicated the containment suit, hanging in its alcove. "In a few days, a week at most, I will put on that suit. I will part the strands of time, and I will step into history. After that, let the Centauri do as they wish—it won't matter! I just need those few days, Koriah. Do you think you can buy them for me?"

"I will try, Karza," she said quietly.

I believed her. But we both knew that she would not succeed.

CHAPTER
TWO

A page from the bridge pulls me from my memories. Koriah is leaning over the communications console, perhaps unaware that I can see her through the eyes of Biotron Unit #31. I accept her call, and her voice echoes around my chamber. Her report comes as no surprise: my enemies wish to speak to me again. I have ignored their last two hails, but there is a fine line between projecting indifference and appearing afraid.

I instruct Koriah to patch their representative through to me. A moment later, her image appears on my centermost, largest monitor. "What is it this time, Centaurus?" I snap, giving her no time to speak. "I thought I had made my position quite plain!"

She is wearing battle armor. Her long face is concealed by a black ceremonial mask, serrated along its bottom edge to give the appearance of fierce teeth. A white fire blazes behind her eye lenses, and steel coils twist down her neck like a proud mane. She folds her bare, muscular arms over a black chestplate. "You are in no position to dictate terms to us, Karza," she says, her tone made all the harsher by mechanical augment-ation. "You are defenseless and surrounded. We could blast you out of the sky with ease!"

"You won't," I counter, "because that would destroy what you came here for. To get that, you'll have to board this station—and be assured that, in such an eventuality, I will trigger the self-destruct system and blow us all to atoms!"

"I don't believe you have the courage to take your own life."

"My work *is* my life. If I lose one, the other has no meaning."

"And your underlings? Our scans indicate a total of nineteen life forms aboard your Astro Station. Do the others share your death wish?"

"They will follow where I lead." Eleven of the Centaurus's "life forms" are Biotrons, but I don't correct her misapprehension. What she doesn't know, I may be able to use against her.

"We will test the veracity of that claim soon enough. I have spoken at length with your Galactic Defender. I know she has communicated my offer to the rest of your staff. Perhaps you would care to remind them that the deadline for acceptance approaches."

"I'm sure they've already made their decisions," I growl.

"Indeed. We look forward to welcoming some of them aboard our Battle Cruiser."

I make a short, precise stabbing motion with the forefinger of my right hand. The nerve impulse is translated into an electrical signal, which travels down one of the wires plugged into my chest to terminate the communication. My central monitor goes blank. I move the image of Koriah onto it, from a smaller screen, by flexing my right wrist and sliding my index finger along the arm of my chair. A tiny, circling motion brings the Galactic Defender into close-up. I study her concern in the lines of her forehead, as she sees from the readings in front of her that contact with the Centauri has been lost. Her hand hovers over the console for a moment, but she chooses, wisely, not to disturb me. She leans forward, resting her chin on her fists. She is troubled, but I can't read her thoughts behind her blank eyes.

I feel a flash of hatred toward her, for putting me in this predicament. Still, her naïve attempts at brokering a peace have bought me some time, though not enough.

The Centaurus was right: I have little choice in this matter. Flattening my right palm, I open a voice channel to all parts of the Astro Station. "As you are all no doubt aware," I announce, "the Centauri have promised safe passage to anyone who wishes to desert us within the next hour. Should any of you choose to accept this dubious offer, you will assemble outside the hangar bay at 0745 hours. I will make my personal shuttle pod available."

Koriah's eyes narrow suspiciously. For her benefit, I add darkly, "Whatever my fate, after all, it will not involve my leaving this station again."

"My little Galactic Defender," I mutter under my breath. "Always so predictable..."

Koriah was the first to appear, of course. She isn't leaving—whatever else she may or may not be, she is no coward—but she will want to oversee the evacuation. She spends as much time meddling in my affairs as she does dealing with the Centauri, the true threat here.

She takes up a position in front of the hangar doors, arms folded. Every so often, she throws a glare at the two Biotrons—#37 and #40, according to the codes in the bottom left corners of their respective monitors—that she found waiting for her. If I didn't know better, I'd swear she could see me through their eyes. Eventually, she says, apparently to herself, "Five minutes to go. I know what you're trying to do, Karza, sending your robots here. But you can't intimidate them. They have a right to leave, if it's what they want."

Over time, I have gathered a team of seven assistants—hopeless drifters, mostly, whose paths have crossed mine and in whom I have sensed a certain potential. I give them a purpose. Some have contributed greatly to the project, allowing me to take strides forward while they attend to the minutiae in my wake. Others are suited only for menial tasks, but they free up my Biotrons for more vital work, and they've become increasingly important to me as my mobility has waned.

My most trusted aide, sadly, is no longer with me. I was forced to send Persephone away, some weeks ago, on an urgent mission, another distraction. I haven't heard from her since—no surprise. Since they closed their blockade around me, the Centauri have been jamming all communications, apart from between us and them. So, now there are six.

They have been debating the Centauri proposal for two days, lurking in dark corners away from the ears of any Biotron unit. What they fail to realize—what nobody knows—is that I have other ways of monitoring what happens on my station. I knew, as soon as I began to take others aboard, that I was inviting betrayal. In this chaotic universe, nobody can be trusted. I had the Biotrons, my only reliable servants, conceal listening devices at strategic points in the corridors, and in personal quarters.

Through these, I have come to know my staff better than they imagine. Last night, I heard Ogwen refer to me as an "obsessive fool." He accused me of chasing the impossible, of hiding from reality—and yet he stays with me because he doesn't wish to return to his old life, to face what awaits him. We have that in common, most of us. A bureaucrat by nature, Ogwen doesn't have the temperament to cope with the tension that has permeated the station of late. It doesn't help that, with communications and supply lines cut, he can no longer do his job. With nothing to fill his time but worry, he has taken to spending days tossing and turning in bed, and nights pacing the corridors with a bottle of methohol. For all his complaints, though, he won't leave. He is too afraid.

Nor will I lose LeHayn. She remained fiercely loyal to me throughout the discussions, sharing my anger and my stubborn refusal to give in to bullies. Wroje was less forthright—my microphones picked up few words from her whispering voice—but she will follow her partner's lead, as always.

Kellesh is harder to read. A young Terragonian—not even a hundred years old—he lost his wife and son to a Repto attack, two years ago. I found him drifting in a life pod, and put his technical skills to good use. Kellesh spends most of his time alone, crawling through ducts, lashing together obsolete systems, but I have never seen him brooding. He throws himself into his work, and maintains a cheerful façade—but sometimes I see a shadow behind his yellow eyes, and I wonder how deep the façade extends.

Two figures pass a Biotron unit in a corridor, flitting across one of my outer screens. A moment later, the units at the hangar door register their arrival. My chest tightens.

The insectoid—its name is a series of clicks and guttural stops—starts at the sight of the Biotrons. Its colleague holds it steady, and Koriah assures the insectoid that she'll keep it safe. Even so, its bulging, multi-faceted eyes stare nervously out of my central screen, its antennae twitching. I won't miss it, I tell myself, my tightening fists belying my silent assertion. In another time, another reality, my only use for this creature would have been on the dissecting table. I'd have liked to crack open its green shell, to expose the secrets of its race—an evolutionary offshoot of the Kronos, I have long suspected—but this is just one of many areas in which I have had to curtail my curiosity.

Veelum, on the other hand, would be a real loss. An old man with mournful eyes, his muscles are still strong, his face grim and determined beneath his short, iron gray hair. He came to me a year ago, having heard rumors about my work and wanting to share my solitude. To my knowledge, he has never spoken of his past. He keeps his own secrets. His thoughts about me, and about the evacuation, have likewise been left unvoiced; he has listened to the others, and made up his own mind. But Veelum is a competent scientist—better than Fzzzpa—and an excellent worker. I won't let him go.

Fortunately, I don't have to. Veelum's clear, rich voice fills my chamber, relayed to me in hollow-sounding stereo. "Where else would I go?" he asks in answer to Koriah's questioning. "I've come to see off the youngster, that's all. He's a bit nervous about leaving."

"Don't be." The Galactic Defender treats the insectoid to a reassuring smile. "I know you haven't been happy with us for some time."

"He's a social creature," says Veelum. "He needs

others of his own kind around him—and more of a purpose in life than we can give him here."

Koriah shoots a guilty look at the Biotrons, surprised that Veelum would speak so openly in front of them. He smiles tightly. "Oh, I'm not doubting Karza. He's quite brilliant, in his own way, and I believe in what he's doing. But you know the situation. We're almost out of time. That's all right for me—I've lived my life—and the others have made their own decisions. We'll see this through to the end, death or glory. But I want more for the kid."

My lips curl into a snarl. Relieved as I am to keep Veelum, his betrayal angers me. Without his interference, his support, the insectoid wouldn't have dared come this far. It doesn't matter, I tell myself as Koriah operates the wall-mounted controls and the hangar door slides ponderously aside. What use is the creature to me now, anyway?

"You sure this is okay?" asks Veelum. "The Centauri will keep their promise?"

"They've no reason to hurt him," says Koriah, "and he's useless to them as a hostage. They...they might want to interrogate him. They'll want to know what defenses we have here, how many people, that kind of thing." The insectoid looks startled. "Don't worry, they know the worst of it already. They know we can't fight them. Just answer their questions, and I'm sure they'll let you go home soon."

The Centauri hope to divide my forces, such as they are. They will be dismayed to find only a single being aboard my pod. I almost wish I could see their faces. Still, even one defector indicates weakness on my part; a weakness I am loath to display.

The insectoid tries to speak, but its meaning is lost in a stammer of nervous *tik*s. "He's worried that

Karza will be angry with him," says Veelum. "He feels he's betraying him."

"Karza will understand." Koriah looks into the eyes of Unit #37, as if challenging me to speak through him, to support her claim. Maybe I should. But my fingers close about the arm of my chair, and my throat constricts as I try to swallow a tide of resentment. All I can see is the masked face of the Centauri representative, laughing at me. Like the insectoid. Like Veelum. The latest in a long line of sneering dolts who have kept me from my work, who have brought this universe ever closer to destruction. No longer can I console myself that they'll suffer for their ignorance in the next timeline. When I look to the future, I see only darkness. The end of my own life. The end of everything.

I should have taken the Emperor's throne. The universe could have known order, for a short while at least. Our existence could have meant something.

Koriah is helping the insectoid into the shuttle pod, setting the auto-navigation system. She looks up as Units #37 and #40 march into the hangar bay behind her. "Karza? Did you want to say something?" A muscle in Veelum's face tightens. He steps forward, as if thinking he can do something. The insectoid swings around to face me, letting out a chittering squeal as it grows larger on my screens.

I issue the order almost without thinking. I don't even remember operating the voice link. I just know that it feels right. It feels good to be in control for once, to know the future for sure. The Biotrons act in unison, bringing up their hands. Koriah sees the nozzles that extrude from their palms, and cries out in horror. She tries to knock the insectoid aside, but, paralyzed with fear, it just falls to its knees. She places herself in front of the cowering creature, her arm-mounted laser pistols flashing. Unit #37 bears down on her, crowding her with his greater bulk and weight, clearing a path for Unit #40 to reach his target.

My central monitor flashes green, washing my chamber in an eerie light. When it clears, the insectoid is a smear of body parts, its shell blasted away, the muscles beneath stripped from its skeletal frame. Its dark green blood has spattered its executioner's face, gobbets of it sliding down the inside of my screen. I picture the Centauri spokesman lying in its place, and feel a thrill of satisfaction.

Abruptly, the output from Unit #37 ceases, leaving me with a screen of crackling static patterns. Responding automatically to his comrade's distress, Unit #40 swings around to afford me a view of Veelum slipping off his shoulders as a scowling Koriah fires another laser bolt into his head. Unit #37 sags, then topples to the floor face-first, with a heavy clunk. #40 brings up his hand, but his targets are registered as friendly in his database, so he waits for me to confirm the kill order.

I almost do it. I almost let Koriah and Veelum die on a whim. I pull back from that brink, reminding myself that I need them. A lump forms in my throat as I think about what I have already done, how I have jeopardized the project. My release was short-lived; now, it has turned into a familiar helpless ache.

I instruct Unit #40 to stand down. Koriah and Veelum are staring at him with mixed expressions of horror and contempt. I feel some comment is needed, but I mustn't show them my uncertainty, my weakness.

I patch my voice through to the Biotron's speakers, and I say in a gruff voice, "Nobody leaves."

I feel some echo of my earlier satisfaction when I face the Centaurus again. Her tone is strident as she reminds me that her deadline has passed, but I sense her anxiety that her threats have not had the desired effect. "Do you think I care for your deadline?" I sneer. "I told you before, my staff is loyal to me. We will fight you to the death!"

The Centaurus lets out a *harrumph*-ing snort. "I wish to speak to your Galactic Defender."

"That is not possible," I say primly. "I have had this station's communications systems rerouted. All incoming messages will be diverted to my chamber. From now on, Centaurus, you deal with me alone."

She rears up onto her hind legs, her front hooves coming into view as they pedal empty air in frustration. I catch a glimpse of her strong black fetlocks. I have no doubt that she would attack me, were we in the same room.

I intend to say more, to extract what rare pleasure I can from my foe's impotence, but I catch a glimpse of movement on another screen. Koriah has grown tired of shouting at a Biotron unit, or perhaps she has just realized that I switched off its audio receptors some time ago. She is marching through the main lab, watched by Unit #30, intent upon the door to this chamber. I cut my link to the Centaurus.

Koriah is separated from me by a single bulkhead. I can't block out the sound of her fists against my locked door. "I know you're in there, Karza!" she yells, somewhat redundantly. Where else would I be? "Face me, you murdering son of a Repto! I want an explanation for what just happened, you hear me?"

In her anger, she hasn't spared a glance for LeHayn and Wroje. They were working at the computer, sifting through this morning's fresh data with hollow eyes, occasionally squeezing each other's hands for mutual reassurance, but too aware of the lurking Biotron to vocalize their feelings. Now, they are watching the Galactic Defender, their faces etched with deep worry lines. LeHayn's thick lips are pursed, her dark eyes hooded in confusion. A day ago, I could have expected her to leap to my defense; now, she is not so sure.

Another monitor shows me Kellesh, as unkempt as ever, his red chin bristling with yellow stubble, lank hair hanging to the shoulders of his green coveralls. He holds a laser driver in his teeth while he prods experimentally at the rotting circuitry of a water-recycling unit with his fingers. He is whistling through his teeth, and I know that, if he's feeling anything at all, then he is blotting it out as usual.

In his quarters, overheard by a concealed microphone, Ogwen is alternately snoring, sobbing, and muttering frenziedly to himself. He sounds quite drunk.

That leaves one person unaccounted for. Opening a voice link to all Biotron units, I say in a soft but commanding voice, "Display most recent sighting of Veelum." A few seconds later, a gentle beep directs my attention to the screen that currently displays input from Unit #23. The oldest and wisest of my Biotrons—I programmed them to learn from experience, to mature—replays a memory of Veelum, marching sullenly toward his quarters. I expected as much. The elderly scientist tends to seek solitude when troubled. I see, from the time code on the recording, that he has been shut away for over an hour. I will give him an hour longer, then I'll send a Biotron for him. I can't afford to leave him idle. I only hope I haven't lost his cooperation. I would hate to employ extreme measures to regain it.

"I'm not going away, Karza. Speak to me, or I...I'll turn my guns on your computer! All your precious data, up in smoke. Is that what you want?"

I sigh heavily. I don't want this confrontation, and I doubt Koriah would carry out her threat, but I can't take that risk. I unlock the door with a crook of my thumb, and it slides open. I close it again as she storms into my chamber; there's no need for LeHayn and Wroje to witness this.

"This project is more important than one life," I say before my visitor can open her mouth.

"Oh, no, Karza, not this time! You've used this 'project' of yours as an excuse for everything you've ever done, but not for cold-blooded murder!"

"You have never understood. It doesn't *matter* what happens in this continuum, girl. I can wipe it all out—all the suffering, the mistakes. The insectoid will live the life it was always meant to live, never experiencing the pain that brought it here. The same goes for Kellesh and Veelum, and for all the others. If I can just make one journey back..."

"And if you can't?"

"Then, in some ways, the insectoid has been fortunate," I rumble. "Its death was quick, and relatively painless. It won't have to bear witness to the end."

Koriah is taken aback, but she soon recovers. "I won't overlook this, Karza," she says in a voice that is quiet but steely with resolve.

She can't see the smile beneath my white helmet, but she can hear the humor in my voice. "And what do you intend to do about it, my dear? Arrest me? You can hardly take me back to your headquarters, can you? Not with a dozen armed and hostile ships gathered around this station. And you couldn't summon reinforcements, even if there were any available."

"I could shut down your project," says Koriah spitefully. "I could hand your equipment to the Centauri in return for safe passage out of here, for us and your staff."

"That is the second threat you have made against my project," I growl. "Make another, and you will learn what a formidable opponent I can be."

"What—you'll kill me like you killed the insectoid?"

"I would deal with you as I would anybody else who stands in my way."

"This isn't over, Karza," she promises—a futile parting shot. I open the door for her, and she leaves with her head bowed and fists clenched in frustration.

I don't know how long I spend after that in deep, sullen reverie, before I'm disturbed by an incoming call. The Centauri representative again. I don't want to speak to her, at first, but she is insistent. And I remember our last conversation, the pleasure I took from my small victory, and I long for that feeling again.

I put her onto the main screen. "Really, Centaurus," I say, in a voice that is studiedly casual, even a little bored, "do we have anything left to say to each other?"

"You lied to me, Karza!" she hisses.

"I don't recall."

"My latest scan of your station finds only seventeen life forms. Three days ago, there were nineteen. Having some trouble with your 'loyal staff,' Karza?"

"Nothing I can't handle," I reply tersely, "as I believe I have demonstrated."

"I must apologize," sneers the Centaurus, "if my offer has caused...unrest among your people. I wonder, if I were to make it again, what reaction I would get this time."

"That we will never know."

"Continue to 'handle' your problems this way, Karza, and you will do our job for us. Your support is crumbling. How much longer do you imagine you can hold out?"

"Never underestimate the power of fear, Centaurus, to keep order."

"I do not. It is your people's fear that will drive them away from you in the end—their fear of dying at your side, or at your hand."

"You're wrong, Centaurus," I say confidently. "They are far more afraid of the consequences of betrayal—and, if they are not, then they ought to be."

Veelum returns to the main laboratory an hour later, after a gentle reminder. He looks pale, and his face hardly forms an expression all day. He carries out his work in a disinterested manner, his lips clamped into a straight line. He spares few words for his co-workers, and when I address him through my supervising Biotron, his replies are perfunctory.

Not that I have much to say. Most of my work is done. My theories are sound—they always have been—and Veelum understands them as few people would. He knows what he is doing. All that is left to me is to wait and watch, confined to this damn seat, while he goes about his business. And that is harder than anything I have had to do.

On Veelum's instructions, LeHayn and Wroje have reopened the Rift. Despite my anxiety, I still feel a tingle in my spine when I look into its emerald light. It recalls my younger days: the excitement I felt when that first Rift shimmered in front of me; the feeling that the fulfillment of all my ambitions was within reach. This current Rift bears scant resemblance to that uneven green sliver, of course. It dominates one wall of the laboratory, opposite the door to my chamber—seven feet tall and three feet wide, it is perfectly rectangular, its energies contained and regulated by dampening devices in a framework of black metal. This Rift can hardly be considered a simple tear; it is a doorway into the past…and my future. We are using a computer-guided probe to plot a safe path through the years, to a particular time, a particular place, but time's tangled strands conspire against us. I seethe as we hit another knot, another dead end, and are forced to backtrack.

Maybe, when I feel the end coming, when I'm sure there is no hope, I will indulge my greatest longing. I will leap into the Rift at long last, let the currents take me and tear me apart, because at least then I will have stepped through that doorway. I will have traveled in time, just once, before time ceases to exist.

A familiar klaxon strikes up from the computer. LeHayn and Wroje leap to their feet and pull urgently on a silver tendril that snakes into the Rift's light; Veelum sighs to himself and shakes his head. By the time the probe is retrieved, it has all but disintegrated. Any information it may have gathered has been lost. My frustration is a prickling ball in my chest. Another day's work for nothing. My one consolation is that the Centauri have not been in touch again. They are biding their time, waiting to see if the situation here will turn further to their advantage. They won't wait long. I don't know how many more days I have left.

I was dreaming again. The galaxy lay at my feet, and I was a good ruler. I brought progress and education to my people, eradicating the superstitions that had held them in thrall. My inventions kept them warm and fed. My soldiers kept them safe. Any hint of insurgence was excised before it could spread. No longer were the worlds of the Empire in decay; I was leading them into the future.

This time, though, it was different. Always before, I had dreamed of the man I would become in the new timeline: A Karza shaped by happier circumstances, informed from the start by the experience of a lifetime. This time, I was not that man. Nobody had whispered in the ear of my young self; nobody had guided me to the throne. I had simply made the most of my opportunities. My dream was of the man I could have been: A man who had suffered, yes, but a man blissfully unaware of the cancer in the time stream; a man who had never been distracted by the futile pursuit of the Time Traveler's secrets. It was not a dream of possibilities, but a dream of regrets, and it left me with a gnawing sense of failure.

Lost in despair, it takes me a moment to realize why the dream ended. A noise outside; I'm not sure what it was. Did somebody call out? And now, some sort of a scuffle. A grunt. A heavy slap as something hits the floor.

LeHayn and Wroje were out there, working through the night, prepping a new probe for launch and trying to reconstruct some of the corrupted data from the old one. It sounds like they're fighting, but I can hardly imagine such a thing. LeHayn, I'm sure, is capable of throwing a punch, but not against Wroje—and she'd be more likely to burst into tears than to hit back. My eyes flick over my screens, looking for the laboratory; my Biotrons are instructed never to leave it unguarded. I am perplexed to find it empty—and a dreadful suspicion washes over me.

"Unit #27, report status. Unit #27…"

There is no response, and a closer inspection of Unit #27's screen shows that its time code has frozen.

A phantasmal hand closes around my heart. Could the Centauri be here? Could they have crept aboard, somehow, without being detected? Urgently, I scan my monitors for the two nearest Biotrons, and order them to the lab—but they're too far away. I fear that they'll arrive too late to do any good. I am halfway out of my seat before I have time to consider the wisdom of my actions. I'm tearing wires from my chest, wrenching tubes from my helmet, until there is nothing to hold me back. I almost fall against the chamber door, feeling blindly for the lock—and only now do I realize the peril I'm placing myself in, because until now I have only thought about the threat to my work.

I stumble out into the lab, my red lenses darkening in response to the clinical white light, so bright after the nighttime gloom of my chamber. The Rift is closed, but its frame is intact. The computer clicks quietly to itself. I see no immediate threat, and nothing appears to be damaged—nothing, that is, except Biotron Unit #27, which stands like a statue, one eye blown out, a faint burning smell issuing from its casing.

The door to the corridor stands ominously open—and there is a body on the floor.

My legs propel me across the room in a lurching gait, my knees dropping rather than lowering me to LeHayn's side. She is dead. Her hammer-shaped head lies at an impossible angle to her body, a line of blood streaming over her fat lip. I smooth back her short black hair to find a bruise on her temple. She put up a fight.

A short, strangled gasp sounds from the doorway. I look up to see Wroje, her saucer eyes round and disbelieving, her scrawny frame trembling, her thatch of violet hair in disarray. "No, no," she croaks. "You can't have...not LeHayn, no..."

I don't register the accusation at first. There's a lump in my throat, and I feel weak. I expended too much energy too quickly. My head throbs. I reach to the only person who can help me. "Wroje...take my hand...help me back to my..."

She flies at me, tears streaming from her eyes, screaming, "You murdered her! She wouldn't do as you said, so you killed her, like you killed the kid!" She is raining punches down on me, but I can hardly feel her weak blows through my exo-suit. Still, I have good reason to be worried. I've never seen Wroje like this before, but I've always known what fury lurked within her. I doubt she has told anybody her secret, maybe not even LeHayn. Her shame has contributed, in part, to her lifelong passivity. My muscles on fire, I drag myself from beneath her. For a moment, our eyes lock, and I am reminded starkly of my father's body beside me. I see my long-gone self in her, railing against the loss of the one person I ever cared for—an injustice that, in my youthful naivety, I blamed on fate.

To my relief, Wroje seems to have forgotten about me. As she sobs over her partner's broken corpse, I search for the strength to stand but can't find it. My head spins, and there is a terrible pressure behind my eyes as if I, too, am about to cry, for the first time in decades. I want to curl into a ball and let unconsciousness claim me, but I fear that, disconnected from my machines, I might never wake again. I will hold on, until a Biotron arrives to take me back to my seat—and then I will know precisely what has occurred here.

Through the chaos in my head, through the blood that pounds in my ears, I am aware of a soft tinkling sound, emanating from my chamber to taunt me. An incoming communication. The Centauri representative. I already know what she has to say.

Two more down. Now, there are only fifteen.

CHAPTER
THREE

The ship appears two hours after LeHayn's death, as the station's clocks edge toward a notional dawn. Unit #39, stationed on the bridge, detects it first and calls it to my attention. I watch its approach, unable to make out any details at first, but tense, almost sick, with hope. It has been several days since Koriah was last able to send a report to the Galactic Defenders—could they have sent somebody to investigate her silence? Or has Persephone returned from her mission at last?

Maybe, I think gloomily, the mysterious ship carries allies of the Centauri.

I think I recognize it. A blocky, gray construct, its proud wings trailing fire, a golden oval jutting out of its front end. I have seen this ship, or one like it, before—but where?

The Centauri have seen it, too. Two of their white Battle Cruisers, bristling with missile launchers and weapons modules, peel out of formation to bear down upon the intruder from each flank. Abruptly, it drops into a barrel roll, and spirals away from them. The Battle Cruisers open fire, silent explosions blossoming against the black void of space. The rogue ship is buffeted, and clipped by a plasma bolt. It shudders, but its shields hold.

That answers one question. Whoever controls that vessel, they are no friends to the Centauri—which means they may prove useful to me.

Ordaal! I remember now. The mercenary had a ship like this one, but why would he have come looking for me, after all these years? We were reluctant business acquaintances, no more—and this for only a short time. He must sense that, somehow, there is a profit to be made from my situation. His loyalty, as always, will be for sale, but, loath as I am to admit it, his resources may be worth the asking price. If Ordaal can buy me the time I need, he can have the Astro Station itself.

I realize that such conjecture is pointless. Ordaal's ship—if such it even is—is in retreat, the Cruisers hard on its tail, fire bolts sizzling past its wings. It is only through superior speed and deft piloting that it remains in one piece. The Centauri break off the pursuit, and retake their positions in the blockade as their enemy leaves detection range. I doubt he will return. My best hope is that he will alert the Galactic Defenders to what he has witnessed, but even then it will take them days to respond. And what if, in the meantime, the Centauri have the same idea? What if they decide that they have to act fast?

By its very appearance, the gray ship may have sealed my fate.

"Where is he?" The nervous, breathy voice belongs to Wroje. "He called this meeting—why isn't he here?"

"He's only a few minutes late," says Kellesh, reasonably.

"What...what if," stammers Wroje, "he just wanted

to get us out of the way? What if he's up to something? He wants us all dead, I know he does."

Ogwen lets out a short bark of a laugh. "The shrimp's right," he says in a voice that is slurred and a little too loud. "While we're sitting here like idiots, all Karza has to do is flood the room with a poison gas, or blow us all out into space."

"He won't do that," says Koriah firmly. "He needs us."

"He needs you," jeers Ogwen, "and Veelum, and Persephone if she were still here. For all he cares, the rest of us can join LeHayn and the kid. He'll probably harvest our organs to build more of his bloody robots."

"Then I'd suggest," says Veelum quietly, "that we stick together."

"Veelum's right," says Koriah. "Right now, we're in the safest place."

"As safe as we can be," mutters Ogwen under his breath, my microphone barely picking up the words, "with a psychopath on board." There's a general murmur of nervous agreement. The Centaurus was right: I'm losing them.

"I think we should remember," says Kellesh, "that Karza denies killing LeHayn."

"I saw him," shrieks Wroje, "kneeling over her body. No one else was there!"

"And the kid?" asks Ogwen. "Does he deny killing the kid, too?"

"LeHayn was angry," says Wroje. "She felt betrayed by...by what Karza did. She was going to say something. I should have talked her out of it. I should have tried harder."

"You think she confronted him?" asks Kellesh.

"It's not your fault, Wroje," says Koriah. "You know

what LeHayn was like when she set her mind on something. None of us could have stopped her."

"I only stepped out of the lab for a few minutes. I shouldn't have left her!"

"It's simple then, isn't it?" drawls Ogwen. "Karza's a killer, and none of us are safe here. I vote we take his pod and get the hell off this wreck while we can!"

"You weren't so keen to leave yesterday," observes Kellesh.

"Of course I wanted to leave! I just didn't trust Karza. I knew what would happen. But now...now, we're all together on this, right? We've got numbers on our side. Five of us, one of him. Let him try to stop us!"

"You're forgetting nine things," says Kellesh. "The Biotrons!"

I have heard enough. I send Unit #40 onto the bridge, his display showing me the back of Ogwen's prematurely bald head as he gesticulates passionately with his wiry arms. He is expounding on how it should be possible to get a distress signal to the Centauri; how Koriah could shoot her way into the hangar; how, if Kellesh could sabotage the computer in the main laboratory, I would be too busy to even notice an escape attempt. Sensing movement behind him, he turns, and his thin rat face blanches as he falls silent.

My staff is gathered around the empty cryo-crypt—once used, I assume, to store specimens for experimentation—that we have come to think of as our conference table. They greet my representative with suspicious glares.

"I assume you're in there, Karza," says Koriah, addressing me through the Biotron's audio receptors.

I speak with his voice. "I will say this only once more. I did not kill LeHayn."

Ogwen lets out a derisive snort, but, from his panicked reaction when I turn the Biotron's gaze upon him, I don't think I was meant to hear it. Wroje doesn't dare say anything; she wraps her arms tightly about herself, and chews on her lip.

Kellesh faces me squarely. "Then who did?"

"There are two possibilities," I say. "One: The Centauri have found some way of striking from a distance, with the aim of both lessening and dividing our forces. I have to say, I find this extremely unlikely, which leaves us with the second option." I pause, inspecting each of their faces in turn on my monitor. "LeHayn was killed by one of you."

Veelum clears his throat. "What about the Biotrons?"

"Impossible!" I snap. "They follow my instructions."

"But they are capable of independent thought!"

"He's right," says Kellesh. "There was a Biotron in the lab. What if it went nuts and attacked LeHayn? She shut it down somehow, but too late."

I can barely contain my impatience at this illogical distraction. Seething, I explain, "Unit #27 was exposed to a virus, which shut down his nervous system. By the time of LeHayn's death, the bioorganic part of his operating system had suffered a catastrophic failure. The only rational conclusion is that he was deliberately targeted by somebody who wished their actions in the laboratory to remain unseen."

"Which would suggest that the murder was premeditated," says Kellesh.

"Not necessarily," says Koriah. "It was late at night, remember? The lab would normally have been empty at that time."

"That occurred to me, too," I say. "I have had Biotrons examine both the scene and LeHayn's body. It appears that she hit her head on the corner of a bench during a scuffle. I suspect she was not the killer's intended victim at all, but rather that she paid a high price for surprising him." Wroje buries her face in her hands and sobs.

"You think somebody tried to sabotage the project," says Kellesh, matter-of-factly.

"Or, perhaps, obtain details that he could sell to the Centauri."

Now, everybody is looking at each other, several pairs of eyes meeting briefly, guiltily, across the cryo-crypt. They are beginning to suspect, to wonder who they can trust. It was easier for them when they could blame me.

"From now on," I say brusquely, "the main laboratory will be guarded by two Biotron units. A unit will also be assigned to each of you, to watch you at all times."

"Now hold on a minute!" cries Koriah.

"Not in our rooms," squeals Wroje. "I can't have one of those things in my room, watching me while I sleep. I can't!"

"Ogwen, you will move into the empty quarters next to Veelum's. That will leave the starboard habitation corridor unoccupied; it will then be sealed off, along with Laboratory Three and the hangar bay." I talk over Koriah's attempted argument. "I am putting these measures in place for your own safety. A smaller area is easier to patrol. Whichever of you is the traitor, he will not get another chance to harm the project or my staff."

"And the Biotrons?" asks Veelum, coolly. "I know you trust them, Karza, but one unit has already been tampered with. It could happen again."

I concede his point. "For the present, the Biotrons

will take downtime only when absolutely necessary, and always under the supervision of another unit."

"Even so," says Koriah, "I think we'd all feel more comfortable if they didn't come into our rooms. Maybe they could stand guard outside our doors overnight."

The suggestion elicits nods from some of the others, so I accept it. It could even work to my advantage. If they think there are still some places in which I can't hear them, somebody might give something away. "I'm also assigning a unit to question each of you about your movements last night," I say. "I trust there are no objections to this?"

Nobody speaks up.

I was right about the Centauri: they are becoming impatient. And, after I ignore their next two hails, they resort to a show of force. They fire on the station.

I am thrown forward in my seat, then yanked back by the wires attached to my chest. My nutrient tube comes loose, and I fumble for it behind me as its sickly green contents ooze out onto the floor. A dozen alarms sound, but I silence them with an irate flick of my wrist. The Time Traveler containment suit flops out of its alcove.

I wait with baited breath, wondering if this is it, if the Centauri have decided that my work is not worth the time and effort required to obtain it, if they are taking their final revenge upon an obstinate foe. But no more blasts come. This was a warning shot.

I look to the screen that shows the main lab. Veelum and Koriah are picking themselves up ruefully, while Wroje cowers on the floor, ashen and tearful. Fortunately, the Rift is intact, as is the latest probe on its tiny, three-legged launch platform. Had it already entered the Rift, had it been feeling its way along the tangled strands of time when its anchor point was shaken so violently, I hate to think what might have happened.

Each of the nine Biotrons confirm systems normal, as does the Cosmobot, although it has toppled over and can't right itself. They also report the survival of Kellesh and Ogwen, the latter bruised and shaken. He had just stepped out of the starboard habitation corridor, carrying his belongings in a single bag, when a section of the hull was blown out behind him. He only survived because his Biotron bodyguard magnetized his feet and seized him, holding him long enough for an emergency bulkhead to fall between them and the rent. Now, Ogwen is jabbering in panic, convinced that the attack was a deliberate attempt upon his life.

I know better. It is no coincidence that the Centauri targeted an uninhabited part of the station. I doubt they care about the lives of anybody on board—but then, I don't think they'll go out of their way to kill, either. Not while they're still hoping to encourage my people to defect to them.

I'm in no mood to face their representative again, so I record a one-way video message to send to her. "You should know," I say, "that I have split my project files between memory storage units in all areas of the Astro Station, particularly those in the remaining habitation corridor. Any further strikes will not fail to destroy irreplaceable data." The bluff should be effective—the Centauri want the secret of time travel almost as much as I do.

Unit #32 bleeps for my attention. I direct his input onto the main screen, to find Kellesh staring out at me. "KARZA IS LISTENING," the Biotron informs the red-skinned Terragonian.

"Just wondered if you want me to do anything about the breach," says Kellesh breezily. "Self-repair systems are working on it, but they're down to about 23% efficiency."

"I have no use for the affected areas," I respond through the Biotron. "I'm sure you have more urgent duties." Let the station fall apart around me—it no longer matters.

Kellesh nods and turns away.

The next person to contact me is Koriah. She wants to speak with the Centauri. "We can't pretend they don't exist, Karza. That shot was a warning. We have to negotiate!"

I assure her, curtly, that I have taken care of it. I see, over her shoulder, that Veelum and Wroje have resumed their work, and this is all I care about.

I watch for the hundredth time as they send a probe into the Rift, holding my hopes on its slender thread. I try not to think about what the Centauri will do next, try to imagine that none of us will be here to see it, but that image no longer comes easily to me as it once did.

Time has defeated me. What I need now is a miracle.

"I need a weapon."

Kellesh's red face crumples into a frown on my main screen. He was repairing a control panel on the bridge, dividing his attention between this task and Unit #34, through which I address him. Now he sets down his tools. "You mean a laser pistol? I can wire one together for you, but it'll mean cannibalizing a Biotron."

I shake my head, though my engineer can't see the

gesture. "Something more powerful. Something that can fire through space."

"If you're hoping to fight off the Centauri…"

"That is not my intention."

Kellesh is confused, trying to guess what I'm thinking. "You've always refused to let Ogwen order weapons for the station, or even a defensive screen. You said we couldn't waste credits on anything not directly connected to the project."

"I know what I have said in the past," I say shortly.

The Terragonian shrugs. "Well, if it's what you want…I have been thinking over a few possibilities since the blockade began."

"I need it now, Kellesh. This takes priority over everything else."

He shakes his head. "It's not possible, Karza."

"The weapon only has to fire once. We don't need to disable the Centauri fleet, we don't even have to damage them—just distract them."

"I don't know what I can do with the equipment we have." His lips twist into a grin, exposing small, sharp fangs in the corners of his mouth. "But leave it with me—I'll work something out."

Two Biotrons stand in the port habitation corridor, alerting me to the fact that Veelum has joined Ogwen inside his new quarters. Almost automatically, I patch the audio feed from the room through to me. Their conversation, however, is mundane: Ogwen was dozing, and is still bleary, when Veelum knocked on his door. The older man is worried that, should we lose another probe, we'd be unable to replace it.

"I don't know what you expect me to do," says Ogwen, dully. "Even if we had the funds for more equipment, the Centauri won't let me contact my suppliers."

"I know that," says Veelum gently. "I'm just suggesting that you update the stores inventory. If it comes to it, Kellesh might be able to lash something together from spare parts and whatever he can salvage from our last few wrecks."

"I'll send the Cosmobot," offers Ogwen.

"It'd be quicker if you both went," says Veelum, pointedly.

"I'm tired. All the excitement last night…"

Veelum sighs. "It might do you good to occupy your mind."

Ogwen responds with an anguished cry. "You don't think my mind's occupied? All day and all night, my head's pounding, filled to bursting with thoughts, with questions…What'll happen to us if we stay here? What if we try to leave? What if the Centauri storm the station? Do you think Karza will carry out his threat—blow us all to hell, just to protect his computer and a few machines? Are you okay with that? Are you?"

"If the Centauri storm the station," Veelum says calmly, "I wouldn't give much for our chances either way. In the meantime, that threat is the only thing keeping them away."

"So, how does this end for us, Veelum? How do we get out of this one?"

"We finish the work in time."

Ogwen snorts. "A pipe dream! Don't you think you've indulged Karza's fantasies of time travel long enough? If the Centauri even knew how long he'd been banging his head against that same brick wall, they'd realize he's never going to get through it. They'd know there's nothing here worth taking!"

I scowl behind my helmet, resisting the temptation

to send a Biotron crashing into the room. I don't need Ogwen anymore, but another death at this point might finish the project.

"Anyway," continues Ogwen, his whiny voice in full flow, "what if you *do* succeed? Karza gets what he always wanted—he travels back in time—and what happens to the rest of us then? Do we get left to the Centauri? Will we even be here?"

"If Karza changes his own past," says Veelum, "he'll change ours, too. We won't ever have met him, at least not under the circumstances we remember. We don't know for sure what will happen to us, then. We may continue as we are, in a redundant offshoot of a new timeline. In that event, we'll have to find some way of saving ourselves without letting the Centauri take the time travel equipment. On the other hand, you could be right. If Karza is careful enough, he won't split time, he'll simply rework its pattern into a single continuum of which we'll all be part. We might find ourselves elsewhere, living different lives. We won't remember anything that happened here because, to all intents, it won't have happened."

Ogwen's reaction is silent—a wince or a pained expression—but it prompts Veelum to comment, "I thought you would have welcomed that prospect."

"If the last few years hadn't…" He fumbles for the words. "I…I wouldn't be the same person. I wouldn't be me. Where would I be? What would I be doing?"

"Didn't you once work in the court of King Atlas?"

"I couldn't go back there!" says Ogwen, too quickly.

A short pause. Then Veelum says, "Kellesh spoke to Karza a few months ago. He asked him to contact his younger self when he reached the past, to warn him about the Repto attack that took his family. Karza promised that, in the new timeline, they wouldn't die. I think he had a similar deal with LeHayn—she asked him to do something for Wroje. If there's something you regret, something that happened before you came here…"

"I…I don't think there's anything he could…Sometimes, I think, if I'd never met her…" Ogwen swallows, and continues plaintively, "But I don't think I could bear that."

I have never revealed the extent of my ambitions to my people. They think I am concerned only with righting one injustice, with saving my father, and with buying another lifetime in which to fight off the destruction of time. Frail as I am in their eyes, I doubt it has occurred to them that I could win the Emperor's throne, even were I minded to fight for it. They don't know me at all. But my rise to power will make their dreams come true. It may take many attempts, but eventually I will have my order. In my universe, no Repto would dare form a pirate band, and Kellesh's family would be safe. King Atlas would be executed—for I know him by reputation, and that he would never bend his knee to me—leaving Ogwen free to court his daughter without fear. And Wroje would be spared a lifetime of abuse, for her mother was unfit and would not be granted a permit to bear children.

"And you?" asks Ogwen, quietly. "What can Karza do for you?"

"Nothing that would make a difference," rumbles Veelum. "To me, one place, one timeline, is the same as another. I don't expect anything to change."

"Then why are you here?"

To my disappointment, he declines to answer that question. The elderly, white-haired scientist lapses into a characteristic silence.

"I still say he killed her," says Ogwen, indistinctly.

Jerked out of his introspection, Veelum has to ask him to repeat the comment.

"All this extra security," says Ogwen, "Biotrons breathing down our necks—he's trying to throw us off the scent, make us suspect each other. I think Wroje was right all along: LeHayn challenged Karza about the insectoid, so he had one of his robots kill her! Now he's got them watching us, in case we step out of line, too."

"You could be right," concedes Veelum, "but what does it matter? Either way, it's clear what we have to do. It's in all our interests for the project to be completed."

"And what if Karza's lying to us? We're helping him to travel in time, handing him the greatest weapon ever created, and we don't know what he'll do with it. He could stop you, me, anyone he likes, from being born—and he'd do it, you know he'd do it. For all we know, we might be better off handing the station over to the Centuari after all!"

Some five hours later, the gray ship returns, as I prayed it would.

Veelum and Wroje have pulled the latest probe out of the Rift for a third time, and are analyzing the information it has collected, still trying to pinpoint the particular knot in the time stream that destroyed its predecessor. Koriah assists Kellesh with his urgent work on the recycling tanks in the station's underbelly. Ogwen nurses a plastic cup, half-full with a murky black stimulant, in the tiny refectory; his hair is disheveled, eyes red-rimmed.

The Cosmobot is in the stores, examining the contents of crates and sorting through burnt-out relays. It works methodically but slowly, and components sometimes slip through its clumsy digits. It was with a certain wry humor that I assigned this plodding, unimaginative robot to my supplies manager, feeling them well suited to each other.

I transfer the view of the oncoming vessel onto my main screen, zooming in as close as I can, my nerves jangling with anticipation. Whether it is Ordaal who commands the ship or somebody unknown, he wants to reach me badly enough to brave Centauri fire a second time. Friend or foe, he will at least change my situation—and he could hardly change it for the worse. I speak through Unit #34. "I need that weapon now, Kellesh."

A scurry of movement from the recycling units. As far as I can tell, Kellesh is paying out wire to a detonator. He waves Koriah into the service elevator, and promises to join her in a moment. My nerves prickle, and my stomach flutters with the fear of failure.

The gray ship comes up immediately behind the greater bulk of the Centauri flagship. At first, I think it is on a collision course, but it banks away at the last possible instant, almost scraping the hull of the white Battle Cruiser. The other Centauri ships bring their guns to bear on the audacious intruder, but they can't fire without risk of hitting their leaders. They break formation, moving ponderously into more advantageous positions. The flagship, buffeted in the hot gases of the gray ship's fuel discharge, spits out bolts of fire petulantly, but its target is too close and moving too fast for it to hit.

Koriah has been joined in the elevator by her Biotron bodyguard, and by Kellesh's. The engineer himself is still working feverishly on his device. "You're out of time, Kellesh," I tell him, trying to keep my voice even. "If you can't make that weapon work now, we're dead."

"Get out of here!" Kellesh yells at Koriah.

"I'm not leaving you!" she cries.

The gray ship loops around and over the top of the flagship, which sways and drops and surges forward, trying to shake off its enemy as if it were some irritating insect. The other Battle Cruisers move around and behind it, surrounding it; soon, there will be nowhere for the gray ship to go to escape their sights—but I think I see what its pilot is doing.

"There's no point in you dying, too!" insists Kellesh.

I agree with him. I instruct Unit #34, standing in the elevator beside Koriah, to take them up to the main deck. He reaches for the control, but the Galactic Defender sees what he is doing and throws herself in his way, raising her right pistol in threat.

"Kellesh," she screams, "get in here now!"

The gray ship shoots out from beneath the flagship, on a direct course toward the Astro Station. Its speed is incredible, but it comes with a price. The fiery discharge from one of its wings turns black with smoke—the final protest of an engine pushed beyond its capabilities. The ship spins wildly, pulling away from us, and two Battle Cruisers drop onto its tail.

In the service elevator, two Biotrons manhandle Koriah out of the way, Unit #35 shrugging off a glancing laser beam as he stabs at the control panel. A pair of steel lattice gates rumble toward each other. Koriah wedges herself between them, but they're squeezing her into an ever narrowing space.

"Now, Kellesh!" I yell through Unit #37. "It has to be now!"

Kellesh throws himself into the elevator, headfirst, knocking Koriah back into the cramped cab so that the pair land in a tangle of limbs. The gates meet with a clang. The detonator falls and skitters into a corner, and Kellesh fumbles to retrieve it. Its wires trail between the closed gates, and, as the elevator begins to rise, they are pulled ever tighter, yanking the detonator across the floor before Kellesh's fingers can close around it.

The gray ship's pilot has regained control, but not before a Battle Cruiser could cut him off from the station. I'm impressed by his flying skills as he takes evasive action, the ship hurtling untouched through a plasma barrage as if he knows in advance where each bolt will hit. Still, his fortune can't last forever.

"Kellesh!" I roar.

He has the detonator. And, in the instant before the upward motion of the elevator yanks the wires out of its back, he operates it.

The Astro Station rocks again, less severely than before, as the backs are blown out of all four recycling tanks. Water and sewage blast out into space, freezing almost instantaneously into mad star formations, shattering against the sides of Centauri Battle Cruisers. The pilots break off their attacks on the gray ship, and raise their shields. A second later, they realize what has happened—that they aren't under threat—but, by then, their target has come around and is barreling past them.

A recycling tank crumples, and is pulled through the rent in the hull behind it. The oncoming ship doesn't even flinch as several hundred kilograms of scrap metal bounces off its oval, golden nose. It is close enough now that I can pick up its ident signal, despite the Centauri's jammers. It is called the *Sunrunner*. I remember that name. It is Ordaal's ship, as I surmised. I curl my fingers, extending the station's landing ramp toward it in silent welcome.

Below me, the service elevator strains to rise against the increasing air pressure that is pulling it back down.

Unit #34 punches out the hatch in its ceiling, and boosts Kellesh up onto the roof. Koriah swarms up under her own power, and blasts the gate to the main deck, just over her head, with both laser pistols. She creates a hole large enough to crawl through, and drags Kellesh up after her. Unit #37 follows, but #34 is still standing on top of the elevator cab when it finally gives up the unequal struggle and plummets. The Biotron leaps for the gateway, and just manages to grab its lower lip with his left hand. The vacuum pulls at him as the elevator cab explodes into debris at the foot of the shaft—but, a moment later, an airtight shutter, no longer blocked by the elevator itself, slides horizontally across the shaft beneath his flailing feet. The Biotron drops safely onto it, and awaits rescue.

The *Sunrunner* is on the landing ramp, being conveyed into the hangar bay. It is a slow process, but, as I expected, the Centauri are loath to fire upon the ship and risk damaging the Astro Station and its contents further. Now I can only pray that I have not made a mistake.

I send all available Biotron units to the hangar doors, to receive our visitors.

They are waiting for us as the hangar doors roll apart to reveal them.

The tallest and broadest of the three figures sees the semicircle of Biotrons awaiting him, and draws and lights an energy sword with admirable speed. He wears black, skintight armor, beneath silver boots, armbands, and a shoulder harness. His chestplate and face-concealing helmet are a livid shade of red, and a pair of angular fins jut from each side of the latter.

To my surprise, I recognize him. We have never

met, but his name is legendary. He is the latest in a line of noble warriors to be given the title of Acroyear. The last I heard of him, he had been defeated, forced into a life of servitude in Micropolis—but then, I have been somewhat out of touch of late. Evidently, things have changed.

Flanking Acroyear are two more beings, both armed with laser pistols, both inspecting their reception committee with worried eyes. The being on the left has pink skin, like mine, and short, brown hair. He looks young, barely out of adolescence—although, until I identify his race, I can't know that for sure. He, too, is wearing a thin suit of black flux armor, as is the final member of the trio, whose purple skin, four arms and gills identify him as a Vaerian, that rarest of species.

The arrival of Koriah, another Biotron striving to match her brisk pace, defuses the tense atmosphere. The three figures relax visibly upon sight of a Galactic Defender. "This is a privately owned Astro Station," she announces, standing before them with her arms folded. "Please identify yourselves and state your business here."

The boy's mouth falls open. He stares at Koriah, and he mouths something to himself—her name, I think. Interesting. She shows no sign of having recognized him.

The Vaerian takes the lead. "My friend here is called Ryan Archer, and he's come a long way to find you. The big guy with the blade and the bad attitude is Acroyear. I'm Ganam Jafain, but you may as well call me Knave—I'm sure you will, anyway."

"We are seeking a man named Karza," says Acroyear.

"What do you want with him?" asks Koriah.

Ryan Archer is still staring. "You're a friend of his?"

he asks hesitantly. "So, that means he's a good guy, right?"

"Our business with Karza is private," growls Acroyear.

"We have some news for him," says Knave, "about a friend of his."

"And we're hoping he can help us with something," adds Archer.

"Go ahead," says Koriah, indicating the nearest Biotron with a sweep of her arm. "He can hear you."

"No!"

The boy starts as I speak abruptly through the unit. I am leaning forward in my seat, alive with curiosity and rekindled hope. I don't know who these people are—although to have an Acroyear on my side would be useful indeed—but suddenly I can almost see the future again. I want to hear their story, and watch them as they tell it, without electronic mediation, this Ryan Archer in particular. I sense something about the boy, something special. I feel as if our destinies are entwined somehow.

"Bring them to my chamber," I instruct.

CHAPTER
FOUR

"You seem surprised," I say.

Archer realizes that he was staring and drops his gaze. "Sorry. It's just, you...you're not quite what I expected."

I look down at the wires and tubes that sprout from my white containment suit. "Pardon me for not rising to greet you, but as you can see, my mobility is somewhat impaired." I fix Archer with a long, appraising look. "But then, if you heard tell of me in Micropolis, you must have known that I am an old man."

Archer shuffles uncomfortably, as I must have shuffled once under the glare of the Emperor's visor. He and his companions stand in a line before me, watched by our Galactic Defender. As a show of trust, I have left my Biotrons in the lab outside this chamber, but they can reach me in a second should I send for them. I am well aware that my visitors are armed.

I glance at Acroyear. "You did come from Micropolis, I presume?"

"We did."

"And this news you have for me, of a friend?"

"We met Persephone," says Archer. "She told us

about you. She was helping us. I…I'm sorry. She died. The Reptos killed her."

"Did she complete her mission?" I ask pragmatically.

"She saved many lives," Acroyear confirms, "and kept the Reptos from taking the Time Traveler's machinery. She died a hero!"

I nod. "Then, that is enough."

Archer is staring again, as if trying to read my thoughts through my shielded eyes. If he knew how I ached at the revelation of Persephone's fate, he would not think me so hardhearted, but we both knew what peril I was sending her into. I deny my feelings, as I have always denied them. Persephone did her duty. She kept the Reptos from hastening the collapse of time with their clumsy interference. She is gone for now, but not forever. In the new timeline, she will be spared, as will LeHayn and the insectoid and the others. I will wash the blood from my hands.

"You also wanted something from me?"

Archer clears his throat nervously. "It's kind of a long story. You see, the reason we're here is that Persephone told us about your work. She said you'd studied the Time Traveler, the guy in the gold and silver suit who hovers over Micropolis, and that you know all there is to know about him. Is that right?"

"It has been my life's work to uncover his secrets."

"Only…the thing is, I think there might be something wrong with time."

I am careful not to react, although my heart jumps at his words. Let the boy keep talking; I want to hear how much he knows.

"The Time Traveler—I think he's the cause of it. He made a mistake, and he wants me to put it right. He's been…this is going to sound nuts, but recently, he's been trying to contact me through my dreams."

"Impossible!" I retort. "The Time Traveler's consciousness is fragmented across decades. He exists in our timeframe for only a nanosecond before passing through on his journey into the past. Even were he aware of the world about him, I have seen no evidence that he has the power to make telepathic contact with you or with anybody else."

"Nothing like keeping an open mind," Knave mutters.

I glare at him. "If my words sound harsh, it's because you disappoint me. I wasted valuable resources helping you to board this station. I was foolish enough to imagine you could help me, but it transpires that you're chasing a fantasy!"

"It's more than that!" protests Archer.

"The Time Traveler has become a symbol," I say. "To many people, he is the future. Dreams about him are extremely commonplace."

"What," says Archer hotly, "even in people who've never heard of him?"

"Everybody knows of the Time Traveler."

"Not where I come from!"

"Archer claims to have been born in a universe outside our own," explains Acroyear.

"I've seen it," chimes in Knave. "A world of giants!"

"When these visions started," says Archer, "I thought they were dreams too. Weird dreams, more vivid than any I'd had before, but just dreams. And then…then the people of your universe came to mine, and I knew they were real. I saw the Time Traveler in my dreams, long before I ever saw him in real life, and I saw Acroyear and Knave and…" He seems to think better of continuing that sentence. Instead, he says, "The visions—the Time Traveler—led me here. He led me to your universe, to Micropolis, and now to you."

I am watching him closely. Archer seems to believe his own story—and, despite its implausibility, I am interested. "Let us say, for the sake of argument, that I accept what you're saying. What, then, does the Time Traveler want of you?"

"I don't know," confesses Archer. "I was hoping you could tell me that."

"What exactly," I ask patiently, "does the Time Traveler say to you in these dreams?"

"He doesn't. Speak, I mean. He shows me stuff. Memories—but memories of things I never did. It's like...I think he's showing me *his* timeline, the way things were before he made his mistake, before he tinkered with his own past."

I lean forward eagerly. "And you meet the Time Traveler, in these 'memories'?"

"Yes! Well, I think I do. There was a desert world. We crash landed: me, Acroyear and Knave here, Persephone, and a couple of others. We found a half-buried pyramid, an old Pharoid temple. It had been cleared out, except...We went down to the basement, and we found these machines, and that's where he was. I have this image of his face—that gold mask—staring at me, but that's where the memory ends."

"You don't know what happened next?"

"I've been trying, concentrating as hard as I can, but it's like there's some kind of barrier there. I can't get past that point."

There is a long silence, then, during which my mind is awhirl with thoughts. Archer's tale sounds preposterous, but he knows too much that he ought not to know. Could it be possible that, somehow, he *has* seen the Time Traveler's reality? Could he have witnessed the start of his journey? Could he have, locked inside his mind, the final piece of the jigsaw, the secret for which I have thirsted these long years?

And, if so, what good could it do me? Archer might help me learn how time came to be in its current tangled state, but will that knowledge enable me to repair it?

"I'm right, aren't I?" says Archer. "There *is* something wrong. The Time Traveler didn't just change history, he damaged it somehow. This reality, this timeline, is unstable."

"Yes," I say quietly, "you're right."

Archer swallows. Acroyear asks, "How bad is it?"

I think carefully before I answer. My gaze lingers on Koriah, who returns it with deep suspicion. "The universe is threatened. Soon, this reality and all realities will cease to be."

Knave whistles through his teeth. "That's bad,"

Archer nods solemnly, as if he expected this. Then he stares straight at me, a look in his eyes that I can't quite read. "How long have you known about this?"

"Most of my long life."

"So, that's why you're here. I mean, that's why you're so interested in time travel."

"At first, it was a means to an end. The Time Traveler gave me the inspiration to seek out the secrets of the fourth dimension. That's how I learned of the instability in the time stream. Since then, my primary goal has been to repair the damage."

"The Time Traveler changed your entire life, just by being there." A smile pulls at Archer's lips; he seems to be enjoying some private joke. "You're trying to save the universe!"

"Correct," I say tartly. "Now I ask that you leave me to think on what you have told me. Koriah here will show you around the Astro Station, and assign quarters to you. Please note that you will be watched by my Biotrons at all times. Do not take this as a personal slight; in these times, with enemies massing at my door, I'm obliged to be careful."

As my visitors turn to leave, Archer sees the containment suit hanging in its alcove, and he freezes. Slowly, jerkily, like a marionette, he moves over to it and runs his hand across its silver mask. He is lost in thought for a moment, but he snaps out of it, glances guiltily back at me, and hurries out after his companions.

Koriah hangs back, still staring at me. I know what she is thinking. "Karza?"

"Later," I say crisply.

"What do you make of him?" The Vaerian's voice, from Archer's quarters.

"I don't know. In some ways, he's so different. In others...the armor...those eyes..."

"Will he help us?"

"I guess," says Archer. "You heard him—he knows what's at stake."

"Yeah. Still trying to get my head around that one."

"I've never thought of Karza as a nihilist. He wants to control, not destroy."

"And what if he can't do either? He's dying, Archer. Maybe he doesn't care what happens to the rest of us after he's gone."

"If that were true, he wouldn't be here. He's spent his whole life fighting this, Knave. I don't think he's about to give up now. He's trying to save us all!"

"And you think he'll succeed?"

"If anyone can."

Archer speaks as if he knows me, although I'm sure we haven't met before. He could have researched my early life—he has revealed no knowledge that couldn't have been gleaned from public records in Micropolis—but I sense there is something more. That strange connection between us again.

I turn my attention to Koriah and Acroyear, deep in discussion on the bridge. It was Acroyear's decision to cut his tour short, keen as he was to be briefed about the Centauri and to discuss tactics. He will be an asset—so long as the Galactic Defender doesn't turn him against me. The Centauri haven't contacted me since the *Sunrunner*'s arrival—I imagine they're still trying to work out what it means to them—but, when they do, I look forward to telling them exactly who has joined my cause.

My spirits are dampened by a report from Kellesh. "Our little stunt with the recycling tanks worked, but it means we have no reserves left. We'll be out of water in about a day and a half." So, even with the Centauri stalled, time is still running out.

I instruct Kellesh to search the *Sunrunner* for anything we can use to keep the project and ourselves alive. As an afterthought, I tell him to obtain Acroyear's permission first.

I rest my chin on my fist, my elbow on the arm of my chair, and I listen as Archer and Knave continue their conversation without saying anything of interest. I want to know more about them. I want to know about the timeline Archer claims to have seen, and his connection, real or imagined, to the Time Traveler. I want to witness the single event that, more than anything, has determined the course of my life, because in so doing I feel I can give my life meaning. And maybe, just maybe, I would find in that event the seed of a solution to my current problem—but what if I don't?

What if my curiosity leads me to waste what little time remains?

Acroyear intrigues me. His confident bearing, the proud tilt of his head, even the way he carries his heavy armor—everything about him marks him as the warrior of legend. If he was indeed humbled by Maruunus Ki—if that story wasn't exaggerated by Ki himself—then clearly he has rediscovered himself. He remains alert, even when he thinks he's alone, his hand never straying far from his sword hilt. I would like to see him in battle. More than that, I wish I had the strength of youth to challenge him myself.

Koriah told him about the insectoid, of course, and about LeHayn. He has spent the past hour exploring the station, shadowed by Unit #40, showing no outward reaction to what he has learned. Finally, he wheels around to face his mechanical escort.

"There is no doubt that it was Karza who had the insectoid killed?"

"HE CONSIDERED IT THE ONLY WAY TO MAINTAIN SECURITY," the Biotron responds loyally. "ONCE KARZA HAS MASTERED TIME—"

Acroyear dismisses the rest of the explanation with a flick of his hand. "What about the woman—LeHayn? Karza denies killing her. I understand all personnel have been questioned about their whereabouts at the time of her death?"

"THAT IS CORRECT."

"I want to hear everything you know."

"REGRETTABLY, I AM UNABLE TO DISCLOSE THAT INFORMATION."

I open a voice link to the unit. "Tell him."

The Biotron hesitates for a moment—a very organic reaction. "I AM IN RECEIPT OF NEW INSTRUC-

TIONS," it reports. Acroyear's helmet hides his expression, as does mine. All I can see is the reflected light from the Biotron's eyes.

"VEELUM AND KORIAH EACH STATE THAT, AT THE TIME OF THE INCIDENT, THEY WERE ASLEEP IN THEIR RESPECTIVE QUARTERS. THEIR CLAIMS CANNOT BE SUBSTANTIATED. KELLESH WAS WORKING LATE ON THE BRIDGE, ASSISTED BY BIOTRON UNIT #32. OGWEN ARRIVED APPROXIMATELY TWELVE MINUTES BEFORE THE INCIDENT, AND CONDUCTED A SHORT CONVERSATION WITH KELLESH BEFORE LEAVING. HE WAS NOT SEEN AGAIN FOR FORTY-THREE MINUTES, AND STATES THAT HE CANNOT REMEMBER HIS MOVE-MENTS DURING THAT TIME. WROJE WAS WORKING WITH LEHAYN IN THE MAIN LABORATORY, UNTIL LEHAYN SENT HER AWAY TO REST. SHE WAS LAST MONITORED APPROACHING HER QUARTERS, APPROXIMATELY THIRTY-THREE MINUTES BEFORE THE INCIDENT. WROJE CLAIMS THAT SHE WAS UNABLE TO SLEEP, AND DECIDED TO RETURN TO WORK, BY WHICH TIME LEHAYN WAS DEAD."

"And Karza?"

"KARZA DID NOT KILL LEHAYN."

"What was she like?"

"PLEASE BE MORE SPECIFIC."

"LeHayn. Was she popular?"

"SHE WORKED HARD, AND WAS EXTREMELY ABLE. SHE WAS ALSO LOYAL TO KARZA. I BELIEVE HER RELATIONS WITH THE REST OF THE STAFF WERE AMI-ABLE. LEHAYN AND WROJE WERE ESPECIALLY CLOSE. ACCORDING TO MY MEMORY FILES, OGWEN MADE A TOTAL OF FOUR DISPARAGING REMARKS ABOUT HER WITHIN HEARING OF A BIOTRON. HOWEVER, IT SHOULD BE NOTED THAT OGWEN HAS MADE SUCH

REMARKS ABOUT MANY BEINGS, INCLUDING THIS UNIT."

"Koriah introduced me to Ogwen, I think. Short, thin, balding, rings around his eyes?"

"THAT IS AN ACCURATE PHYSICAL DESCRIPTION."

"And yet LeHayn struggled before she died—and I understand she was strong."

"HER MUSCULATURE WAS WELL-DEVELOPED, AS I BELIEVE IS NORMAL FOR HER SPECIES."

"So, could Ogwen really have killed her?"

"IT IS NOT MY PLACE TO SPECULATE, BUT THE POSSIBILITY CANNOT BE DISCOUNTED—PARTICULARLY IF, AS KARZA BELIEVES, LEHAYN'S DEATH WAS ACCIDENTAL. OGWEN SPENT LAST NIGHT IN AN ADVANCED STATE OF INEBRIATION. I WOULD VENTURE, HOWEVER, THAT IN A CONTEST OF STRENGTH, NONE OF THE STATION'S STAFF COULD HAVE BETTERED LEHAYN."

"Not even the Galactic Defender?"

"I WOULD SAY NOT, THOUGH I HAVE NO DOUBT THAT KORIAH IS A SKILLED COMBATANT."

"She also wears laser pistols," mutters Acroyear.

"THERE IS NO EVIDENCE THAT A WEAPON WAS FIRED."

"The Biotrons are armed, too," notes Acroyear, "and strong enough to snap LeHayn's neck, especially if one of them took her by surprise."

"THAT POSSIBILITY HAS BEEN CONSIDERED," says Unit #40 stiffly, "AND DISCOUNTED."

"Is it true?"

Koriah has sought out Veelum, ambushing him as he leaves his quarters. Fired up with determination, she doesn't spare a glance for the Biotron units that accompany each of the pair, doesn't seem to care that I might be watching.

Met by Veelum's nonplussed reaction, the Galactic Defender expounds, "I thought Karza was building a time machine. I thought that was why we were all here: because he wants to go back in time, and change whatever it is he doesn't like about his life. Now, I find out he's trying to—what?—save the universe? That, if his project fails, we're doomed?"

Veelum's expression darkens, and the only comment he can manage is a leaden "Ah."

"You knew about this? You must have known! You've worked more closely with him than…LeHayn knew, too, didn't she? And the others?"

Veelum shakes his head. "They don't know."

Koriah cries, "Why didn't you tell me?"

"Would it have made you feel better?"

"That isn't the point! I might have acted differently. I may have been able to get reinforcements. Has Karza told the Centauri? Do they know what they're risking?"

"They wouldn't believe him," says Veelum. "Nor, in Karza's opinion, would the Galactic Defenders. He has been dismissed too often, denied funding by too many eminent scientists who simply didn't understand the patterns of time as he does."

"But you believe him?"

"Oh yes," says the old man quietly. "I believe him."

"And if Karza reaches the past—he can save us?"

"Karza is a brilliant man," says Veelum. "Our galaxy has never known another like him. Only he can halt the destruction of time…but he has little time left. He plans to deliver his research notes to his younger self."

"Is that possible?"

"He believes so."

Koriah's jaw drops in awe, her yellow eyes misting

over. "He can buy another lifetime to further his work—and then another, and another. A never-ending loop."

"No," says Veelum, "not never-ending. The cancer that's eating away at the time stream does so in all eras simultaneously. Eventually, it will catch up to Karza, even in the past."

Koriah turns away from Veelum, chewing her lower lip in anguish. "I misjudged him. I thought he was only concerned with saving himself."

"That may be how it began," says Veelum gently, "and I believe it's still Karza's ultimate goal to rewrite his own tragic history. But he can't do that if there's no history to rewrite."

The Galactic Defender's habitual confidence seems to drain from her. She sags, resting her forehead against the corridor wall, and she says three words, in a voice barely loud enough for the audio receptors of the nearest Biotron to detect it:

"This changes everything!"

The gloom of artificial night envelops the corridors of the Astro Station, darkening my monitors. However, a light burns again in the main laboratory, the glow of the open Rift chasing shadows from the corners. Veelum is working, assisted by Archer, who professed himself untired, his body clock set to a different schedule from ours. Units #31 and #35 have been assigned to stand guard, but the latter has taken this opportunity to switch to downtime.

The probe sinks into the Rift again, Veelum using the computer to navigate it along its tortuous path. Archer stands by to pull it out of the light should it encounter difficulties, but he stands close enough to Veelum to watch over his shoulder. At first, he is bemused by what he sees, his questions indicating a lack of understanding. In short order, however, he assimilates the basics of the project—and, within an hour, he's making suggestions.

"Wouldn't it be faster," he says, pointing to the tangled, incomplete map of time that rotates slowly on the computer's main display screen, "to go through this area here?"

"Faster, yes," rumbles Veelum, "but more dangerous. We've lost four probes trying to take that particular route. That's where the strands of cause and effect are at their most knotted, where the Time Traveler's presence has done the most damage."

"So, you're trying to plot a course around the blockage," Archer deduces.

I interrupt through Unit #31. "The Time Traveler has been visible to us for decades. The effect of his presence in this timeline has multiplied exponentially. Effect becomes cause, and breeds a new generation of effects. It is almost impossible to work backwards, as we are forced to do, to follow the strands to their starting points."

"So, you're trying to…to feel your way around the blockage, to find the parts of history that haven't been changed, and to trace them back…"

"Indeed. Once we have found a route to the past, it will be a simple matter to make our way forward, past the Time Traveler's appearance, to our destination point."

Archer shakes his head. "You don't have time."

Veelum raises an eyebrow.

"You think you're almost there," says Archer, "but you haven't seen the Time Traveler's reality. You can't imagine the effect he's had, how different things were in this galaxy before he set out on his journey. He's changed everything!"

He drops into a seat and squints at the thin green lines of the map, each representing the broad flow of history, each formed in reality by the woven threads of billions of tiny decisions, impossible to chart with any accuracy. "There's no way you can reach the past without encountering more obstacles, and with each second that passes, things move farther away from how they were meant to be. The path is becoming more tangled." He is tracing a line with his forefinger, almost absently, into the dark space at the map's heart. He lets his hand fall away from the screen, and stares at it with narrowed eyes.

"I can do it!" he announces. Veelum frowns. Archer pushes back his chair, and leaps to his feet. "Let me program the computer. I can guide the probe, I know I can."

"You hadn't seen this equipment an hour ago," Veelum reminds him. "It's a lot more complicated than it looks."

"But I've seen the past!" insists Archer. "The real past, I mean. The Time Traveler's past. I know where the threads ought to be. Maybe that's why I can…I can't explain it, I just…" His voice tails off as he realizes that Veelum is still skeptical. He puts a hand to his forehead and grimaces, as if trying to keep the knowledge therein from exploding outward. He casts a glance at the door to my private chamber, makes a decision, and starts toward it. "I'll speak with Karza."

"You're already speaking to me," I tell him.

He stops in his tracks and looks askance at the Biotron through which I spoke. No doubt he is reassessing our earlier conversation, the one he thought he was sharing with an artificial intelligence. "Your idea has merit," I say, "but, as Veelum has explained, it has been tried before—and, with resources dwindling, I won't risk another probe."

78

"I can do it," says Archer stubbornly.

"So you've said, but I would like to see evidence of that claim."

He spreads his arms wide, helplessly. "I don't know how to prove it. It's just…all my life, I've had this instinct about things. I can understand foreign languages, computer systems, alien technology, in minutes, because it's like I have this voice in my head that tells me what I have to do to get where I need to be."

A thought occurs to me. "Then, it was you who piloted the *Sunrunner*?"

"No. No, that was Acroyear, but I was standing at his shoulder, telling him which way to turn, where the next bolt was going to hit."

"And what is the origin of this 'instinct' of yours?"

"I don't know."

I scowl. "Have you no scientific curiosity? You have lived with this phenomenon all your life, and yet you have never investigated it?"

"It's not that simple," says Archer defensively. "I thought I was just…you know, normal, a fast learner. It's only recently that my world's gone crazy, and I've had to trust to these instincts to keep me alive. So far, they've not made a bad job of it. I'm still here, anyway—and I know you won't believe this, but I think it's the Time Traveler."

"You're right," I growl. "I don't believe it."

"Who else knows the future? Who else could be guiding me through it?"

"He knows *a* future, not this one. Take my word for it, Archer, the Time Traveler has not communicated with you. He isn't watching us now, and he never has."

"Then why do I keep seeing him in my dreams?"

"A salient question," I say, "and one to which I would like an answer. I would like you to undergo a full physical scan, and psychometric testing."

Archer pouts. "I thought we were in a hurry here. I can finish your work, I can guide your probe—does it matter how and why I can do it, so long as I can?"

He is impatient, as am I, but experience has taught me to suppress that emotion, to deny my hopes and proceed with caution. "I appreciate your confidence in your abilities," I say. "However, before I stake the survival of the universe on one man's intuition, I would like a better assessment of the odds against me. Does that sound unreasonable?"

"No," says Archer with a resigned sigh. "I guess it doesn't."

Kellesh appears at his door in response to Unit #37's insistent knocking. His yellow hair is disheveled, his red skin dark around his bloodshot eyes. The Biotrons tell me that he finished his work on the bridge less than three hours ago, but I don't apologize for waking him. I simply explain that I need him again. As always, he accepts this without argument.

"Some years ago," I say, "I constructed a device to augment brainwaves and convert them into broadcast signals."

The Terragonian nods blearily. "The mind probe. I've seen it in the stores." And tried it out, no doubt. Kellesh's insatiable curiosity is one of his most admirable traits.

"Its intended use," I say pointedly, "was to help me visualize my own thoughts, to draw out connections and possibilities that I may not have consciously recognized." I am being disingenuous. I was well aware, of course, of the machine's potential as an interrogation tool; had I not been, I wouldn't have wasted my time on it. It is only because Ogwen's predecessor turned out to be a hopeless diplomat that my blueprints were not sold to three different races, to do with as they wished. I didn't get the extra funds for which I had hoped—and, after using the machine three times on myself, I concluded that it was too slow, its results too imprecise, to be worthwhile, and I abandoned it.

"You want me to dust it off, clean out the circuitry, see if I can get it working?"

"You surmise correctly," I say.

Kellesh nods. "I did think about suggesting it myself," he says, nonchalantly. "If anything can root out the killer…"

I smile to myself. Kellesh is shrewder than he sometimes appears, but not as clever as he thinks. "I already know who killed LeHayn," I take pleasure in informing him. "I require the 'mind probe' for a different purpose altogether."

Archer lies, bound by his wrists and ankles to a trolley in the medical bay—a tiny alcove off one corner of the bridge. He is staring at the patch of lime green gel that spreads across his chest and is crawling slowly up his body. The gel seeps through his black armor, in search of biological matter. Archer is trying to be brave, but he shivers at its touch and, as the gel extrudes a slimy tendril toward his chin, he screws his eyes shut and clenches his fists.

A minute later, he is smothered, a green mask clinging to his face, rippling as it assimilates every facet of his being. The medical computer—an archaic contraption—clicks and whirs as the protoplasmic creature sends information to it along two wires sunk into its shifting mass. Finally, a dark stain appears at the creature's heart, and spreads outward. It shudders as it dies, leaving a dry, black husk, which Archer shakes from his head in revulsion. He is gasping for air, having held his breath by reflex, unable to accept my advice that the creature was porous. "Can...can you get me out of these straps now?" he pleads.

Biotron Unit #35 moves to oblige as the medical computer ticks away ponderously, analyzing its fresh data. My eyes drift across my other screens, as my staff begins to stir in the light of early morning. Veelum is still in the lab—he doesn't seem to need much sleep—joined now by Wroje, whose puffy eyes suggest that she spent the night crying into her pillow. She is wearing a loose-fitting, short-sleeved smock. As it slips down her shoulder, I catch a glimpse of the tattoo at the base of her neck: the silhouette of an Equestron head, crowned by a proud fin. The symbol of the Order of Oberon.

Kellesh is in his quarters. I can't see him, but I don't doubt that he is carrying out his duties with his usual diligence—in secret, as I requested. Ogwen has joined the Cosmobot in the stores, as if remembering that he has a job to do—not that he's doing much more than supervising, and this mostly from the floor with a bottle of methohol. I wonder how he'll cope when his supply dries up.

Koriah arrived on the bridge an hour ago, carrying out routine scans in a desultory manner. Only when Acroyear sought her out to discuss tactics again did she regain some of her usual spark. The Vaerian joins them as they are studying a plan of the station, picking out the best defensive positions to take in the event of a hostile boarding, but he has little to contribute, other than glib remarks.

It bothers me that our visitors have taken so quickly

to our Galactic Defender. They seem to trust her, alone of my people. It might simply be that they respect her rank—and perhaps Acroyear feels a kinship with a fellow warrior, but I feel there's more to it than that, something I've missed. A snatch of whispered conversation as Archer and his colleagues left my chamber—too soft for me to hear, but I'm sure Koriah's name was mentioned.

A chiming signal echoes through my chamber. I am being hailed by the Centauri again. Their representative sneers at me from my main screen, as I shift the feed from the medical bay aside. "We grow tired of this game, Karza!"

"I warned you at the start, Centaurus, that you would find no easy prize here."

"Your stubbornness will be your downfall!"

"It has kept me alive so far."

"We will have your equipment and your research, Karza, or we will have your corpse. There can be no other outcome."

"If there's one belief that drives me," I growl, "it's that anything is possible."

The Centaurus snorts. "We are well aware of your ongoing efforts to complete your work. You think you can escape us by fleeing into the past–but you're still here, Karza. You have devoted your life to the study of time, but you don't have the intelligence to master it!"

I seethe at that insult, feeling my bile rising. "If you think so little of my intelligence, then why are you here?"

"Oh, we don't doubt the value of your work, as far as it goes. Your findings will provide a solid foundation on which superior Centauri minds can build."

"You'd better hope that's true, Centaurus. You'd better hope I never reach the past—for if I do, I swear,

I will take the utmost pleasure in visiting your world in its primordial era, to poison the misbegotten slime that birthed your loathsome race!"

"An empty threat, Karza. Your project is doomed, your station crippled, and your staff no longer trusts you. It is time to end this. Prepare to be boarded!"

I feel a pang of fear in my stomach. "I've warned you before, Centaurus, what will happen if any of your kind set hoof aboard this station."

"And I think you were bluffing, but it matters not. The troops we are sending are expendable. Destroy them, if you must, and yourself in the process—but for what? You would only delay our triumph, not prevent it."

I have nothing to say—nothing that would make a difference. The Centauri have made their decision. Even the presence of an Acroyear, my trump card, would not dissuade them now; best to keep that secret in reserve, for what good it will do me.

"Our troops will be dispatched in one hour. You have that time to think about what I've said. We are still happy to accept your unconditional surrender. Failing that—goodbye, Karza. Our conversations have been…stimulating."

The Centaurus cuts the link, leaving me to stare at a blank screen. I feel numb. I knew this moment would come, but now that it's here, I can't accept that this must be my fate. There must be something I can do, some way to buy more time.

In the medical bay, Archer rises gingerly, as if expecting his legs to be weak. He runs his hands down the front of his armor, and is surprised to find it clean and dry. A thoughtful expression crosses his face, and he turns and examines the medical trolley as if for remnants of the green gel, proof that it existed. He rolls the trolley from side to side on its castors. I'm staring at Archer's back, through a Biotron's eyes, and I think about the false hope he gave me, the precious time wasted because I wanted to believe him.

"Unit #35," I say in a husky voice. My mouth feels dry. Am I making a mistake? Does it matter? There is no time for indecision. All my life, I have denied my desires, forcing myself to be patient, methodical. No longer. I think about what I plan to do, and I can't think of a single reason not to do it.

"Unit #35," I repeat—and I hesitate for a long moment, before giving the order. "Kill him! Kill Ryan Archer!"

CHAPTER
FIVE

Unit #35 lumbers forward. His metal hands come into view as he extends them toward Archer's neck. Oblivious, the boy is still playing with the medical trolley, as if he has discovered a fascinating new toy. The back of his head looms large on my screen.

There is no indication that he has sensed his peril. He does not stiffen, doesn't turn, doesn't let out a gasp. He simply twists aside, at the same time giving the trolley a push toward his advancing killer. Normally, I would expect a Biotron to avoid such a clumsy obstacle, but the trolley hits its legs without warning, at the most inopportune moment. He topples onto it, and is conveyed into the wall. Fighting to free himself from a tangle of metal, he catches sight of his target's flushed face, his hands raised in apology. "I...I'm sorry, I don't know what happened, it just slipped out of my..."

The Biotron raises his right hand again, the weapon attachment emerging from his palm, and Archer's eyes bulge as he realizes his predicament. He races for the archway that leads to the bridge, but comes up short before he reaches it. His hesitation saves him, as the Biotron fires and the archway is washed in a green cloud of lethal radiation.

Archer flattens himself against a wooden shelving unit as Unit #35 bears down on him. Glass containers fall and shatter around him as he tries to back away, but finds he has nowhere to go. He fires his laser pistols into the Biotron's chest, to no avail. "Acroyear!" he screams. But although the warrior is nearby, he can't possibly reach him in time.

I have seen enough. I speak through the voice link to Unit #35 again. "Your last order is rescinded. I repeat, your last order is rescinded. The boy is not to be harmed."

The Biotron retracts his weapon, and lowers his hand. The relief in Archer's eyes is overtaken by confusion. And, at that moment, Acroyear and Koriah come crashing through the doors from the bridge, Knave keeping pace with a curious springing gait.

Acroyear's energy sword is drawn. He looks for a foe, sees only the Biotron, and interposes himself between it and his friend. Koriah is only a little slower, demanding to know what's happening as she brings her laser pistols to bear, liquid metal hardening into its usual bubble shape over her head.

"He—it—just went crazy, attacked me for no reason," reports a shaken Archer.

"Karza?" snaps the Galactic Defender. "Can you hear this?"

"I can," I reply through Unit #35, "and there is no cause for concern."

"Sure," says Knave uneasily. "Killer robots we deal with every day."

"Despite the rumors circulating this station," I say, "my Biotrons are not out of control. Unit #35 threatened Ryan Archer on my orders."

"Well, that makes me feel a whole lot better," comments Knave.

"What are you playing at, Karza?"

"A small experiment, my dear Koriah—nothing you need concern yourself with."

"You...you tried to kill me," says Archer incredulously, "as an *experiment*?"

"I needed proof of the unerring intuition to which you lay claim. I am still awaiting the results of your medical scan, of course, but an unconscious part of you knew what the Biotron was going to do before I had given the instruction. I am satisfied."

"And what if you'd been wrong?" storms Koriah. "We'd have had another corpse on our hands, another sacrifice to your obsession!"

"Events forced my hand—or perhaps you have already forgotten the stakes here."

"I haven't forgotten anything, Karza. I just happen to believe that life is sacred—even one life! I don't care what you think you're fighting for—you've gone too far!"

"You'd weigh one life against the whole of Creation? I knew you were naïve, Koriah, but I didn't think you were so stupid! Or perhaps you're feeling guilty?"

"What events?" Acroyear's voice is a quiet rumble, but it cuts across the escalating argument. "What are these events that forced your hand?"

Suddenly, everybody is silent, waiting on my word. As I relate the details of the Centauri's new ultimatum, they exchange nervous glances, and Knave stares down at the floor.

For a moment after I have finished speaking, there is silence. Then Acroyear hefts his sword and says grimly, "Koriah and I have been working out our strategy. If our enemies think they can take this station without a fight, they will learn their mistake."

"Excellent," I say gratefully. "Then I suggest you continue."

"We will require as many personnel as you can spare. That includes the Biotrons."

"I need Veelum and Wroje. I doubt they'd be of much use to you, anyway. Kellesh is engaged in vital work for me, but I'll have him join you as soon as he can."

"What's more important than saving all our butts?" asks Knave.

"We can't beat the Centauri," I assure him, "only delay them. Repulse their first invasion force, and they will send another, or destroy us from afar. Work on the project must continue—every second is precious! I'll send Ogwen and all available Biotrons to the bridge to await briefing. Archer, you will report to the main lab."

"Alone?"

"I'm ready to test your theory that you can guide my probe to its destination."

"He's going nowhere without an escort," states Koriah.

I take a deep breath. "Archer is in no danger from me. Quite the contrary—I believe he is now our best hope, perhaps our only hope."

Archer looks to Acroyear for his cue. The warrior thinks for a moment, then nods. With a brave smile, Archer heads for the door. Unit #35 makes to follow him, but Acroyear restrains him by the arm, and glares into his eyes.

"If you lay a finger on him, Karza," he says, "I will kill you."

I don't doubt that he means it.

It begins as a green spark, dancing in the air, deeper and more intense than any natural light. To our eyes, it appears flat, but this is an illusion. The spark is merely the mouth of a tunnel, which winds through dimensions invisible—and once unknowable—to us.

Archer operates the computer control system, and the spark pulsates and suddenly explodes. It tears through the reality we know and the boy flinches, throwing a hand over his eyes in fear that the expanding light will wash over him, leaving him blind.

It is caught, of course, by the containment grid. As its tendrils touch the black metal frame, they crackle and recoil. Eventually, like a living being, the spark resigns itself to its confinement. Its turbulent, flaring surface settles–and the Rift is open.

Archer stares into the green light, awestruck, hardly listening as Wroje explains how he should have decreased the power of the energy dampers more gradually for a smoother initialization. "It's beautiful!" he whispers.

"To me," I say through Unit #35, the only Biotron I've retained in the lab, "it is the possibilities that the Rift represents that are beautiful."

Archer screws up his face; the light is beginning to hurt his eyes, but he can't turn away from it. "I...I think I know what you mean, but it's more than that. I feel like...like the light is calling to me, like it's my destiny to go through that doorway..."

Suddenly, he's on his feet, taking his first step toward the Rift as if hypnotized. I am about to order the Biotron to restrain him when he shakes himself out of his trance.

"Step into the Rift now," I remind him, "and it will tear you apart."

"I know, but it's what the Time Traveler wants," Archer says confidently. "He wants me to go through the Rift—not yet, but soon. I've felt like this before, back on Earth."

"Your homeworld?" I have never heard the name before, but then I have been out of touch for a long time. "The Acroyear said you came from beyond our universe."

Archer nods. "That's right. There was a Rift there, too, that opened up—or was discovered, I was never sure which—by this guy called Ordaal."

"The bounty hunter?"

"You know him?"

"We have had dealings," I confirm.

"I ignored the feelings at first. I thought they'd go away—I mean, hell, what reason did I have to go chasing after a dream in another dimension? But they got stronger. In the end, I had no choice, I mean that's how I felt. I took off in the *Sunrunner*, and just hoped for the best. And when the feelings led me to the Time Traveler, that's when I knew for sure they were real, that he was guiding my actions. Now, I feel—I *know*—that somehow he's waiting for me, on the other side of that Rift. I have to go to him!"

I choose not to contest Archer's unlikely beliefs again. Partly, this is because it would be a waste of time, but I'm also beginning to see how he has reached the conclusions he has. "You should return to your work," I say quietly. "You have a great deal to learn." Fortunately, the boy learns fast. I estimate that, in less than half an hour, he will understand the workings of the probe, and its control computer, at least as well as anybody but me.

A wave of weariness breaks over me, and I close my eyes. Behind my eyelids, red and silver patterns coalesce, and I am confronted by the familiar image of the Time Traveler, my lifelong companion—the stranger whom I came to think of as a friend, but now suspect could be my greatest enemy. "What haven't you told me?" I yell at him with the full force of my mind. "Why are you still keeping secrets from me?"

As always, the enigmatic figure gives no answer.

"I won't do it, you can't make me do it!"

Koriah lets out a long-suffering sigh, trying and failing to restrain Ogwen as he marches past her again. The bureaucrat's words are gabbled, eyes wild and red-rimmed, hands a flurry of motion as if he can't decide what to do with them. He makes another sudden turn and approaches the Galactic Defender again.

She steps into his path and waves a laser pistol under his nose—one of several from the *Sunrunner's* stores. "You're being stupid, Ogwen."

"I don't want to fight. I can't! I can't even use one of those things, and anyway, Acroyear said I could coordinate the defense from here."

"We don't know what the Centauri will throw at us. If they get past us, if they make it here to the bridge, you need to be able to defend yourself."

He rounds on her, voice rising in pitch. "If they get to the bridge, we've already lost! But if I'm not armed, if they can see I'm no threat, maybe *they won't kill me, maybe they'll*–"

"Ogwen!" Koriah has him by the shoulders, shaking him. *"Ogwen!"*

He slumps into one of the seats on the operations platform; it spins a quarter-turn under his sudden weight. He's breathing deeply, in and out through his nose, trying to bring himself back under control, to conquer the effects of the stimulant that Koriah pumped into him.

She leans over him, speaking through clenched teeth. "The Centauri aren't interested in accepting your surrender. Even if they were, their troops are likely to be drones, programmed for nothing more than mindless slaughter. A laser pistol could give you the seconds you need to get out of here. It could save your life!"

"For how long?" asks Ogwen, suddenly melancholy as the drug continues to play with his chemical balance. "I've been staring death in the face for days. I've had enough. Maybe it'd be better to get it over with. At least, then, it'd only hurt for a second."

"Take the weapon, Ogwen," growls Acroyear, marching onto the bridge and immediately sizing up the situation, "or I will personally run my sword through your spineless body."

Ogwen glares mutinously at him, but doesn't argue; apparently, he's not as prepared to die as he insists. With bad grace, he snatches the laser pistol from Koriah. She curls her lower lip, apparently disgruntled at having been undermined. If Acroyear notices, he gives no sign of it. Accompanying him are Knave, three Biotrons, and—to my concern—Veelum. The old man, Acroyear tells Koriah, volunteered his services as soon as he heard about the imminent attack.

I lean forward, and speak through Unit #34. "No, that is not acceptable. I need him."

With an arched eyebrow, Veelum responds, "Wroje can operate the computer as well as I, and you have Archer to plot your course now. I'm sure you can spare me for a while."

"I can't lose you, Veelum!"

Koriah pushes him aside angrily and addresses me through the Biotron. "If we can't defend this station for want of numbers, Karza, we all lose!"

Veelum's eyes alight upon the small pile of laser

pistols, which lies atop the cryo-crypt. He takes one and straps it determinedly to his arm. "I won't hide in my room, Karza. So long as I have the strength to fire one of these things, I'll fight to protect my friends."

"Then I instruct you," I bark, with a petulance that doesn't become me, "all of you, to protect Veelum at all costs. Give your life for his, if you must. The project depends upon it!"

"Talk to me, Karza."

The request comes as a surprise. Sweat beads Archer's brow. The rigid posture of his body, hunched over the computer's main console, further betrays his tension. He sent the probe into the Rift some two and a half minutes ago. Wroje is watching, offering quiet guidance whenever the boy hesitates. Unit #35 stands by the anchor line to retrieve the probe manually in case of trouble—although, by then, it will almost certainly be too late.

I patched the computer's visual output through to my main screen: A tiny red spot, indicating the probe, inches its way into a cluster of green lines so tightly entwined that I can't see a way through them. I, too, have shuffled forward in my seat, wracked with suspense. Archer's hands jerk uncertainly across the controls, as if each move he makes is the result of a huge effort of concentration. With each passing second, I have wrestled with the thought of aborting the mission—this was a mistake, he isn't ready—but somehow, incredibly, the probe remains intact, and threads its way onward.

"I can only do this if I rely on instinct," pleads Archer. "I'm thinking too hard, trying to second-guess myself. I need you to distract me. Please!"

Not without misgivings, I cast around for something to say. A number of questions hurtle to the forefront of my mind—and one in particular—but I don't want to provide *too* big a distraction. Carefully, I venture, "You have met Koriah before, I assume?"

"No. I told you, I'm new to this neck of the cosmos."

"And yet, you told your companions that she could be trusted."

A tiny hesitation. "She's a Galactic Defender."

"I think there's more to it than that. If you haven't encountered her in this reality, then perhaps in the old one? Your dreams—your visions of the Time Traveler's continuum."

Archer clamps his mouth shut. Perhaps I, too, should say no more, but his hands are beginning to move more fluidly, more confidently, and the probe indicator is picking up speed. I push the computer feed to one side and bring the laboratory onto the main screen, to study the boy's reactions more closely.

"You say you've been having these dreams for many weeks. You must have seen a great deal of that other reality."

"Bits and pieces," he admits. "Just snatches here and there, like...like buried memories, slowly coming to the surface."

"You seem reluctant to discuss it."

"It's not that. It's just..." Archer's hands are shaking again. He stabs at a key, then catches his breath and flurries to reverse his mistake.

"The Time Traveler's universe must have been quite similar to our own," I remark, changing the subject tangentially.

"What makes you say that?"

"You saw both Acroyear and the Vaerian in your

visions. A remarkable coincidence, would you not say, that you should meet them both in the flesh thereafter?"

"I went looking for Acroyear. We were...I remembered us being comrades, friends. We fought side by side. I thought he could help me."

"You weren't looking for Koriah, and yet you found her, too. How many familiar faces have you seen since leaving your homeworld?"

"What are you suggesting? Don't you believe me?"

"Oh, I believe you," I say quickly, before I cause another accident. "I'm simply musing aloud about the workings of time. The Traveler's presence has changed billions upon billions of events—some important, some barely measurable. And yet, Acroyear is still here, Knave is still here, Koriah is still here, and all of them still recognizable to you."

"I see what you mean," says Archer, more thoughtful now than wary, and making good progress with the probe as a consequence. "I guess, when you think about it, the odds that all those people would still be born, that they'd be the same, that we'd find each other..."

"One might almost believe there was some kind of intelligence at work—a guiding hand, trying to push history back onto its right course, as far as it will go."

"The Time Traveler?"

"Or time itself, trying to heal the damage that has been done."

"You believe that's possible?"

"I have to, otherwise travel into the past couldn't be undertaken, without all being destroyed by paradox."

"I guess not."

"Of course, not everything is unchanged. You ought

to be wary, Archer, of judging people in this reality by half-remembered experiences of them in another."

"The Time Traveler hasn't led me wrong so far," he says guardedly. "Acroyear is still the best man you could hope to have on your side in a fight; Knave still knows how to lift our morale..." A little more subdued, he continues, "Ordaal was still a mercenary, interested in no more than the bottom line; Nova still a sadist..."

"And Koriah?" I ask softly.

"In the old timeline," says Archer, "she was the last of the Galactic Defenders. It didn't matter. She stayed true to their ideals. I didn't know her for long, but I know this: She risked her life, and damn near lost it, to save mine."

"So, in this timeline, you trust her with your life."

"Yes!"

"Even though you know there's a murderer on board."

"It couldn't have been her," Archer says confidently.

"I'm certain that, in fact, it was."

"No!"

"She had the opportunity, and she had the motive."

"What you said to her, about feeling guilty..."

"Note that she didn't challenge me. She didn't ask me what I meant by that comment, because she already knew, and she didn't want to air the subject in front of you."

"That's not proof!"

"Ask her! She's on the bridge; you can contact her through Unit #35. Ask her if she was responsible for the death of LeHayn."

"I don't have to ask her," insists Archer. "She couldn't...she wouldn't..."

"You don't know Koriah, Archer. You only think you do."

"I...I..." Archer grits his teeth, and shakes his head as if in pain, his hands hovering uncertainly over the controls. "I can't go on. I have to pull the probe out."

"There's no time!" I bark automatically.

"We don't have a choice! I'm losing it! If I don't pull out now, you can scratch one probe from your inventory."

The red indicator light is already moving backward as the probe retraces its steps. I bite my tongue, annoyed with myself. I couldn't resist the temptation to rile the boy, and this intolerable delay is the result. Still, I tell myself, the probe must have collected a great deal of useful data in the last few minutes—almost a day's worth. This way, we can download into the computer, keep it safe, before we venture any further.

"Karza, what happened to Wroje?"

Unit #35 lost sight of her, his attention trained on Archer. With a start, I have him pull back and scan the laboratory, but the boy is right: Wroje is no longer present.

I feel a familiar churning in my stomach, although I don't know what harm she, of all people, could do. It is simply that I dislike losing control; I hate the feeling that things are happening on my own station of which I am unaware. Fortunately, a Biotron unit saw Wroje shutting herself into her quarters a short time ago.

Slowly, I realize what I said in front of her, without even thinking about the effect it would have, and I curse my indiscretion again. Still, Wroje is redundant to the project now; Archer can cope without her. No harm has been done, other than to her feelings.

The Rift flares bright and green on my main screen, and I am drawn once more into its depths. I remember what Archer said about the light calling to him, and I, too, feel that tug on my heart. But I lack his certainty of a presence behind the light, his belief in a tangible connection to the Time Traveler. Perhaps that's why I told him about Koriah, why I tried to shake one of his certainties: because I find myself jealous of him.

The Time Traveler hasn't chosen him—the rational part of my brain is sure of that. So, why does the same anguished question keep running through my head? Why do I keep asking myself: Why Ryan Archer, why this slip of a boy, and not me?

They emerge from the lead Battle Cruiser, an hour to the second after my last contact with the Centauri. Antrons, as I might have expected–purple skin, tiny Sharkos fins jutting out from behind their shoulders, six sinewy limbs each ending in four claws. Their heads are lumpen and bald, blank eyes devoid of intellect, mouths leering open as if they aren't quite large enough to contain their dagger-pointed mandibles. There are at least a hundred of the creatures. They swarm across the void toward us, propelling themselves with the thrashing of their limbs. They look like they're swimming.

Knave watches through the bridge's forward portal, his dark eyes glistening as he shakes his head and murmurs to himself, "Antrons. Why does it have to be Antrons?"

The rest of my would-be defenders are similarly frozen by the sight of the forces set against them. They don't act until the first Antron hits the screen in front of them, limbs splayed, and sets about burrowing its way through the barricade with claws and teeth.

Calmly, Acroyear gives the order, "Lower the shield!"

Ogwen, seated at the main control panel with the others ranged behind him, is paralyzed, staring. He doesn't respond until Koriah snaps his name. He stabs at a button, and a thick sheet of steel drops slowly in front of the wide portal. The bridge is safe. Would that the rest of the station could be similarly reinforced.

There is a short, heavy silence, then Acroyear asks, "What are they doing?"

Koriah inspects the readouts over Ogwen's shoulder. "According to external sensors, they've split into three groups. One outside the hangar, another coming up from the recycling bay, the third...they're still clambering over the hull, I think they're headed for...yes, yes, the starboard habitation corridor."

"They've targeted our weakest points," growls Veelum.

"Makes sense," says Kellesh, almost admiringly. "It's what I'd do."

"Don't forget," says Koriah, tightlipped, "we've prepared for this. We're ready!"

"Ogwen," barks Acroyear, "you know what to do."

"We're relying on you," Koriah reminds him, "to make sure the station doesn't depressurize. Acroyear doesn't think you can do it. Prove him wrong!"

Ogwen nods, his expression doleful. He starts work at his console, as Acroyear turns to the others. "Koriah, Knave, you take the lower decks; Veelum and Kellesh, the living quarters. I'll defend the hangar bay myself."

They split into their assigned teams, and leave at an urgent trot; Acroyear has had them for only an hour, but they're responding like a well-drilled squad. I allow myself to believe that there is hope for them—for all of us—after all.

The Biotrons, who had been standing silently in

shadow at the rear of the bridge, peel off and follow them. Only one remains to watch as Ogwen glances back over his shoulder, then tears the laser pistol from his arm, resentfully, and hurls it into a corner.

"When first we spoke," I say, "you claimed the Time Traveler had made a mistake, that he wanted you to correct it."

Archer gives a distracted murmur of confirmation.

"Do you believe he wishes to restore his timeline?"

"Maybe."

"And you would do that for him, if you knew how? You would sacrifice the life you have, everything you have known, for the world of your dreams."

"I didn't say that," protests Archer. "I don't know."

I am concentrating on him, in the center of my bank of monitors. I am trying to ignore the fleeting purple shapes that flicker around him. Many of the station's external cameras are non-functional, and few can be trained upon the hull—so, other than the odd glimpse of a claw or a misshapen head, I have to rely on sensor data to track the Antrons' progress. I see, to my dismay, that they have almost gnawed their way into the hangar bay.

"The Time Traveler's reality—was it a better place than this?" I ask.

Archer thinks long and hard before he gives an answer. "Some people thought it was."

"But you aren't so sure." Archer doesn't respond. Narrowing my eyes, I prompt him, "You have endured the misery of Micropolis, encountered the Reptos, been prey to mercenaries, and now you are threatened by another malignant product of the chaos that infests this galaxy. For all the efforts of the Galactic Defenders, and those like them, the rule of law means nothing here; such monsters can do as they wish, because nobody has the power or the courage to stop them. We need guidance—the firm hand of leadership."

"You had leaders once. Were things any better, then?"

"The Pharoids were weak, unwilling to do what had to be done."

"Then, you'd rather the Emperors hadn't fallen?"

I laugh. "I took the last Emperor's life myself. He was a fool."

"So, let me guess: This leader you think we need—that'd be you, right?"

"Why not? I understand the patterns of cause and effect better than anyone. I could create order. I could design machines to enrich the lives of my subjects."

"Yeah? And what about those who didn't want to be your 'subjects'?"

"There was an Emperor, then? In the Time Traveler's reality?"

He has all but told me what I wanted to know. Realizing this, he hesitates, but only for an instant. Warm to his theme, he stumbles on, "Yeah, sure, there was an Emperor—and he was the biggest monster of them all!"

"Did he bring order?" I ask eagerly.

"If you want to call it that. He was a tyrant! He wanted control over everything we did, everything we said—and he almost had it. And, yeah, he brought progress—he made the rocket tubes run on time—but I saw the other side of his regime. I saw the cells, the people murdered for associating with suspected dissidents, and I saw the byproducts of the Baron's experiments on races he considered inferior." Archer shudders at the memory.

"Perhaps he simply believed, as I do, that sacrifices must be made for the greater good."

"And I bet that's what the Emperor before him believed, too. I bet, when he wiped out your people, the Pharoids, he thought he was doing it for 'the greater good.' Not so cool when you're one of the sacrifices, though, is it?"

I bristle at the accusation, tightening my fingers around the arms of my chair to keep from trembling in anger. I must not respond. I have said too much already; Archer is upset again, the movements of the probe becoming spasmodic in response.

I search for another topic of conversation, something to calm him down, but then I find my eyes focusing again upon the virtual map of the time stream, and I see something that, in the heat of debate, I hadn't seen before. "Archer...what do you think you're doing?"

"What does it look like?" His voice is strained again, his confidence lessening as he returns his full attention to his task. "I'm trying to keep your probe in one piece!"

"You are meant to be guiding it into the past!"

"Isn't that what I'm doing?"

"You are moving across time, not along it." My voice has a faintly hysterical edge. "You are no nearer to your destination than when you started."

He risks a quick glance at the map in front of him, taking his eyes off the controls. "I don't understand, I thought..."

"Take a ninety degree turn downtime."

"I can't, I...I don't know how!"

"Then reverse your course. I won't risk another probe for nothing!"

"This is what the Time Traveler wants. I can feel it!"

"Pull that probe out, Archer!" I yell. "Now!"

Too late, I realize how flustered the boy has become. I need to calm myself, to offer him reassurance, but I'm lost for words. And then the Astro Station shudders.

It takes me a moment to realize what has happened. An alarm klaxon is sounding, but the import of that washes over me, as if my mind is protecting me from it. The Antrons have broken through the transparent hull of the hangar bay. Air slams into them, dislodging several of the creatures and sending them tumbling end over end. The station was buffeted by the initial recoil—its gyroscopes should have compensated, but with a chunk taken out of its right side and its bowels ruptured, the structure was already unstable.

The red pinpoint of the probe on my monitor flares and dies.

The station's self-repair systems groan into sluggish action, pumping white sealant foam into the hull breach. The invaders are already scrambling on board, my control board lighting up intruder alerts by the dozen. An external camera gives me a clear view of the hindmost creature, blasted farther than its comrades by the out-rush of air and floundering in space. It recovers itself, flips over, and scuttles forward again. It dives into the white foam even as it fills the station's wound, but it's trapped as the substance hardens around it.

The other Antrons have crossed the hangar, and are scrabbling at the internal bulkhead. Beyond this, through the eyes of Units #34 and #40, I see Acroyear standing like a statue, sword ready. "As soon as the hangar re-pressurizes," he instructs Ogwen through a wrist-mounted communicator, "I want you to open this door!" I will get my wish to see him in action, but I fear that even he will be overwhelmed.

Elsewhere, more Antrons have swarmed into the open starboard habitation corridor. Tracking their progress from the bridge, Ogwen has trapped them between two bulkheads, but they don't care about turning back, only going forward. They must be clambering on top of each other, to attack the surface of the obstacle before them in as many places as my sensors suggest. They'll have burrowed their way through it soon—though they'll find Veelum, Kellesh, and two Biotrons waiting for them.

The third Antron squadron has done as Acroyear and Koriah predicted: Penetrating the station through the holes left by the detonation of the recycling tanks, they have taken the path of least resistance. They swarm through the battered service elevator and up the shaft, their tapered digits sinking into the walls to create handholds for them. Once again, Ogwen has closed shutters above and below them so that, when they dig through the former, they won't expose the rest of the station to space. Koriah, Knave, and two more Biotrons have wrenched open the gate to the main deck, and are waiting with weapons raised for the first Antron head to show itself below.

That klaxon is still shrieking, the sound of it like a drill penetrating my eardrums.

Wroje has just left her quarters, face streaked with tears, the skin around her eyes blotchy. She walks straight-backed, with a determined stride that I haven't seen from her before.

Archer is on his feet, his expression taut with anguish, but he doesn't know what to do. Unit #35 is hauling on the anchor line, and I feel numb with dread.

It takes the sight of the smoldering, twisted probe emerging from the Rift's light to bring it home to me. I knew my hopes were desperate, foolish, but I clung to them all the same. Now, the last grains of those hopes slip through my fingers, and I'm left feeling empty. I must face what I have long shied away from: The project, my life, is over. There is no time.

I clench my fists, throw back my head, and let out a curdling, keening scream that can be heard across the station.

CHAPTER
SIX

The beleaguered hangar door groans aside in fits and starts. Behind it, a pyramid of Antrons collapses, and the first of the creatures spill, startled, into the station proper.

Acroyear is among them in an instant. His flame-edged sword leaves flaring trails on my monitors as it rises and falls, sometimes cutting through three bodies in a single swipe. Even as they are decapitated, the Antrons remain mute. They show no pain, no fear, no hesitation, just a single-minded determination to advance. I despair at the speed with which they adapt to their changed circumstances, rushing their new enemy as one, heedless of what might happen to their front ranks. Acroyear can't repel them all; in a moment, he is lost beneath a mass of purple muscle. The Antrons are clawing, biting, trying to pry his armor from his body; I know enough about his kind to know that, if they succeed, it will be the end for him.

Fortunately, he isn't alone. Units #34 and #40, ignored for as long as they remained still, step forward in unison. Swathes of creatures fall under their radiation fire, bodies blackening, dark purple pus seeping out of their joints.

Without seeming to communicate in any way, they divide their forces. A dozen Antrons leap onto Unit #40, bearing him down under their combined weight. His video feed goes off-line as his head is torn from his neck. Through the eyes of Unit #34, I see that the fallen Biotron is still struggling, arms thrashing in a blind, automotive response.

At least the pressure has been taken off Acroyear. His muscles rippling beneath the skintight parts of his flux armor—in which, I notice, there are now several ragged tears—he throws Antrons from him until he has room to swing his sword again.

I can see into the hangar bay, over his shoulder. A white sealant stain spreads across the clear hull, blotting out the stars. Trapped in the center of this is the lone Antron straggler, pedaling the air in frustration with the only one of its limbs that isn't held. Its mouth works ceaselessly, its mandibles clacking together, but it can't turn its head far enough to attack the trap that holds it. The sight brings a shiver to my spine.

Ryan Archer sits hunched in a chair, cradling the half-disintegrated probe in his lap, staring at if as if he can't believe what he has done.

"Antrons," spits Knave, peering gloomily down the service elevator shaft. "I hoped I'd never see their kind again."

Koriah has no words; she resorts to an awkward, sympathetic smile.

"I shouldn't hate them so much," sighs Knave. "Most of them didn't have a choice in what they became. It's nobody's fault that we Vaerians were born with a—how did that biosmith put it?—a 'uniquely adaptable cellular structure.' If it hadn't been for the circus, if I hadn't had the dumb luck to get out, chances are I'd have ended up the same way. I'd have sold my body, and my soul, to the crime syndicates to survive a few more miserable years."

"Seeing them must bring back some bad memories."

"That's only the half of it. It isn't the past that scares me, Koriah. It isn't even the future—I've always taken that as it comes. Ever since we arrived on this station, people have been talking about time travel, about other realities, about what we could have been. Well, that's my alternative reality, right down there. That's me, scratching my way through that bulkhead: a lobotomized zombie!"

"I don't believe that! Archer knew you in another timeline, right?"

"So I'm led to believe."

"And he knew you as the man you are now—as Ganam Jafain, not as some soulless monster. That can't be a coincidence. That isn't just 'dumb luck.' You're a survivor, Knave! Whatever the circumstances, you'd never have let them turn you into…into *that*."

Sentimental rubbish, of course. Another of my regrets is that, in my long life, I never found the time to study the Vaerians. I recognized the potential they had as genetically modified soldiers long ago, although I would have left them with some intelligence. Mindless drones have their attraction, but an inability to take the initiative will always undermine them.

I shouldn't complain—I'm counting on that weakness to save me. Not that it matters. I feel no connection to the events unfolding on my monitors. I no longer care if my defenders win or lose; they can only delay the inevitable. They can buy me a few more hours, but what would I do with them? For the first time in my life, I am without purpose.

"You know there's nothing left of them, don't you?" Koriah says to Knave, gently. "They aren't your people any more—they're just killing machines!"

The Vaerian nods, and responds in a quiet voice, "I know."

And, at that moment, a single word rings out along the corridor behind them: "*Koriah!*"

I catch my breath. I didn't recognize the voice at first; rarely before have I heard it raised to more than a whisper. Wroje's eyes are aflame and fixed on the Galactic Defender. Koriah frowns, sensing something amiss but not realizing the danger she's in.

Wroje's purposeful stride breaks into a run, and then a charge. I watch with detached fascination as the tattoo on her neck glows white, even through her clothing, and her body begins to transform, like putty molded by unseen hands.

She has unleashed the rage within her, at last—but I can see from her expression that she has not lost control; rather, she has made a cold, rational choice to do this.

Wroje's smock tears down the side as the lower part of her body expands. Two extra legs have grown out of her hips, and a tail swishes angrily behind her. For an instant, she resembles nothing more than a Centaurus, her torso protruding from the body of a quadruped, the symbol of Oberon glowing brighter than ever. Then, the last part of her that was recognizably Wroje is gone, shrinking down into the creature's elongating neck. Her shocking violet hair fades, and grows into a mane, and I am looking at the tattoo made real: A proud white steed, galloping to the attack.

She launches herself at Koriah, her eyes red, her nostrils flared. The girl is caught by surprise, still stunned by what she has just witnessed. Her uniform helmet is only half-formed, and the creature that was Wroje strikes through the soft liquid metal with her front hooves, landing a glancing blow to her head.

She reels, and staggers backward into the elevator shaft. Almost without my seeing him move, Knave is behind her, catching her and simultaneously pushing her to safety. "Did you know she was a Panzeroid?" he cries.

"News to me," responds Koriah, tightlipped.

The Vaerian is in Wroje's path now, but she is more than willing to go through him to reach her true target. He throws up two of his four arms, and her hooves slam into his laser pistols, denting them. From behind him, Koriah recovers her wits and fires with both barrels. Wroje shrugs off the blasts, only appearing further enraged.

My Biotrons haven't yet joined the fight. There are three units present now, #23 having followed Wroje here; each has asked for instructions, needing my authorization to act against a crew member even in such an altered form. I open a voice link to them, but close it again. A certain voyeuristic part of me wants to see how this scenario will play itself out.

"Knave—look out!"

The Antrons have broken through the shutter. The first of them are emerging from the elevator shaft, their claws already snatching at Koriah. Thanks to her warning, Knave is able to squirm out of their reach. With an impressive leap, he flips over Wroje's finned head, and lands in a crouch behind her. He spins around, brings up his pistols and aims for the back of her head, hoping to distract her--but only one of his damaged weapons fires. Wroje tosses back her head and lets out a whinnying howl of pain, but she doesn't turn. She remains intent upon Koriah.

The Biotrons, faced with an unambiguous enemy at last, lurch into action. They fire their blasters in tight beams, picking off Antrons one by one, but only when they can target them without risking harm to anybody else. It isn't easy: Like their comrades elsewhere, the Antrons fight at the closest possible quarters. Koriah, already injured by Wroje, is borne down and buried. The snarling Panzeroid lashes out with teeth and hooves, trying to get to the Galactic Defender through the creatures—it looks like Koriah might actually benefit from Wroje's animosity toward her. But suddenly the Antrons are atop her too, climbing onto her back where she can't reach them, pulling at her lustrous mane and sinking their mandibles into her neck.

The Antrons have focused their attentions upon Acroyear's sword, which has claimed so many casualties. They may not be smart, but evidently they have rudimentary reasoning skills. They gnaw at the warrior's hand, prying the sword's hilt from his fingers, and they don't care how many of them taste its blazing edge in the process.

Suddenly, they have their prize. Acroyear's weapon drifts away from him on a purple tide, but it proves too heavy for the Antrons to carry. It drops into the throng, and the creatures scramble to escape its fire. Acroyear seizes his opportunity to lunge after it, but his enemies are everywhere, tripping him, blinding him.

A sudden movement draws my eye back to my main screen.

Archer is crossing the lab, headed for the outer door. "Stop him!" I instruct tersely.

Unit #35 steps into the boy's path. He tries to go around him, but the Biotron extends a metal arm as a barrier. Frustrated, he appeals to me, "There's nothing I can do here now. My friends are out there, fighting for us all. I should be with them!"

"Do you realize what you've done?" I growl. It is the first time I've spoken to him since the accident, the first time I have been able to bring myself to address him.

Archer has the decency to look shamefaced, at least. "I'm sorry. I know I let you down."

"You have done more than that, boy!" I roar. "You have failed every being that lives, that ever lived or might have lived, and this is all you have to say for yourself?"

"If you hadn't wound me so tight, if the station hadn't shook when it did…"

I ignore his pathetic excuses. With a flick of my wrist, I summon the least of my mechanical servants.

"You disobeyed me!" I snarl. "You sent the probe along the most treacherous path possible, and with no intention of finding the past. Your arrogance has doomed us!"

"The Time Traveler—" he bleats.

"I will hear no more about the Time Traveler! He doesn't speak to you, Archer; he never has. The results of your scan confirm it. The ability to intuit the future, to predict the outcome of your choices, is intrinsic to you."

"What…what are you saying? What do you…?"

Calming myself down, I explain, "You have a unique gift, Ryan Archer. Your brain is unusually attuned to the basic structures of reality. Instinctively, you sense the patterns of time: You know how the threads fit together, and where they will lead."

"You're saying I'm some kind of fortune-teller? That's crazy!"

"You do not literally see the future—at least not under normal circumstances. Your gift is confined to a subconscious part of your mind. You simply know, without understanding why, which course to take, which threads you have to pull to create the pattern most advantageous to your needs. You will agree, I think, that you have clearly demonstrated this ability."

"Under normal circumstances?" repeats Archer.

"Time is in a state of disrepair. Its patterns are unraveling, unreadable. It is little wonder you have felt confused. You've been predicting patterns that are no longer there, seeing futures that can no longer be—and those futures have begun to intrude upon your dreams. In your search for an explanation, you've fixated upon the most prominent image in those dreams—the man who, your senses are telling you, is the cause of the discontinuity."

"So, he's not real after all?" I know how Archer feels. I have destroyed the single certainty that has kept him going. He feels like I did, when first I discovered the cancer in the time stream—and, before that, when the Emperor killed my father. That's why I didn't tell him any of this earlier; he needed to have a clear head to operate the probe.

My gaze flickers to the gold and silver containment suit. "No, Archer, the Time Traveler is real—it is your claimed link with him that is fantasy."

"But I knew him. I met him, I'm sure of it!"

"I don't doubt it. Were you not destined to encounter the Time Traveler, in the old reality, you would not see him in your visions now. That's why

I can't let you join your friends, Archer, why you mustn't put yourself at risk. Your mind holds the key. Only you can unlock the Traveler's secrets, and show us how this sorry state of affairs came to be."

"But…but what good would it do? It wouldn't save us. It wouldn't change anything."

"It would satisfy my curiosity," I growl.

The door to the laboratory swishes open, to reveal the peeling bright hues of the Cosmobot. Its arms are outstretched, and a long black box rests upon its clamp-like hands, nestled in a tangle of wires. Protruding from the top of the box are two silver control rods, tapering like horns. Archer can't know what it is, but he blanches at the sight of it. His intuition again, or simply a reaction to the tone of my voice and the device's stark, straight-edged design?

"I've told you everything I know," he insists. Amusingly, he seems to have mistaken the device for an instrument of torture—and he doesn't doubt that I would employ such a thing.

"You came face to face with the Time Traveler. I must know what happened."

"I don't know! I told you, I can't get past that point. I've tried!"

"The information may be stored in your subconscious. Failing that, your extraordinary mind is surely capable of finding it, with the right…stimulus."

Archer eyes the device suspiciously, beginning to see its true purpose. "Will…will it hurt?"

"Yes."

"I don't know about this, Karza. I mean, sure, I want to know where the Time Traveler came from, as much as you do, but we can worry about that later. It'll come to me! I'm sure it will. We don't need any machine, we just need a little more time."

I laugh out loud at that. Then I instruct Unit #35 and the Cosmobot to bring Archer to me.

The first Antrons are breaking out of the starboard habitation corridor. They squeeze their curious heads through the holes they've gnawed and clawed in the emergency bulkhead, to be met by a fusillade of laser pistol fire from Veelum and Kellesh. It doesn't deter them. The creatures clamber eagerly over their own dead. They continue to attack the bulkhead until it all but disintegrates, and a tidal wave of purple comes crashing through it.

With admirable aplomb, the two men follow Acroyear and Koriah's plan, withdrawing and allowing the Antrons to follow them. Therefore, several dozen of the creatures are trapped in one stretch of corridor when Biotron Units #31 and #32 appear to each side of them.

For several seconds, all I can see on two screens is a bright green glow, in which the faint impression of flesh being stripped from twisted, crumbling skeletons may only be a trick of my own imagination.

Archer puts up a fight. Unit #35 tries to restrain him, but as before, the boy senses his opponent's movements before he has made them. Still, the Biotron won't let him reach the door—and, outnumbered, Archer can't stay out of his clutches for long.

The Cosmobot joins the fray. Archer leaps out of the way of another lunge by the Biotron, and straight into a flailing yellow arm, which strikes across his temple.

"Don't damage his head!" I yell through my voice link. "Or the machine," I add, wincing as the black box slips out of the clumsy robot's hands to hit the floor with a resounding clang.

Reeling, Archer stumbles into the Biotron's grasp, and two steel hands tighten around his shoulders. No matter how he kicks and squeals, he can't tear himself free.

Wroje's transformation is working to our advantage after all. No matter how many Antrons pile on top of her, they can't keep her down. She bucks and kicks and sends them flying away, only to right themselves and dive back into the melee.

This gives Knave something of a respite. He uses it to set his sights on Koriah. He wades toward her, kicking Antrons aside. Several purple heads turn toward him, but none of the creatures attack. I think they're confused by the Vaerian's resemblance to their own kind.

He reaches the Galactic Defender and begins to pull attackers from her, hurling them away with as much force as he can muster. An Antron squirms about in his grasp and tries to bite him, its mandibles snapping together an inch from his throat. Alarmed, he drops the creature, but it lands on its feet and is leaping at him again in an instant. Knave brings up his functioning laser pistol just in time and drills a hole through its head—in the process, erasing any doubt that its comrades may still have had about him.

They come at him individually at first, each distracted from its previous victim by the enemy that is suddenly in their midst. Knave greets them with a flurry of limbs—twisting, gripping, throwing—denying them a chance to fasten themselves onto him. I seem to recall that the Vaerians' four arms, and their natural agility, make them ideal studies in the so-called "lost" martial art of Laen Ka. Antron after Antron hits the unyielding hull of the Astro Station, sometimes breaking their bodies and sliding into bloodied heaps at its base.

More and more of the creatures are turning to Knave, now, but they pay the price for presenting their backs to Wroje, when the Panzeroid's vengeful hooves stave in their skulls. Meanwhile, Biotron Units #23, 30 and #39 are still picking off any Antron foolish enough to leave itself exposed to their radiation blasters.

Koriah, no longer a threat, has been abandoned, as no doubt Knave intended. Unnoticed by all but me, she lies in a crooked shape on the floor, bleeding into her helmet.

Incredibly, the Antrons are still surging forward, through the Biotrons' green fire. They pick up the blasted corpses of their fallen, using them as shields. As if connected by one instinctual group mind, they focus upon one of their two attackers.

Unit #31 makes to back away, to allow Veelum and Kellesh to fire their laser pistols from behind him as planned, but the Antrons are too fast. Suddenly, they're atop him, boosting each other up his metal casing, pinning his arms to his sides, trying to twist his head from its neck socket. Unit #32 holds his fire, for fear of harming his colleague. At the opposite end of the corridor, Veelum and Kellesh, neither of them warriors, exchange helpless looks.

"Don't let up! The robot's done for, anyway." Kellesh's voice, coming even as I was about to take control of Unit #32's voice box to make the same point.

Veelum's only response is a grim nod. Four laser

pistols flash, so brightly and repeatedly that Unit #32 is almost blinded. His eyes polarize in response. By the time my decrepit monitor adjusts to the change in lighting, Unit #31 is down, his silver head held aloft in the hands of four victorious Antrons, and the rest of the creatures are swarming down the corridor toward their next targets.

Unit #32 fires his weapon again, and more of the invaders die in eerie silence. The blast, however, is not as fierce as usual. His ammunition is spent.

Veelum and Kellesh run for it, and the Antrons stream after them. They round a corner, leaving my sight, but I hear Kellesh yelling to Ogwen over his wrist communicator, instructing him to lower another bulkhead as soon as the pair have passed beneath it.

I know the layout of this station like the back of my hand. They won't make it in time.

The Cosmobot pushes Archer onto his knees in front of me. Unit #35 enters the chamber behind it, carrying the mind probe device in his safer hands. He offers it to me, and I take it and begin to untangle its wiring.

"There's no need for this, Karza," insists Archer, pale with fear and with the pain of metal fingers digging into his shoulder blades.

"The less you resist," I inform him tersely, "the less it will hurt. Hold his head still." This last is directed at the Cosmobot, which releases Archer's left shoulder and takes a rough hold of his chin. At the ends of two wires, I have found a pair of needles, so thin as to be barely visible in the dim light. Archer's fearful gaze locks onto them. "I am about to insert these sensor devices into the frontal lobes of your brain," I tell him. "I suggest you don't struggle. Should my aim be even a millimeter off, I may cause irreparable damage."

He freezes, teeth clenched in anticipation as I lean forward and carefully position the needle points to each of his temples. I push them home simultaneously, sinking them into the boy's head up to the wires that link them to the black box in my lap. Archer won't have felt any pain, but he winces, belatedly, with the realization of what I have just done. He remains paralyzed, as if fearing that any motion might cause the slivers of metal to move inside him, to tear through tissue. The Cosmobot transfers its grip back to his shoulder.

I activate the device, and Archer shudders as an electrical tingle leaps through his brain. I unthread another wire and hand a two-pronged jack to Unit #35, instructing him to plug it into my communications array. The monitor that once displayed the live feed from Unit #40 lights up with a dancing, crackling static pattern; I move it to the central screen and peer closely, eagerly at it. I can see shapes shifting in the gray snowstorm—sometimes, I think I can make out a face, or the silhouette of a man, but whenever I try to focus upon it, it shifts and blurs and scatters into random dots.

I twist the horn-shaped controls on the top of the black box. "The device is calibrating itself to your brainwave patterns," I tell Archer. "The process will take a few minutes—but then we shall see exactly what you have been keeping from me."

"Acroyear! Acroyear! Can you hear me? Veelum and Kellesh are dead. There's a squadron of Antrons on their way up to the bridge. *Acroyear!*"

My two most faithful employees. An hour ago, news of their passing would have been devastating; now it hardly matters. I see their bodies on the feed from

Unit #32, as it lumbers past them in hopeless pursuit of the creatures that pulled them apart. I feel nothing.

Through Unit #36's eyes, I see Ogwen on the bridge, pink and sweating, squealing into the communications console, and my only thought is that I'm glad the Antrons have prioritized the bridge over the main laboratory and my adjoining chamber.

Acroyear is no position to help the harassed bureaucrat. I can't pinpoint him at first, smothered as he is by Antron bodies—but, like a juggernaut, he keeps on going, and the odds against him are slowly but surely lessening. I wonder how much longer his considerable strength will sustain him; already, I detect a certain weariness on his part, whereas the Antrons appear as fresh and eager for the fight as ever.

The creatures, however, have made one fateful error. They are all but ignoring Unit #34, convinced that the Biotron is the lesser threat to them now that his blaster is exhausted. They are caught unprepared when he marches forward, seizes two Antrons by their fins, hoists them above his head and slams them into each other. Still, the rest of the creatures continue to concentrate on Acroyear, and their efforts pay off: like a mighty oak tree cleaved by an axe, he is finally toppled. He breaks his fall with hands and knees, and a horde of delighted Antrons leap onto his back, pinning him down. In a moment, he will be buried again, and probably suffocated—but, in that moment, Unit #34 reaches the energy sword.

He flips it into the air with a blue-booted foot. Antrons dive out of the way of its spinning, blazing blade. Relieved of their weight, Acroyear pushes himself up from the floor as his attackers tumble from him. He raises a gloved hand, and his fingers close around his weapon's hilt.

"They're at the door!" wails Ogwen. "Acroyear! Koriah!"

Acroyear takes advantage of his momentary respite to snap into his wrist communicator, "Extend the landing ramp!"

"Are you insane?" cries Ogwen. "The hangar door's still open. You'll—"

"If you want me to stand a chance of reaching you, you'll do as I say!"

On the bridge, Ogwen looks like he's about to argue. But then he glances back at the armored bulkhead that is the only thing separating him from the station's invaders, and sees it trembling as the Antrons from the starboard habitation corridor hurl themselves at it. He lets out a sob and practically throws himself at the control console.

In the hangar bay, a large, square section of the transparent hull peels back, like cellophane exposed to a harsh flame. With a heavy clunk of gears, the landing ramp is lifted from its position flush with the floor and slowly unfurled. The station shudders again, and Acroyear is snatched away on a hurricane-force wind. With his left hand, he grabs onto the hangar bay doorway as he's pulled through it. His right hand holds tenaciously onto his sword, his legs caught in the wind and streaming behind him. Taken by surprise, Antrons fly past him, and into him, threatening to dislodge him. Some try to hold onto him, to save themselves, but he shrugs them off. My shuttle pod provides an anchor for the lucky ones, as does Koriah's Rhodium Orbiter; many more are ejected into space.

Unit #34 cranes forward, reaching with both hands but just unable to reach Acroyear. He can barely stay upright himself—he has magnetized his feet, but he can't take a step without sacrificing his balance.

"You can...retract it again...now, Ogwen..." Acroyear's voice is strained, his words whipped away almost before his open communicator can catch them.

Half-extended, the landing ramp jerks to a reluctant halt, then, slowly, tortuously, reverses its course, folding back up into itself.

Acroyear loses his uneven struggle, and is torn from his handhold. He hurtles across the hangar, twisting in midair, reaching for something to save him but finding nothing. He skims across the landing ramp as it settles back into its housing, and then there is nothing between him and open space. I don't know if his armor will protect him out there; even if it does, he will be at a disadvantage, his enemies used to zero-gravity conditions.

The hull reforms, a nanosecond before Acroyear slams into it.

Outside the station, the expelled Antrons are already regrouping, preparing to attack again. Inside, those that remain are picking themselves up, regaining their orientation. They are fast, but Acroyear is faster. He rushes a cluster of them with a blood-chilling war cry that gives even these dumb creatures pause for thought. His sword dices four more of his foes without his even breaking step. He races past Unit #34, firing a terse instruction at him. Obligingly, the Biotron places his bulky form in the hangar bay doorway. Pouring after Acroyear, like iron filings drawn to a magnet, the Antrons leap upon this new obstacle, but they are too few now to pose a serious problem to him.

Elsewhere on my monitor bank, I see Koriah through

Unit #23's eyes. He managed to drag her away from the battle outside the elevator shaft, and has removed her helmet and dispensed a thin layer of plasti-skin to the cut on her head, staunching the bleeding. Fortunately, I equipped all my Biotrons with first aid equipment and skills some years ago, when my body began to fail. Extruding a needle from his forefinger, #23 shoots a stimulant into a vein on Koriah's neck. Her shallow breathing gives way to a startled gasp, and her eyelids flutter and snap open. It takes her a second to adjust to her new surroundings—the dingy storeroom in which the Biotron found safe haven for her—and then she hauls herself to her feet and makes to leave.

"IT IS MY RECOMMENDATION," says the Biotron, "THAT YOU REST UNTIL YOUR HEARTBEAT AND RESPIRATION FUNCTIONS REGAIN THEIR NATURAL RHYTHMS."

"Are…are you telling me the Antrons were defeated while I was out?"

"I DON'T EXPECT SO."

"Then I have work to do."

Groggily, she stumbles through the door and flinches from the low light of the corridor outside. She slumps against the wall, putting a hand to her wounded head. I am disappointed, but not surprised. For all her bravado, I always knew that this girl was no warrior.

The Antrons are on the bridge.

Ogwen lets out a high-pitched squeal as the bulkhead falls, and leaps out of his seat, scrambling for the discarded laser pistol. "Save me!" he implores his attendant Biotron. "You have your orders, keep those things away from me!"

124

Personally, I would value the half-life of any of my Biotron units over the continued existence of the pointless Ogwen. Still, Unit #36 has already come dutifully to his defense, making himself the Antrons' primary target as his radiation blaster scythes through them.

He doesn't last long. The creatures pry open his red chestplate, yanking out wires and arteries alike, until, in a shower of sparks, he falls still. His internal camera continues to transmit: I can still see Ogwen, fumbling with his pistol, crouched beneath the bridge's main console as if it can hide him. His hands are shaking, and he can't fasten the strap around his arm. He fires the weapon twice—almost, I suspect, by accident—each of the bolts going wild. Then he forgets it altogether, letting it slide to the floor, as the Antrons come for him.

"Oh, no," he groans, in the moment before he's engulfed, "oh, no, oh, no, oh, no."

And that's when Acroyear arrives.

Unit #34 has dealt with the Antrons in the hangar bay, rending and mauling until all that remains of them is a heap of tangled corpses, a few limbs twitching spasmodically. Their comrades outside the station, however, are seconds away from breaking in again. Their numbers are diminished: there can't be more than twenty of them left, but it's still too many.

The Biotron operates the wall-mounted controls and the hangar door slides along its runners, locking into place an instant before my sensors tell me that the hull has been breached for a third time. I don't have to see through the steel shutter to know that the invaders are swarming toward it, resuming their efforts to dig their way through.

On this side of the door, Unit #34 awaits them, prepared to defend my station to the end.

"They're losing," moans Archer. "The insect creatures, there's too many of them." He has turned as far as he can in the Cosmobot's grip to look at the screens behind him, distracting himself from what's happening in his head. He looks back at me, a desperate plea in his eyes. "I could help them. I could make a difference. Don't you see, Karza? If you let me go, it might save the station. Then you'd have all the time you need to…to rummage in my mind. I'll help you. We'll find out about the Time Traveler together."

"I don't think so," I say. I flex my wrists, and all but the centermost of my screens go blank.

"What are you doing?"

"Events outside this chamber are a distraction I can ill afford. Either the Antrons will reach us, or they won't. In the meantime, I will learn as much as I can from you."

"You're insane!" whispers Archer.

"That is entirely possible," I concede. "Obsessed, certainly." I smile. "But I rather think it is too late for me to change now."

On my main screen, the static is beginning to clear. An image is forming: a shadow, I think at first—but as it gains definition, I realize that it is a being. A face, masked by a black helmet. The helmet's lower half is a series of vertical slats, giving the impression of bared teeth, and its crown is ringed with stubby horns. A chain mail curtain falls behind the head, draped over a pair of armor-plated shoulders. And those eyes…

Triangular red lenses, glaring at me, burning into my soul, reawakening the fevered nightmares of my childhood.

They are the eyes of the Emperor.

CHAPTER
SEVEN

The black face blurs and dissolves, although the eyes linger in my mind.

A dizzying succession of images takes its place: people, places, shapes and colors, some recognizable, even familiar, others gone before I can make out what they were. Acroyear, Knave, Koriah, even my own face stares back at me. I see Reptos, Membros, and Kronos creatures, and something that looks very much like a Lobros. Glimpses of the Micropolis skyline bring back unpleasant memories of my youth. There is a woman with purple hair and glider wings flaring from her back—and a man in golden armor whom I think I know, but the perspective is all wrong. He appears again, and I recognize my old acquaintance, Ordaal, rendered from the point of view of somebody to whom the mercenary is a giant.

Archer lets out a moan. "Try not to resist the probe," I advise him. "It will hurt less."

"It feels like something's crawling around inside my brain," he complains. I feel it best not to tell him that that's exactly what is happening. The needles in his head have sprouted organic filaments, which I am guiding via the twin levers on the control box.

Persephone. I linger on her face—her long blonde hair, the haughty tilt of her head—until it slips away from me. I can hear sounds now: fragments of words, the stuttering wail of a klaxon alarm, and a heartbeat thumping, thumping.

I see the Time Traveler many times. I see him floating in Micropolis's polluted sky, and I see him rising from the blackness of sleep with his urgent message.

I move down from the surface layer of Archer's consciousness, teasing the horn-shaped control levers like a pilot guiding his ship toward the landing pad. The pictures are clearer here, Archer's memories more ordered. He's in a sterile, multi-layered white chamber, looking at another Rift. White energy flares inside a rectangular white construct that can only be a primitive version of my own containment grid. Tiny figures flit about the chamber on blue energy wings; it is only when I see the *Sunrunner* sitting on a landing platform, looking to Archer like an oversized model kit, that I realize they are beings from my own universe.

A world of giants, Knave said. I wish I'd been able to visit it, to study it. A familiar frustration builds in me. So much time wasted, so much I'll never know.

The image crackles, fades and skips. Now I'm looking at a mech. Its head is a golden oval, its white torso plugged into a set of wheels. It has two flexible arms, and three digits on each hand. *»MICROTRON UNIT REPORTS ALL SYSTEMS FUNCTIONAL,«* it chirps—and the image stutters again. *»MICROTRON UNIT…MICROTRON UNIT…MICROTRON UNIT…«* Before I know it, my probe is pulled down an associative pathway in Archer's mind, and suddenly the screen is filled with flames, my speakers popping with the fury of an explosion, and I'm staring down at that golden head, half-melted, on the floor of a litter-strewn alleyway.

"Ryan? Ryan? What are you doing in here? Ryan!" A middle-aged man, with a full beard, and brown hair swept back from his forehead. He wears a padded blue protective suit, its helmet hanging loosely around his neck. He's striding across the chamber toward the screen, toward Archer, the deep lines of his forehead folded into a scowl. *"I told you not to come here…what did you think you were doing…what is this, some kind of childish joke?"* The face looks familiar, particularly around the eyes. Could this be Archer's father?

Another association. Suddenly, we're in a room that is similar but different. The Rift is still present; the *Sunrunner* is not. The white light has turned a fiery yellow, and five figures erupt from it. Black and silver armored suits, golden faceplates. I can hear Archer's voice, the way it must sound in his own head: *"Oh my God! Dad!"* The bearded man is down, helpless on his back, a blaster aimed at his chest. Archer himself is held by an iron arm, being dragged into the light. And then there is a flash of flame, and everything goes black.

I think I had it: an image from the other timeline, but it slips away from me. And Archer screams. His eyes are sweating and sightless, but I have no doubt that he can see what I'm seeing. I don't know which is the greater for him—the physical pain of the probe or the emotional pain of its revelations.

"I told you," I say without sympathy, "try not to resist."

He shoots me a glare. "I'm doing my best," he says through gritted teeth.

"Talk to me," I suggest. "Tell me what you can see."

Deeper, ever deeper.

There's a girl with a tiny metal ring through her nose, and hair gathered into bunches. Archer identifies her as "Connie." A series of flash-frame images suggest that he was intimate with her, but he's resisting again, groaning as he tries to block the memories from my sight. I smile to myself at his coyness and move on.

I am at once intrigued and despairing at the state of the world called Earth. I see overpopulated streets and ugly, angular stone buildings reaching for a polluted sky. It reminds me of nothing more than Micropolis under its current leaders. Archer seems comfortable talking about his home, and I linger on these images for longer than I should, asking him many questions. I tell myself that my curiosity is justified if it puts the boy at ease. A calmer mind is easier to negotiate.

I'm in a small, sparse room, looking across a table, meeting tiny eyes sunk into a fat, red face. "That's Roger Delaney," offers Archer, with evident distaste. "The Mayor of Angel's Gift. That's the town where the Rift opened, where the Micronauts came through."

"Mayor?" I frown, wondering if I've understood the term correctly. "Another leader? Another ruler to add to your congressmen and presidents and governors and kings? Your people seem obsessed with creating layers of bureaucracy—and yet, as I understand it, you have no Emperor, nobody to take overall control."

"We like it that way. Ruling the world—it's too much power for one person."

"Too much?" I cry, incredulously. "One paltry planet? And that is your human philosophy? Little wonder, then, that so many of you are impoverished, that your science is still so primitive. You bicker among yourselves, squander your resources, and all for want of somebody who can see the bigger picture. You could be so much more than you are, but you have given yourselves over to chaos!"

"It's called freedom," snaps Archer, "and it's worth the sacrifice!"

"Maybe that is what they teach you on Earth," I retort.

Another glimpse of the Time Traveler's reality. Armored men rampaging through the Rift chamber. Blue-suited scientists cut down, blood bubbling and steaming in their open wounds. The bearded man is yelling at Archer, *"Get out of here! Quickly!"* but he doesn't respond, and I can only imagine the fear that grips his stomach and freezes his legs. I remember how I felt, when similar monsters descended upon my world, my father.

And then the picture breaks up again—but I've found my key.

The father's name is Dallas. His face recurs frequently in my subject's memories, weathering with time. Often, though, he is a cool and distant figure, a source of affection that the young Archer feels unable to access. I think about the unwanted attentions of the Emperor, and wonder which of us was the more fortunate.

Still, I detect the bonds of love in the way that Archer talks of his parent and, each time I lock onto his image, I find it easier to trace a connection to the images that the boy doesn't want to—or can't—acknowledge. The father, yelling at his son to escape while he still can. The father, recoiling as a console explodes in his face. The father, writhing in the blast field of an alien weapon as his son is snatched away to another universe.

"Get out of here! Quickly!"

"Oh, my God! Dad! No! Daaaaaaaad..."

A choking sob escapes Archer's throat. There are tears on his cheeks, but already a new picture is beginning to form. A subconscious memory of a predictive dream.

Archer's first sight of another world: A magnificent palace, lifted on a flaming podium, curved spires thrusting upward like the twin prongs of a tuning fork, black against a red sky...

...A dark cell: A glowing energy chain, anchored to a disc-shaped base unit, and a broad-shouldered figure in the shadows, a hint of red metal...

...A pen full of creatures, their species varied but each dressed in the same mauve and faun fatigues, like prisoners, bathed in green radiation fire, screaming and dying...

I see the man in the black helmet again, his red eyes burning—but only in glimpses. As I lose him a fourth time, I look to Archer, and see the pain of effort in his expression. I suspect he's blocking the memory of the black-clad man from me, fighting the probe to turn his mind to other thoughts.

And, always, there is the Time Traveler. It seems that every memory the boy has of this long-gone timeline contains a shortcut to his golden-masked face. I try to bring it into focus on my screen, but, ubiquitous as the image is, it's also elusive. My eyes return to Archer, to see if he is keeping this from me too, but all I can see in his face is fear.

"Please, Karza," he begs in a deathly whisper, "don't do this. Don't make me see!"

"We're almost there," I reassure him gruffly. "The probe has located the part of your brain that can interact with the alternative universe."

"You don't understand! There's something terrible coming, I can feel it."

"The images aren't real, Archer. They can't hurt you."

He cries out, "I don't want to think about it! I don't want to see!"

I tighten my grip on the control levers, and flatten my dry, cracked lips into a pitiless line. "You have no choice," I snarl.

"It's a way out. It could be our only way out."

A group of figures treks across the desert, beneath a yellow sky.

Archer is accompanied by Acroyear and Knave, and others I can't see. He must be weary, because his eyes are forever downcast, watching his own feet rise and fall through fine brown sand. It takes me some time to put together the jigsaw shapes in his peripheral vision, to recognize the mech that called itself Microtron, and, much to my surprise, Persephone. I hadn't realized that she, too, was part of Archer's experiences in the old timeline; he didn't say. I'm not sure what this means.

And there is someone—or something—else: a hulking, mechanical creature, three or four times Archer's height, bringing up the rear of the party. I see it for only an instant, and then as no more than a vague impression and a lingering after-image of its shadow, after Archer glances over his shoulder and is dazzled by twin suns behind the giant's head.

Twin suns. Brown sand. "Where are we?" I ask, already sure of the answer.

"I...don't know," says Archer, through heavy breaths. "The world was meant to be dead. I never learned its name."

"Throne-World," I rumble, half to myself. "The city that became Micropolis."

"Yeah. I figured that, too."

"In the old timeline," I deduce, "the Emperor never came here. There was no Time Traveler, nothing to bring this mud speck to his attention, and so he built the seat of his power—the heart of his Empire—elsewhere, on a world more suited to his needs." And did that Emperor, I wonder, still wage war on my people? Did he single me out to be taken under his dark wing? Did he take me to his new Throne-World, and if so, what did I find there?

"How did you come to be here?" I ask.

"Shot down," murmurs Archer—and the screen shows me an associated image: the burning bridge of a ship that might be the *Sunrunner*, the brown planet spinning crazily on its forward screen. "We were on our way to rendezvous with Koriah. She'd been setting up contacts, and we...we'd had our own problems. Nova ambushed us. Azura Nova."

"You've mentioned her name before."

The purple-haired, winged woman. Archer sees her as he first sets foot on a new world, his hands shackled in front of him; she takes flight like a golden angel, and soars toward the castle in the red sky...Then, she is in the prisoners' pen, standing over a defeated Acroyear, clearly enjoying her power over him although her frozen face shows hardly a hint of emotion....She is cradling the stump of a severed arm, and there is a hint of a black-clad figure beside her....Finally, she is a face on a communications screen, sneering as she demands the surrender of her foes, and the release of their hostage.

Acroyear stabs angrily at a switch, and cuts her off in mid-transmission.

...and Archer runs, Acroyear pulling him along by the hand, both men struggling to make headway across the clinging, shifting grains underfoot, both flung into the air by the force of an explosion behind them. Both buried, facedown, in the sand...

Knave: *"Looks like the perfect vacation spot to me. Sun, sand...more sun, more sand..."*

Persephone: *"Are you insane? We don't have any supplies. We have no shelter. How long do you think we can last on this ball of dirt?"*

Acroyear: *"Your father has no mercy, and I will not go back to his pens."*

Acroyear again: *"They will be carrying out sensor sweeps of the surface. We have to get away from the wreckage."*

"I HAVE DETECTED NO LIFE SIGNS AS YET. HOWEVER, THERE IS A LARGE, MANMADE STRUCTURE SOME 17.6 KILOMETERS FROM OUR PRESENT POSITION." I know that voice.

The desert again. Archer must have spent some considerable time tramping across it. Here in my chamber, he squirms uncomfortably. My screens give me access only to the sights and sounds of his experience—an experience he never had—but he must also remember his weariness, the taste of sand in his throat, and the heat of two suns searing his skin.

On the screen, Microtron is beginning to flounder; it tries to speak, but emits only an electronic squawk. *"He's got sand in his casing,"* observes Archer.

"Doesn't he have filters against foreign matter?" asks Persephone with disdain.

"He probably didn't expect to be buried up to the diodes in the stuff."

"I WILL CARRY HIM, UNTIL HIS SELF-CLEANSING SYSTEM CAN CORRECT THE PROBLEM."

Archer's giant companion bends into view, lifts Microtron in his huge, metal hands—and my suspicion is confirmed. "A Biotron!"

"Um, yeah," says Archer. "I've been seeing him a lot. He was one of us, I think."

"Your group of misfits. You led me to believe you were outsiders, rebels."

"We were!"

"On the run from this Nova woman?"

"You saw for yourself."

"And her master?"

Archer doesn't answer. I prompt him. "The Emperor. Persephone's...father?"

The picture on the screen flickers again. A suggestion of red eyes.

"It's a way out. It could be our only way out."

"You can't be serious, Archer!" snaps Persephone. *"This machinery is ancient, untested. It could spread our molecules from one end of time to the other."*

"Worried there won't be enough of us left to stock your father's bio-vaults?" sneers Knave.

"DESPITE ITS AGE, THE SYSTEM APPEARS FUNCTIONAL," reports the Biotron.

"Nova will have found the wreck of the Sunreaver *by now,"* considers Acroyear. *"She knows we have no means of escaping this planet. She will search until she finds us."*

"So, you think you can hide in the past?"

"Works for me," says Knave.

"You imbeciles! We'll be just as trapped there as we are here. We'll still have no ship, no communications devices, no water."

"I've been trying to figure out these controls," says

Archer. *"I think we can set spatial, as well as temporal, coordinates."*

He turns as Microtron trundles up beside him. Behind the diminutive robot, I glimpse three consoles through the gloom, arranged in a triangular pattern. *»I'VE REACHED THAT CONCLUSION, TOO. UNFORTUNATELY, THE SYSTEM HAS A RANGE OF ONLY A FEW HUNDRED MILES—CERTAINLY NOT ENOUGH TO REACH THE NEAREST INHABITED WORLD.«*

"So, we're stuck on this planet," says Archer. *"What if we go further back—to a time when this temple was new, before the Pharoids abandoned it? They must have had technology—devices that could help us. If we could only get a message to our past selves somehow, warn them about Nova's ambush, we wouldn't be in this mess."*

"So, now you're talking about creating a paradox!"

"I suggest you hold your tongue, Princess," snaps Acroyear, *"unless you'd rather we shackle you again."* He turns to Archer. *"Is it possible, to rewrite history in such a way?"*

The boy's response is non-verbal, so I can neither see nor hear it from his point of view. I think it was a shrug.

"The Emperor had a special interest in you, didn't he?" I'm manipulating the controls of the mind probe device, pushing deeper into Archer's subconscious, seeking out what he doesn't want me to see. "He sent his troops to your world, to bring you to him—but somehow, you escaped. With the assistance of Koriah and Acroyear, I expect. You set yourself up against the established order. Why, Archer? Who was this man? What was his connection to you, and what turned you against him? Tell me!"

At last he cries out again, throwing his head back and striking it against the unyielding Cosmobot. And I lean forward, shivering with anticipation, as the black-clad man, the ruler of a galaxy, shoots into focus on my screen.

"Within the chest of weakness, beats the heart of imperfection...I've carved that defective heart from its cavity and extracted order! My order."

I planned to study the Emperor; instead, I find myself distracted. In this memory, Archer stands on a hovering disc, above a city I have seen before, have known all my life, but only in dreams. I am looking at a city of steel and lights, of breathtaking, innovative architecture, in which form and function are nevertheless perfectly balanced. Far below, beings move through the streets and along rocket tubes in a steady, clockwork flow, like miniscule components of a great machine.

The sky has a familiar red hue, and I realize that this is the world I glimpsed before, where the Emperor's palace floated in the sky. Throne-World. I am in awe.

"You, Ryan, are one of the strong."

Archer turns from the city to look at the Emperor. I meet his red eyes unblinkingly, staring as if I might see through them, see the face behind them. The helmet modulates and amplifies his voice, making it cold, mechanical, unrecognizable. I can't be sure...

The memory-scene skips. Red eyes flare, and I shame myself by falling back into my seat, startled. The picture is blurred, but for a second it seems that the Emperor is wreathed in angry scarlet energy. It streams from his eyes, and coalesces about his fists. And then Archer throws his hands in front of his face—in life, reflexively, as on the screen—and my view is blocked, although I can see the boy's bones through his flesh, washed in red.

"Not very smart, are you?" Archer is being pushed along by a thug in black and silver armor. *"Angering the Baron. Save yourself some misery and tell him what he wants."*

The prisoners' pen. We've been here before. I need to go back.

I try to retrieve the memory of the Emperor, but, aggravatingly, I can't find it again. I don't know if this is Archer's doing, or a limitation of my own equipment. I could ask him to help me, to guide the probe toward the memory—I could hurt him, if he refused—but I don't want to betray my interest. Not yet. I can't voice my mad suspicion, my hope; I don't wish to look foolish. So, I let the currents of Archer's mind return me to the desert.

I'm looking at a pair of stone doors, engraved with pictograms. I recognize the mark of the Pharoids...

A moment later, we're back in the prisoners' pen, where Acroyear is helping Archer to his feet...

A shape in the distance, something protruding from the brown sand...

The tip of a pyramid. It stands about Archer's size, but with the promise of greater volume beneath the surface. Archer runs a hand along its crumbling stonework. Persephone is scornful, almost to the point of hysteria: *"You mean we've come all this way—you've dragged us across this godforsaken planet, you've let us burn—and all for some ancient, half-buried ruin?"* The giant Biotron confirms that this is indeed the construct he detected.

"Like a marker," Archer mutters to himself, although

I'm not sure that anybody else hears him. *"Like it was left for us to find."*

…He's climbing down a ladder, into the darkness, and an indefinable instinct tells me that this is it, that we're almost there…

Then we're back on the ship, and Persephone is yelling, *"Pull up, you imbecile! You've got to pull up!"* She's shaking Archer, shouting over the noise of the screaming engines and the wailing alarms, *"Surrender, you fool! My father wants you alive."*

"You, Ryan, are one of the strong."

Persephone: *"…want us to start digging, now?"*

"Biotron can do most of the work," says Acroyear patiently, *"and he can fuse the sand with his blaster, to shore up the walls of the pit."*

"IT WILL NOT BE A PERMANENT SOLUTION," warns the bio-mech.

"For now, my primary concern is finding shelter—and that means locating the entrance to this building. If the sands cover it again thereafter, then maybe that will be for the best. It will afford us additional concealment."

"So, this is your great plan—to evade Nova by burying ourselves alive?"

"Better buried," growls Acroyear, *"then dissected on the Biosmith's table."*

The scene shifts again. Knave kneels in front of a chest filled with gold coins. He's running his four hands through them, letting them slip through his fingers. *"Perfect!"* he comments, in a voice laden with irony, *"now I get to be rich."*

…Lights flicker across the underground chamber, streaming from its three consoles, driving out the darkness and the dust. A shape is forming at the chamber's heart. A miniature version of the stone pyramid, this one comprised of white light...

"I can't," whimpers Archer, as static crashes onto the screen. "Can't go any further. It's coming. I...I don't want to see..."

...the Time Traveler is staring out of a stone sarcophagus...

And, while the boy is disoriented, I twist the controls and yank us back to the Emperor.

"Clichéd as it may seem, the strong are indeed the only survivors when it comes to my order." On the floor in front of me, Archer takes a shuddering breath. *"You, Ryan, are one of the strong."* His eyes are sightless, forehead drenched in sweat, fists clenching spasmodically. *"Your place is at the side of one such as I, who can guide that strength."*

My heart freezes. I have heard this speech before, or one like it. The words have changed, but the sentiment is the same. The Emperor's image becomes clouded and is lost, but I have seen all I needed to see. Another tyrant, doing to Ryan Archer what was done to me: trying to manipulate him, mold him, make of him a son and heir. I see, now, why the boy had to get away, had to throw off this Emperor's influence. We are more alike than I imagined...

Back at the foot of the ladder, with the three consoles. Archer is inspecting the pictograms on their surfaces, translating them with a process that is one part deduction, one part intuition and one part assistance from Microtron—a mobile notepad and calculator. The boy turns to his companions, and I am disappointed not to see the Time Traveler among them. *"A time machine,"* he breathes in a voice full of wonder. *"I think it's a time machine."*

I knew this already, of course.

My attention is reserved for the looming Biotron. Apart from his scale, and the absence of an identifying number on his shoulders, he's identical to my own units—but I designed them myself. Could it be that, in another reality, another man came up with a concept so similar? I don't think it can. Am I looking, then, at the product of another Karza's genius? And, if so, what does that say about my life in this universe—the life I would have lived, *should* have lived, were it not for the Time Traveler's interference?

I thought I knew what Archer was trying to hide. In my hubris, I expected to see proof that I was destined to rule. Instead, I find vague connections to a doomed rebellion and no indication that my life made a difference.

Ryan Archer, I'm sure, is aware of my fate in that other timeline. If I applied enough pressure, I could make him reveal it to me.

The trouble is, I'm no longer sure I wish to know.

"Even if we could warn our past selves of the ambush," reasons Persephone, *"what do you think would happen? We'd never have come to this benighted world, we could never have found this machinery, never gone back in time to warn ourselves of the ambush, ergo we wouldn't have avoided it. We'd create a never-ending loop of cause and effect. We can't even guess what the consequences of that would be."*

"The Grandfather Paradox," nods Archer. *"What happens if you go back in time and kill your own ancestor?"*

"Maybe it's time we found out," says Acroyear. *"Our immediate situation aside, I will not turn my back on an opportunity like this. This machine could be the*

weapon we have been searching for. With this, and the riches we found on the upper level, we could break the Emperors' hold on our galaxy forever."

"THE PHAROIDS CONSTRUCTED THE MACHINE," says the Biotron. "PRESUMABLY, THEY ALSO STUDIED THE THEORETICAL IMPLICATIONS OF ITS USE. THEY MAY BE ABLE TO ADVISE US."

"*If we can reach their time in one piece,*" says Persephone, archly. "*Hasn't it occurred to any of you that they abandoned this heap of junk—this entire world—for a reason?*"

"*Perhaps they had no choice in the matter,*" Acroyear says darkly.

»*I CAN DATE THE COMPONENTS OF THE MACHINE WITH 93% ACCURACY,*« offers Microtron.

"*So, it should be possible to drop in on the Pharoids just after they built it,*" says Archer.

"*Cool,*" grins Knave. "*So, we pay a quick visit to the past, get some advice; worst that can happen is that the Pharoids send us back here. Hell, even if they can just give us a lift off-planet, if we're stuck hundreds of years before any of us were born, at least we'll be alive.*"

"*Not 'we,' *" rumbles Acroyear. "*It doesn't make sense for us all to risk our lives. I will go alone, in the first instance. I will send word via the machine, if it is safe to follow.*"

"*No can do, I'm afraid.*" Archer has been studying pictograms again. I already know what he has learned. "*Only one of us can make this trip—and that's me.*"

Archer groans, and doubles over in pain. "It's here!" he whimpers. "Please, Karza, enough. Can't...mustn't...go further." The picture on the screen is dissolving, as fear gives him the strength to wrest control of his thoughts from me. A barrage of images: the Time Traveler, Acroyear, the Emperor, the Time Traveler, Dallas Archer, the Time Traveler. A room filled with treasures—exquisitely crafted pots, jeweled scarabs, gold and emeralds glittering in the light from Acroyear's sword. A trapdoor, concealed beneath a stone sarcophagus. Twin suns, brown sand. The Time Traveler. Pictograms on stone doors: An ancient warning, not understood at the time, and not heeded.

With a sadistic snarl, I increase the power to the mind probe.

...The Time Traveler stares out from the sarcophagus. Archer reaches for him...

...climbing down the ladder...

...He's standing before the pyramid of light, raising the golden mask to his face...

...explaining to Acroyear, *"Your armor might protect you, but it might not. The containment suit is designed to withstand the pressures of the time stream."*

...The Time Traveler crumples, as he's lifted out of his stone casket. An empty suit, resting in dust...

...In the treasure room, Archer regards his reflection in the back of a gold locket. The blank eyes of the Time Traveler stare back at him...

"The suit won't fit you, not over your armor—and it sure as hell won't fit Biotron. Knave's got too many arms, Microtron too many wheels. That leaves Persephone and me—so, unless the Princess has a sudden change of heart..."

"Acquires a heart, you mean," Knave comments.

...standing before the glowing pyramid, and now he's walking toward it...

"What if this basement didn't exist, all those years

ago?" asks Knave. *"What if it hadn't been carved out yet? Archer might materialize in solid rock."*

»I CONSIDERED THAT POSSIBILITY,« Microtron assures him. *»BIOTRON AND I CALIBRATED THE MACHINE TO DEPOSIT RYAN ABOVE GROUND, SEVERAL HUNDRED YARDS FROM HERE.«*

"What are your instincts telling you?" asks Acroyear.

Archer's voice: *"I don't know. Nothing good. This doesn't feel right, but then it doesn't feel right to just wait here. Either way, we're screwed. I guess we've nothing to lose."*

Walking toward the light, he takes one last look back at his companions…and then it's enveloping him, welcoming him. For an instant, all I can see is a pure, blinding white, so bright that I can't look directly at it, and then my main screen flares and blows out.

I throw up a hand to ward off a hot spray of glass—and, in the here and now, the reality that suddenly seems so distant to me, I can hear Archer screaming his throat raw.

The screaming stops, eventually, and Archer begins to sob quietly. I have the Cosmobot release him, and he rolls into a tight ball on the floor, as if he can shut out his pain, as if it comes from without. I turned off the machine some minutes ago, and removed the needles from his temples; I'm not sure he has even noticed.

In time, the boy's whimpering subsides, too, but he doesn't stir from his prone position. There is silence, now—not just here in my chamber, but throughout the Astro Station. A total, heavy silence, almost unnatural. My hearing has become hypersensitive, the sound of my labored breathing like the crashing of waves in my ears. I'm accustomed to continual background noise, reports from my Biotrons on my monitors. Do I dare reactivate them? Am I ready to learn the fates of my would-be defenders? They must have triumphed, else the enemy would have knocked down my door by now—but at what cost, I wonder?

"Happy now?" While I was distracted, Archer raised himself to his knees. I didn't expect him to recover so suddenly, wasn't ready to talk to him. It takes me a moment to gather my thoughts. "Have you got what you wanted?" he asks bitterly.

I meet his cold, steady gaze, and answer truthfully. "No."

"You were right," he sighs. "The Time Traveler: He was—he *is*—me. He wasn't trying to contact me, I was just seeing my future. Or, I guess, in a way, my past."

"It's perfectly simple," I say. "You ought to have heeded Persephone's advice. The Pharoids' abandoned time machine was unfinished, imperfect. It sent you into the past as directed—but, instead of guiding you along the threads of time, it tried to force you through them. You remained partially tangible in these three dimensions, throughout a journey that endured for centuries but at the same time for no more than a nanosecond. It's likely that you reached your destination, in the end, but you were torn apart in the process—and you left a trail of devastation behind you."

"I changed history," Archer whispers, ashen-faced. "These dreams, everything I've seen…that's the way it should have been, but I changed everything."

"In a sense," I say quietly, "you created the universe we know."

I surprise myself with my detachment. I should be feeling something, but I don't know what. It's all too much to take in. The Time Traveler, the man who determined the course of my life, is here in front of me, and he is no more than a child who made a mistake. The fate of everything, of worlds long gone and those yet unborn, hinged upon one bad decision.

Part of me wants to kill him, to fasten my hands around his throat, for his presumption in tampering with forces he didn't understand. Another part is grateful, because without him, I would be another man, perhaps a lesser man, and even now I can't stand the thought of that, of surrendering all I have been in my life.

And then I think about my situation. I think about my dreams, and how I was forced to set them aside. I think about the cancer eating at the time stream, and my ultimate failure to halt it.

"You created the universe," I whisper, my breathing quickening, my heart racing as the import of my words settles upon me. "But you also destroyed it."

CHAPTER
EIGHT

The Centauri haven't contacted me yet. It's been an hour since the last of their invasion force died, since their sensors would have reported their failure to them. I imagine they don't wish to face me, any more than I wish to speak with them. Neither side has emerged from this skirmish victorious. The Centauri have tasted the resolve of my defenders and, with no more disposable Antrons on hand, they'll be asking themselves if they can afford a second engagement. Whatever the answer, they won't back down now. They are too proud.

For my part, I know we can't withstand another attack. Veelum is dead. Kellesh is clinging to life, unconscious, his breathing controlled by the medical computer. I have lost four of my nine remaining Biotrons. And my work, my lifelong project, is in ruins.

I could let them take the Astro Station; I wouldn't be handing over anything of value. Let them have my research. Let them see how they are doomed. Let them live with that knowledge, as I have lived with it, for no Centauri scientist could do more than I have already tried to avert the destruction of everything.

However, I will not surrender. I won't give those

creatures the satisfaction of executing me. I promised
them that I'd destroy this station rather than see it
captured. I will keep that promise. I, too, have my
pride.

One last act of defiance. That's all I have to look
forward to.

For the past thirty minutes, I have been replaying
my Biotrons' records of the battle: Something to
occupy my mind, because I fear that if I think too
hard, it may drive me insane.

I watched the defense of the bridge, where Acroyear
was just in time to save Ogwen's worthless skin. He
fought like a madman while the bureaucrat cowered.
When it looked like the odds against the warrior were
too great, Unit #32 arrived from the starboard habitation corridor. The Antrons didn't know which way
to turn. There weren't enough of them left to over-
power the Biotron, but they couldn't get near
Acroyear without his whirling blade cutting them to
pieces. I became entranced by the warrior, his movements so swift, so self-assured, and yet so precise that
they looked almost choreographed.

Ankle-deep in purple corpses, his armor blood-
stained, Acroyear relaxed his muscles at last, and
spared my Biotron a nod of respect for a worthy
comrade. He didn't see the last Antron behind him.
It launched itself at him, mandibles trained on his
neck, where his helmet had been partially torn from
the rest of his armor. The sight was enough to bring
Ogwen out of hiding at last, a laser pistol on his arm.
His eyes burnt in his red face, and he let out a raw
scream of anger as he fired. He hit the back of
Acroyear's head. The warrior rolled with the blow,
dropped, spun, and saw the attacking Antron sailing
over him with an expression of almost comical surprise on its face. He skewered it through the stomach.

Elsewhere, the transformed Wroje dealt with the last Antron from the elevator shaft, seizing it with her teeth and tossing it over her finned head. Casting around for her next victim—most likely, searching for Koriah—her eyes alighted upon Knave. He tried to placate her, raising his hands, but she reared onto her hind legs and howled an angry lament for vengeance unsatisfied. By the time she landed, she had reverted to her normal, slight form, the change rippling over her so quickly that I almost missed it. For over a minute, she stayed on her hands and knees, panting and snorting like an animal, pupils dilated, her clothes torn so that the white tattoo on her neck was starkly visible, highlighted by a faint residual glow. Then her eyes rolled back into her head, and she fainted.

The last Antron squadron chewed its way out of the hangar. Unit #34 put up an impressive fight, but soon the creatures were swarming toward the main lab. They found Acroyear, Knave, and four Biotrons in their path—even Koriah did what she could, although she was still shaken and weak from blood loss. The fight was long and hard, but conclusive.

I keep replaying the moment of Veelum's death, as captured by the eyes of a Biotron unit that couldn't reach him in time. The picture is indistinct and jerky, both Veelum and Kellesh glimpsed only briefly beneath a mass of purple, until the Antrons move on and leave their victims like broken rag dolls in their wake. It would take a full autopsy to reveal which of the old man's many cuts and gouges killed him.

I didn't think I'd care. With the project dead, what is Veelum to me? I respected his intellect, and his pragmatism, but never called him a friend. With all I've lost, what is one more death? And yet, there is a space inside me that aches to be filled. Maybe it's the absence of something familiar, a part of my life that I'd come to rely on, to take for granted. Maybe it's because, for the first time, I know that this death is absolute. There will be no reordering of history, no reprieve for Veelum in the past. I mourn for all the people I've known, all those who gave their lives for me and will not now get the second chance I promised them.

Acroyear brings Wroje to the bridge. She has spent the last hour in her quarters. She cried a lot. My microphones also picked up the sound of her vomiting. She is pale and trembling. When she sees Koriah—the Galactic Defender spins her chair around to face her as she enters, greeting her with a sad appeal in her yellow eyes—she flinches, and shrinks closer to her escort's side.

Archer and Knave perch awkwardly on the conference table, the former inspecting his feet studiously. Ogwen leans against the hull, his arms folded, brooding and obviously drunk. "Well?" he snarls in Koriah's direction. "We're all here now. Maybe you'd like to start."

She gives him a withering look, which quickly fades as she catches sight of Wroje again. She closes her eyes, takes a breath, and nods. She lifts herself from her chair with some difficulty, using the console behind her for support. Somehow, she finds the strength to stand unaided, to face the suspicious gazes of her erstwhile comrades squarely.

"I'm sorry," she says.

"So, it's true, then," says Ogwen. "You murdered LeHayn!"

Wroje bursts into tears, and Koriah's face crumples. She reaches out to the young woman, and starts toward her, but thinks better of it. "It was an accident,

Wroje, you must believe me. I didn't mean to kill her. I didn't want to hurt anyone."

"You're a Galactic Defender," says Ogwen. "You're supposed to protect us."

"I know that," snaps Koriah, without looking at him. She pleads with Wroje again. "We were fighting. LeHayn slipped. She hit her head. I'd give anything for it not to have happened, Wroje. I wish Karza's time machine worked, so I could go back and stop myself."

"Why were you in the laboratory?" asks Acroyear, cutting to the crux of the matter.

"Isn't it obvious?" sneers Ogwen. "Karza was right all along. She's a spy. She wanted to steal his work for the Centauri!"

"No," says Koriah firmly. "I'm not working for them."

"Why should we believe you? You're probably not even a Galactic Defender. That was just a cover story to get you on board, to make us trust you."

"I only did what I thought was right. At the time. If Karza had told me the full story..." Koriah's voice trails off; nobody seems game to prompt her.

Impatiently, I break the silence, speaking through my watching Biotron. "Tell them, girl. Tell them why you came here."

She chews on her lower lip. "When we got your message, when you asked for our help..." She falters, and turns to address Wroje again. "We'd heard of Karza, and we'd heard rumors about his project. We should have investigated long ago, but there are so few of us now, so much to do. This seemed like a good opportunity."

"You weren't sent to defend us against the Centauri at all," Ogwen realizes.

"Don't you understand? We're talking about time

travel here. We're talking about the ability to step into the past and change what has happened, what was *meant* to happen. With a time machine, you could destroy your enemies before they even become a threat to you. You'd have the power of life and death—literally, because you could decide who was born, even which worlds spawned life." Koriah is becoming more confident, more passionate, as she fights her corner. "What Karza is building here—*was* building—could be the most powerful weapon created. That's why the Centauri want it—so, yes, that was the first part of my mission: to keep it from them."

"And Karza?" asks Acroyear.

"I had my doubts. I saw what he did to the insectoid, the way he treated his staff as if they were disposable." She turns to Ogwen now. "I know you felt the same. Ask yourself, Ogwen: Could you live in a world that Karza created? Do you trust him enough to give him that measure of control? Are you sure he'd use it for the good of all?"

Ogwen stares back at her, red-eyed, for a few seconds. Then he lowers his gaze in defeat, murmuring something that my Biotron's ears don't pick up.

Koriah's satisfaction is short-lived. Shamefaced, she continues, "I didn't know about the rest of it. I was following orders. No, more than that, I believed in those orders. I was given the authority, if I thought it necessary, to terminate the time travel project. I didn't know LeHayn was working that night. She must have stepped out of the lab. She walked in on me. I tried to explain, but she..." She swallows. "I fought back. I couldn't let her stop me. I was fighting for the greater good...so I thought. I was doing my job, living up to my title—but LeHayn was determined. I know why now."

153

She teeters dizzily, puts a hand to her head and screws her eyes shut. Archer leaps to his feet, slips an arm around the girl's shoulders and guides her back to her seat. Clearly, her tale has swayed him. I don't know why that should irritate me, but it does.

"I must correct one detail of your account," I say tersely. "None of this, nothing you have experienced in your miserable life, was 'meant to happen'."

"I think we should continue this later," says Archer pointedly. "Koriah needs rest."

"I'm feeling a bit sick myself," burbles Ogwen, sinking to the floor.

"I'm okay," says Koriah bravely. "If there's anything else you need to ask…?"

All eyes turn to Wroje. Uncomfortable with the attention, she steps away from Acroyear. Her tears have dried, but still she can't look the Galactic Defender in the eye. "I…I'm sorry too," she says softly, breathily. "When I…change, when I become that…I can't control myself. I've kept it inside for so long, but…but…"

"You don't have to explain," says Koriah.

"There is one thing. What should Karza have told you? What did LeHayn know that made her fight you?"

Awkward glances are exchanged across the room. Only Ogwen remains oblivious, resting his head on his knees. Wroje nods to herself. "You don't have to tell me. LeHayn thought she could keep it from me—she always tried to protect me—but I knew. Perhaps she's the lucky one, after all. She got out before it happened. She…she didn't have to see the end coming."

Life goes on—isn't that the cliché? And soon, life returns to the Astro Station.

Acroyear prowls the corridors, assessing the damage, doubtless running through battle scenarios in his head. He won't accept defeat until he is dead. Koriah is on the bridge, keeping watch, although she looks weaker and weaker. With only five Biotrons active, and most of them engaged in repair work, I can't keep track of everybody. Eventually, however, I glimpse Knave, tinkering with a damaged life support unit, and a hidden microphone betrays Wroje's presence in the medical bay, talking softly to the unconscious Kellesh. Twenty minutes ago, she reported to the main lab, but I sent her away. I told her there was nothing she could do.

I was wrong. This isn't life, just a hollow approximation: People doing what they can to feel useful, when there's nothing to be done. Striving for an illusion of normality, because the truth would drive them insane.

What can I do? What is *my* normality? Without the project, what remains? My body may be all but immobilized, but I've always had my dreams. Now even they are too painful to offer refuge, tinged with the taste of defeat and the knowledge of consequences to come.

I had a Biotron bring me the remnants of the last probe, to confirm what I already knew. It cannot be salvaged. Turning the rusted, crumbling wreck in my hands, I made the surprising discovery that its memory wafers are intact. A final cosmic joke at my expense: Archer's vaunted instinct allowed him to pull the probe back fast enough to save his useless data. His futile, dead-end route across time is recorded forever.

Snarling, I fling the probe into the farthest corner of my chamber.

"Knave said you were sick."

"It's nothing. It's just, my head's buzzing. Tension, I expect."

By now, the voices of Acroyear and Archer are familiar. I tune into their conversation by habit, although nothing I could hear would benefit me now.

"It is getting to all of us. I should leave you to your rest."

"No. No, I've tried to sleep, but I can't. I just keep going over and over everything in my mind. I can't take it all in. I mean, I've come all this way, I've left my home and my family, and I never knew why, exactly, but I always thought the Time Traveler would guide me. I thought, when it came down to it, I'd know what to do for the best, you know?"

"I know."

"Yeah, well, it turns out there was no Time Traveler after all, just me, so what do I take from that, huh? That the guy who's dragged me to the far end of space is just as much of a screw-up as I am? I mean, the universe, damn it. Everything! It's all going to die, and somehow it's all my fault even though I didn't do anything, and…and…"

"As I understand it," says Acroyear, "the universe has some time remaining to it yet."

"But the project…maybe we had a chance before, but I just…I ruined everything."

"There must be another solution. We will find it."

"How? Karza's spent his whole life looking, and he's, like, a genius."

"Maybe, but I have learned to trust in your intuition. The Time Traveler may not have brought you here, Archer, but your instincts did. I believe there is something you can do, some way you can make things better, and I believe you'll find it. You still have your guide, Archer; you only have to listen to him."

A moment's pause, then Archer asks quietly, "What about the Centauri?"

"They are my problem," says Acroyear.

"You ran the blockade once!"

"From the outside," says Knave, "when the Centauri weren't expecting it—and, even then, we'd never have got through without Kellesh's help."

Ogwen isn't ready to give up. "We can arrange another distraction. Maybe we can send out Karza's shuttle, or Koriah's Orbiter, on autopilot. The Centauri will go after them, and we can make a break for it."

"A decoy. Sure, that'll fool them."

"Right." Apparently, Ogwen didn't hear the sarcasm in Knave's tone. "Their Battle Cruisers, they're built for firepower, not speed. Once we're past them, they'll never catch us. Let them have the station. It's worth a try, isn't it? It has to be better than waiting here to die! What are we staying for, anyway? There's nothing left to defend!"

"Karza still has data that the Centauri want," says Knave. "Right now, I'd say that's the only thing keeping us in one piece."

"You think we're safe here?" shrieks Ogwen. "They won't go away! You killed their entire army—they won't be happy until we all pay for that!"

"They still have Acroyear to contend with."

"He's only one man. He can't save us! It'd be best for all of us if we handed him over—him and Karza both. They're the ones the Centauri want. Maybe we can cut a deal."

"I'm sure it won't come to that," says Knave dryly. "When we have your sunny disposition to keep morale high, how can we lose?"

"I didn't want to do it, Kellesh." Wroje's voice, from the medical bay, where I have no Biotrons to watch her. "I swore it wouldn't happen again, and I believed that. I thought I had the beast contained, but it never went away. It was always there, lurking under the surface. LeHayn could tame it, but now she's gone, and then…then, I heard it was Koriah who…well, I could feel it inside me, rising. It whispered inside my head, begging me to let it go because what harm could it do now? How could it make things worse?

"Mom was right. Everything she said, after they took me and…and gave me this mark. The hurtful things…I tried to convince myself that it wasn't my fault, I didn't choose this, but I know—I've always known, deep down—that a part of me wanted it. I wanted to feel strong. Today, I needed that feeling, needed it more than ever, and the beast offered it to me.

"I told Koriah, I told all of them, that I couldn't control it. But the truth is, in the end, I gave in. I was tired of resisting, of being hurt. I knew it would make me feel better if I let the beast out, and the awful thing is that it did.

"I don't know if you can hear me. I don't know why I'm telling you all this. Maybe it's because I know you won't judge me. I…I don't mean that to sound heartless. I just…I know we've never been too close, but LeHayn's gone, now. And Veelum—that poor, sweet old man—he's gone, too, and that means you're the only friend I have left, and I...I know this sounds selfish, but I just want you to wake up, even if it can only be for a short time.

"Please, Kellesh, wake up. I need you. I don't want to die alone."

Archer is in the laboratory, banging on the door to my chamber with his fists. "I know you're in there, Karza," he calls, stating the obvious. I am in no mood to speak with him. "I just want to talk, that's all. About what we saw, what it all means."

Unit #35 is observing in silence. Realizing that I can see him through the Biotron's eyes, Archer redirects his appeal toward him. I should probably turn off his audio receptors, but even that simple gesture seems too great an effort. I let the boy's words wash over me instead. "We can't take this lying down, Karza. If we put our heads together, between the two of us, surely we can find some way to...some way out. But it has to be soon, I think. I'm not sure, but...but that last vision, prediction, whatever you want to call it—the one where I...I used the time machine—I think that's going to happen soon. I mean, it *should* happen soon. Would happen, if the timelines hadn't been...you know what I'm saying."

I know. I am just not interested.

"We're coming to the point in time, the moment, when the Time Traveler...when *I* should set out on my journey. The moment when history gets royally screwed over because one of the big events that made it, the Time Traveler's appearance over Micropolis, doesn't get to happen. I...it's not like I remember seeing a calendar or anything in my visions, I just feel...the date...I think it's soon, Karza. Today. Maybe only a couple of hours away. I mean, that makes sense, right? I only started seeing this other timeline, this other future, a few weeks ago. I don't figure I can see all that far ahead, do you?"

I am impressed, in a small way. Archer is working his way toward a logical conclusion. I reached it before him, of course—but the solution won't help me.

He scowls at my intransigence, then turns away and pulls at his lower lip, deep in contemplation. A few minutes later, he marches out of the room without another word.

I lose track of Archer for some time, then—until he and Acroyear pass Unit #30 in a corridor, apparently wandering without aim. I have the Biotron follow them at a discreet distance, his audio receptors set to maximum gain.

"I've been thinking a lot lately," says Archer. "I've been thinking about what I'd do if I had to face a choice: this timeline or the old one."

"You thought the Time Traveler would have the answer to that problem."

"Yeah. I thought I knew what he wanted, you know? I thought he'd brought me here to put things back the way they were, to rewrite history somehow."

"It would be natural for him—for you—to desire that," says Acroyear guardedly.

"I guess. I know he made a mistake, and if I were him—which I kind of am—I'd want to put it right. Thing is, I keep thinking about this guy, this Ryan Archer who found a Pharoid time machine and became the Time Traveler, and he just doesn't feel like me. I mean, I've seen through his eyes and I understand him, I know why he did what he did, but I can't imagine being him, actually *being* him. His world, his life, it seems so far away, so long ago, and I keep asking myself, what if we're better off this way? What right does this guy, this stranger, have to expect me to sacrifice everything I know? He made the mistake, not me."

They round a corner, and their footsteps come to a halt. Unit #30 waits out of sight and listens. There is a long pause—so long that I wonder if Acroyear will answer Archer at all. Then, in a subdued tone, he says, "I am afraid, too. Logically, I know that, if the Time Traveler's timeline were restored, I would endure; my memories may even be happier. My memories, however, are a part of me. Were I to lose them, I'm not sure who I would become. Certainly, there would be no continuity of self between me and this alternative Acroyear. I fear that, in a very real sense, I would no longer exist."

Archer sighs. "Me, too, pal. Me, too."

Another pregnant pause. Then Acroyear rumbles, "You have seen both timelines: the one before the Time Traveler made his journey, and the one after, the current timeline. Maybe you are the only person who can choose which is the preferable."

Archer's voice is anguished. "Oh, God, don't say that! Don't you think I've thought about that, Acroyear? And, whenever I do, I turn cold. I'm not a...We're talking about two universes here, billions of lives, and I'm supposed to decide who lives and who dies? How can I do that? How could I live with myself if I did that?"

"If the only other option is that both universes die..."

"You've been through a lot, haven't you?" sighs Archer. "All that time in Micropolis, working in the mines for Maruunus Ki. I just keep thinking of all the...all the evil we've seen—the Reptos, the Centauri, what Ordaal and Nova tried to do on Earth, what Ki did to you—and I wonder if I'm being selfish."

"Selfish?"

"I could change all that. I could put it all right, I could prevent so much suffering—but I…deep down in my gut, I just…I don't want to."

"I am sure the other reality had its share of tragedy."

"I guess. I mean, yeah. They killed my dad. The Harrowers, they came through the Rift, and just…just gunned him down. I watched him die. And then, then I was catapulted into this…your galaxy, and we were on the run, always looking over our shoulders, always having to fight. I keep seeing the Emperor, the ruler of that place, and he scares the spit out of me."

"Then maybe you have your answer," says Acroyear. "Whatever the imperfections of this life, at least we are free now. I have sworn I will not be subjugated again."

"That's kind of what I figured," Archer says quietly. "It's just…I was thinking about the people Ordaal killed, back on Earth. I was asking myself what makes them less deserving of life than my dad is. And Karza…he was so sure that any order is better than chaos, that being ruled by a tyrant is better than having no leadership at all. I just needed to know that…that somebody agreed with me, that I'm not just taking the easy way out."

"I doubt anyone would describe your situation as easy."

"I've got butterflies in my stomach. Great big butterflies. I feel like I'm about to hurl. And my head's still pounding. Am I doing the right thing, Acroyear?"

"Perhaps the old reality has simply had its day. The here and now is more important."

"I guess that's it, then," says Archer. "The decision's made. For better or worse."

"And you can act upon it? You can save us?"

"I'm not sure. I have an idea. I need to...I think, maybe..."

"I knew you would find a way," says Acroyear.

The Cosmobot has finished piling up bodies in the hangar bay. As it turns to leave, the Antron caught in the hull swipes at it with a claw. The Cosmobot turns slowly, processes the sight of the helpless creature before it, and cracks its skull between its metal fists.

It stomps out into the corridor, closes the auto-repaired door, and opens the hangar to space. Hundreds of dead Antrons spin out into the void, many of them glancing off the shields of Centauri Battle Cruisers as they begin their uncontrolled voyages into infinity. This defiant gesture gives me some small satisfaction. I expect—almost hope—the Centauri representative to break her sullen silence, to vent her anger at me, but it doesn't happen.

My instruments tell me that Wroje has the medical computer scanning Kellesh for a third time. Under better circumstances, I would have been forced to berate her for this waste of resources: The computer has delivered its diagnosis, and is doing all it can, synthesizing drugs to pump into the Terragonian's bloodstream. If he is still slipping away—and his monitored life signs suggest that he is—then there is nothing more to be done about it.

On the bridge, Koriah is slumped unmoving over her console. I can see that she is still breathing, but I don't know if she is unconscious or simply in a deep sleep. It bothers me that the supervising Unit #32 hasn't gone to her assistance—the health of the Galactic Defender is of little concern to me now, but the suggestion of a systems error in another Biotron is worrying. Indeed, as I watch, his output flickers and dies. I scowl. He must have been more damaged than I thought during the fighting.

I think about sending another Biotron to investigate. Before I can act, however, the door to the laboratory flies open, and Archer strides in. "I need to use your computer," he says to me through Unit #35; it is not a request.

"I think I know what you're planning," I say. "A brave, but foolhardy, decision."

He seems surprised that I have acknowledged him. He hesitates, but only for a moment. He takes a seat at the computer's main control panel, his hand moving briefly to his temple as his eyelids flutter. "Yeah, well," he says, pulling himself together with visible effort, "it doesn't look like I have a whole heap of options, does it?"

"Tell me, Archer, how did you change so much?"

"I…As the Time Traveler, you mean? I don't know. I don't know everything." I took him by surprise. He is being evasive again. Interesting. "I mean…the old Emperor built his Throne-World around him, we know that much."

"A change of location, no more. Surely time could have smoothed over such a minor inconsistency? Instead, we have a history in which the Emperors were felled, in which an entire galaxy was given over to anarchy."

"Maybe…I don't know, maybe he picked the wrong neighbors."

"*I* deposed the last Emperor."

"I know," says Archer woodenly.

"Then, am I to conclude that my life is important after all? I made a difference?"

"I'm sure lots of people made a difference. I don't…"

"When I was a boy," I recount, "the Emperor killed my father and massacred my people. Only I was spared. He took me to his Throne-World. That was where I first saw the Time Traveler. How might my life have turned out, I wonder, had there been nobody to see, had the sky above the Emperor's palace been empty? What might I have achieved had I not been distracted by the near impossible task of saving a universe that you placed in jeopardy?"

"Pretty full of yourself," mutters Archer.

I can see through his bitter words. "Arrogant as it may seen, I have always believed myself destined for greatness. My dreams have been of bringing order to this galaxy, and perhaps beyond. The Emperor—much as I despised him—saw that potential in me. He raised me to take his place. I could—should—have ruled."

"I'm not sure what you're getting at."

"I think you know what became of me," I growl, "in the old timeline."

"No."

I clench my fists in frustration. "Don't toy with me, boy! You have been keeping that knowledge from me since we met. Why? What do you fear I would do with it?"

"I don't…I just think that, sometimes, it's best not to know."

"You expect me to accept that? I have devoted my life to the pursuit of knowledge!"

"I won't tell you!" vows Archer, with a sudden display of spirit.

"Then I shall rip the truth from your mind!"

"Tried that already, remember?" His tone is mutinous, but he betrays himself with a flicker of his eyes, checking that he can reach the door before my Biotron does.

"At its highest setting," I tell him, "my mind probe can broil your brain in its casing."

"You can't!" he protests. "Listen, Karza, you don't understand! The Time Traveler, the old timeline, who did what to whom, it doesn't matter. All that matters now is that this universe is dying, and I can save it. I'm sure I can! I'm the only one who—"

I laugh. *"Now* who is displaying his arrogance?"

"You don't understand."

"Oh, I understand, Archer. You plan to reenact your other self's folly. As the Time Traveler, he changed his own past. He created a reality in which his journey never took place, in which the myriad effects of that journey were left without cause. You intend to provide that cause, to gather the flapping strands of time and to knit them together—to complete the loop."

"You plotted the Time Traveler's cause," says Archer, "by analyzing the destruction he created. I know you have that data; it's stored in your computer."

"As I said, brave but foolhardy. You would don my containment suit and step through the Rift, knowing the consequences. You would allow your molecules to be spread across time, knowing that the merest echo of that pain almost broke you."

"That's right," says Archer, pale but defiant. "And God knows, the idea of it terrifies me, but what else can I do? This is for everything, the whole ball of wax. I caused this problem—I accept that—and I'm the only one who can solve it. I have to do this, Karza, don't you see?

"I have to become the Time Traveler."

CHAPTER
NINE

I gave Archer permission to use the computer. I felt I couldn't refuse.

He was wary at first, forever glancing over his shoulder at my Biotron. In his position, I would have asked Acroyear to stand guard over me; I can only assume that he isn't ready to tell his friend about his planned sacrifice, doesn't want to face the inevitable questions and soul-searching.

It didn't take him long to lose himself in his work, to forget about me. The rhythmic click-clacking of the computer keyboard could almost be soothing, but I have a sick feeling in my stomach. I'm sure—as sure as I can be without empirical data—that Archer's plan will work. He can save the universe. I feel somehow churlish that that thought bothers me.

The boy has been on this station for a day, and already he is close to doing what I have striven to do for more years than he can imagine. It will be he, not I, who is remembered as a hero, the savior of everything. My feelings, however, run deeper and are far more complex than mere jealousy.

Archer has deduced nothing that I haven't long known. Why does he think that, when I prepared my

containment suit, I modeled it after that of the Time
Traveler? The suit, with its blank mask, conceals its
wearer's identity. Archer thinks it has to be he who
steps into the Rift, who gives his life. He is wrong.
Time needs its Time Traveler, but the suit is all that
matters. Many times I have thought of donning it
myself, when the time was right. It was always a last
resort, of course, a way of snatching at least some
achievement from defeat. It was a possibility about
which I told nobody, a choice I never expected to
have to make.

A decision I could still take.

I have run many simulations of this scenario. They
all brought me to the same conclusion. Archer won't
repair time this way—the damage is too extensive—but he can patch it up. He can halt the cancer.
He can keep time alive, but in a fragile state. Travel
into the past would be as difficult as ever; to visit any
of the days of the Time Traveler's life would be to
unwind the fabric altogether. I will never whisper
those words into my younger self's ear. I will never
have my order. I will die soon, my destiny unful-
filled—and, if I must leave the universe in its present
state, then what is the point of leaving it at all?

Part of me—a voice inside me, one I have rarely
heard—urges me to do the noble thing. Archer is
young. I could take this burden from his shoulders.
I could be the hero.

And life would go on without me, in chaos.

The sound of the computer keyboard seems to fill
my chamber. But now, it feels like a quiet countdown
to my doom.

It took me some time to piece together what happened
next.

Wroje noticed it first. She read the latest medical report on the unconscious Kellesh, compared it to the first two, and was alarmed by what she saw. My first intimation that something was wrong came when she raced out of the medical bay, onto the bridge, calling to Koriah for help. She let out a gasp of horror as she saw the Galactic Defender's condition. She tried to get my attention through Biotron Unit #32, before realizing that he was dead.

I heard a series of scuffling sounds. I think Wroje started to move Koriah, maybe toward the medical bay, before she thought better of it and opened the station's intercom system. "Please," she called plaintively, "everybody come to the bridge. Something's happened. Kellesh and Koriah...help, please!"

By then, the sickness was well advanced in her, too. Knave would arrive to find her short of breath, and doubled up with stomach cramps.

Meanwhile, Archer leapt to his feet, and asked me what was going on. I told him, honestly, that I didn't know. At that point, I hadn't thought to read the report on Kellesh. I didn't know that his cell tissue was decaying, ravaged by a type of radiation I hadn't encountered before.

Acroyear had had his suspicions. He'd heard Archer's complaints of feeling ill, and had realized that he was sickening himself. Unit #30's log would show that the warrior had asked him to scan the station for hazardous substances. He had found nothing—a mark of how devious the Centauri had been.

One of the Antrons must have placed the device. It is small—the size of an egg—and stuck well to the underside of a console. The radiation it spews has grown stronger, more harmful, by the second. It was difficult to find, of course; fortunately, Acroyear realized that it was the people nearest to the bridge who had suffered the most, and this told him where to start looking. He had the others carry Koriah and Kellesh to the farthest point of the station—my main laboratory, as it happens—and began the search alone.

I sent Unit #23 to watch him. Mindful of #32's fate, however, I let him go no farther than the doorway to the bridge. Even when Acroyear requested his help, I refused it. "He is a bio-mechanoid," I explained. "His organic components make him as susceptible to this malaise as any of us."

"He's a robot, Karza!" Acroyear snarled. "He's expendable!"

"Remind me to debate the definition of life with you," I said, "if ever we have time."

I withdrew the Biotron after that, and was forced to rely on my listening devices and secondhand accounts to learn what happened next. I know that Archer and Knave returned to the bridge, overriding Acroyear's perfunctory objections. I know that Archer soon succumbed to the sickness, and was carried back to the lab by the Vaerian. And I know that Acroyear eventually found the device, too late.

Later, Knave would confess his shock at returning to his armored comrade to find him sprawled across the floor. Acroyear had seemed so strong, but it had been sheer resolve that had kept him upright as his muscles had weakened.

I had already accessed the medical computer remotely, and set it to work on the problem. It's still processing, still trying to extrapolate the properties of the unknown radiation from its effects upon Kellesh. I can only hope that the task of so doing, and of synthesizing a cure, is not beyond it. I have shown no symptoms yet—maybe my containment suit has protected me—but I need to be sure. I won't die that way. I won't give the Centauri that satisfaction.

Ogwen hadn't been seen for some time. I heard a sickly, gurgling groan from his quarters—about the same time that Knave was straining to pull Acroyear's metal-clad frame into the corridor—and then nothing more. Back in the laboratory, Archer was starting to come round. Wroje didn't know what to do. She'd been pacing, often starting towards the door but stopping herself. Acroyear had told her to stay put. She'd fetched water from the dispenser in the corner, dampened a handkerchief and soothed the brow of the unconscious Kellesh. She had also done the same for Koriah—I'm not sure I could be so forgiving.

She turned, lighting up with hope, as the door opened. Units #23 and #39 entered, the former carrying Acroyear slung over his broad shoulders, the latter allowing Knave to lean on him. I sealed the room behind them, knowing it would do little to protect us.

Acroyear's powers of recuperation are miraculous. No sooner had he been lowered to the floor than he was trying to haul himself to his feet. He had to settle for landing heavily on a wooden stool, which almost splintered beneath his sudden weight.

"You can't go back in there!" Knave is telling him now.

"Somebody has to," grunts Acroyear, his voice dry and cracked.

"Whatever that thing's giving off, it's getting stronger. I could feel it. Even the Biotrons couldn't get within ten feet of it now. Look at you, you can't even stand!"

Of course, that only gives him an incentive to try again, to prove the Vaerian wrong.

"Evacuate," murmurs Archer, his head lolling on his shoulders. "Only chance…"

"That is what the Centauri want," argues Acroyear. "They will be ready to gun down our ships as they appear."

"Leaving the Astro Station deserted," muses Knave, "but its contents undamaged."

"We aren't safe in here. We have to jettison that device—and the longer we leave it, the more difficult it will be." Knave reacts with alarm as Acroyear teeters toward the door—but, finding it locked, the warrior can muster no more than a feeble slap to its surface.

Unseen by anybody but me, Wroje is scratching the tattoo on her neck, nervously. I know what she's thinking, but the beast inside her can only be unleashed by anger, not fear, and then its rage would be unpredictable, impossible to direct. It can't help us.

"I hate to sound like our friend Ogwen," says Knave, "but I think we're dead!"

He underestimates me. As soon as Acroyear relayed the position of the device to the others, I sent a servant to deal with it: The only one who could hope to withstand its intense radiation for long enough to reach it, let alone remove it.

There's a certain irony to this, I suppose. I've always dismissed the Cosmobot as a plodding automaton, precisely because of its lack of biological components. Its vice-like hands are the perfect shape to pry the Centauri device from its hiding place. It holds it pressed to its chest, trying to smother it. Unfortunately, such close and intense exposure has its consequences. The Cosmobot stomps off the bridge, with its usual slow, clumsy gait, but the metal of its casing is already starting to bubble. It doesn't give up, of course; its programming won't allow it.

By the time it reaches the airlock, I'm amazed it can function. Silver rivulets run down its expressionless face, and its hands have melted into a shapeless mass around the device. I can almost hear its processors wheezing as it staggers over the rim of the circular hatchway—and then, finally, its limbs lock, its purple and yellow colors running together until it resembles nothing more than a mass of congealed candy.

Not without a twinge of sadness, I close the airlock door, and expel the Cosmobot into space.

I could almost admire the Centauri. Lethal as the radiation from their device was, it is easily dealt with by the station's atmospheric scrubbers. Soon, it will have dropped to safe levels, even on the bridge. Had it not been for the Cosmobot—had we all been dead by now—I've no doubt that my enemies would already be preparing a boarding party.

For now, everyone remains confined to the main laboratory. Even Ogwen arrived a few minutes ago, seeking help, unaware of everything that has happened, complaining that he was dying. The medical computer—patched through to the main computer in the lab—has dispensed pills that should alleviate the immediate symptoms of radiation poisoning; the long-term consequences remain to be discovered, but I'm sure they can be managed.

Koriah has surprised me with the speed of her recovery. Kellesh is still unconscious, wired up to the computer again, but his prognosis has improved considerably. Archer is growing twitchy, impatient for the Terragonian to be returned to the medical bay so that he can resume his work here. One unexpected benefit of this diversion is that it has given me time to think about the boy's plan. I know what I have to do now. My greatest concern is that I have only four Biotrons remaining to me; I will have to be circumspect in my approach.

"I have something to say." Archer's voice, and the sound of him clearing his throat, cuts across the hum of conversation, and all eyes turn toward him. I half expected this. Impatient to be doing something useful, he has decided to confront the one task he has been putting off. "There's something I think you should all know."

He tells them his plan. He tells them that he intends to become the Time Traveler, to give his life for them all. And they listen intently—Acroyear, Koriah, Wroje, Ogwen and Knave—but, when the boy has finished his explanation, not one of them has a word to say. It is too much for them to take in. They've endured so much already, and this latest development leaves them nonplussed.

Disconcerted, Archer breaks the silence with an appeal to Acroyear. The warrior thinks for a moment, then asks, "Are you certain this is the only way?"

"It's the only way I can think of."

"Then I understand," says Acroyear. And Archer smiles.

Ogwen, too, has sifted through the information presented, and found his usual angle on it: his own self-interest. "How does that help us?" he blurts out.

Knave frowns. "Perhaps you weren't listening. The universe; the end of all that is…"

"But it won't get us out of here, will it? We'll still be at the mercy of those creatures!"

Wroje shakes her head excitedly. "No. No, we won't. With the timelines straightened out, Karza can do what he promised. He can go back into the past and change what's happened."

Acroyear turns to the nearest Biotron. "Is that true?" he asks, skeptically.

"Regrettably," I answer, "that is quite impossible now."

Wroje looks crestfallen. Acroyear just nods. "Maybe," says Koriah, in a quiet voice, speaking for the first time since she woke, "maybe that's for the best. We've seen the consequences of meddling with time. Maybe the past should be left as it is."

Ogwen opens his mouth to protest, but Acroyear interrupts him. "We can still win this war, in the present."

"Are you kidding me? Have you looked out of a porthole lately?"

"We have taken all the Centauri have to throw at us so far. We are still here."

"Tell that to Veelum," the bureaucrat grumbles. "Or LeHayn. Or—"

"Is there some way we could mask our life signs?" asks Knave, thoughtfully. "Make the Centauri think their radiation doohickey finished us all off?"

"It's possible," says Koriah, "but I don't think it'd do us much good. Whatever their sensors tell them, the Centauri aren't likely to board the station without taking every precaution against an ambush."

"Still," says Acroyear, "we should take every advantage we can get, no matter how small."

"You want another fight with those creatures?" cries Ogwen. "You're crazy! We can't fight the Centauri. The only options we have are to deal with them or run!"

"A deal is out of the question," growls Acroyear.

"Why?" asks Ogwen hotly. "You heard what Karza said. Once Archer's taken the big leap, and...and done whatever it is he thinks he has to do, this project—the time machine—it won't be any use to anyone. Why not hand it over? Okay, maybe they'll kill Karza, maybe they'll just lock him up—but he's an old man, he doesn't have long left, and the rest of us…if we plead with them, tell them how he wouldn't let us leave…"

It's a measure of how far my reputation has fallen that Ogwen, of all people, would discuss me in such terms, knowing that I can hear him. Fortunately, the others pay him no heed. He lets his voice trail off, and shuffles uncomfortably.

"I hate to admit it," says Koriah, "but I think running may be our only option. Your ship, the *Sunrunner*, can outpace the Battle Cruisers, right?"

"We'd need one hell of a diversion," says Knave, "to get past them a second time."

"How long do we have?" Acroyear's question is directed at Archer.

"Um, well, I haven't finished analyzing the Time Traveler's path yet, mapping it onto our dimensional coordinates. I think, if I'm to recreate his journey…well, I'm not sure I have to leave at the precise time he did, not to the second, but the closer the better, I guess. So…"

"Approximately?"

Archer takes a deep breath. "About two and a half hours."

"Then we shall have to hope the Centauri don't attack again within that time," says Acroyear. Turning to address the others, he adds, "And we must be prepared. As soon as Archer steps into the Rift, we make our move."

"Why wait?" protests Ogwen.

"Because Archer's mission is paramount. We must protect him until it is completed."

"We'd protect him just as well by drawing the Battle Cruisers away from the station!"

Acroyear shakes his head. "We can't guarantee that they'd follow us for long. In any case, Knave was right. We need as big a diversion as we can muster."

"The Astro Station," gasps Wroje. "You're going to blow up the Astro Station!"

"Unless you have a better idea," says Acroyear.

Kellesh is back in the medical bay. Archer has resumed his work at the computer in the laboratory. Of Koriah, Ogwen and Knave, I have lost track, but I can see Acroyear and Wroje on the bridge. The warrior has called up a plan of the Battle Cruisers' current positions, and is scribbling on a data pad, occasionally asking Biotron Unit #30 to provide a calculation for him. Wroje entered a few minutes ago, but didn't dare disturb him. She hovers in the doorway, waiting for him to notice her. At last, she takes two steps toward him and clears her throat timidly.

"I brought you this," she says, displaying a light strip of gray plastic into which is set a metal disc. "It has circuitry inside it; I cannibalized it from the backup communications systems. It gives off an inaudible signal that should baffle the Centauri's sensors. I've made one for everybody, including the Biotrons. I just have to give Kellesh his, and find Koriah."

"Good work," says Acroyear as he takes the band and fastens it around his wrist. It is only just long enough.

Unit #30 proffers his hand, and Wroje digs another baffler out of her pocket and ties it around a thick metal finger. As Acroyear turns back to his work, she asks hesitantly, "What...what are you doing?"

"I am calculating our optimal flight path," he says. "The intention is to go out with all guns blazing. We target this Battle Cruiser here." Wroje peers curiously over Acroyear's shoulder as he indicates a scrawled X on his pad. "With surprise on our side, I hope to be able to keep its pilot on the defensive, too busy trying to return fire. In the meantime, we will be keeping the Astro Station between us and these ships here." He circles five more Xs, his light pen leaving a white impression on the black surface. "These four—" another circle "—are unlikely to fire on us for fear of hitting the station."

"But that still leaves two," Wroje points out.

"Yes. Well, that is where we must trust to the *Sunrunner*'s shields, my piloting skills, and a certain amount of fortune."

"What about the station's self-destruct?"

"It will be timed to activate as we reach this point here."

"Isn't that too close?"

"Any farther, and we'd be in the sights of at least six Cruisers. Our only chance is to ride out the explosion. It may even give us a little extra momentum."

"Or it might just tear us apart," shrills Wroje.

"It is a risky plan," Acroyear concedes, "almost suicidally so, but it's all we have—unless you think we are up to the task of luring a Battle Cruiser on board and hijacking it."

"No!" says Wroje quickly.

"Try to have faith, Wroje. If this works, the Centauri will be disoriented. The debris from the explosion will make it almost impossible for their weapons to lock onto us, at least for a few seconds. That could be all we—"

A chirruping sound cuts across him: a page from the hangar bay. I have no Biotrons there, and can't see what is happening, but I recognize Ogwen's voice, hoarse with barely controlled panic, as Acroyear accepts the call. "Koriah, Acroyear, somebody...can you hear me?"

"I can hear you."

"Oh, thank goodness! I need...the hangar...there's something in here. One of those creatures. An Antron! I saw it. I can hear it, crawling about in the dark, around Koriah's ship. It's between me and the door. It's waiting...Please, help me!"

Acroyear outpaces my Biotron on his way to the hangar, so again I must piece together a picture of what is happening from the audio feed: A yelp of surprise from Ogwen, a brief scuffle, a discharging laser pistol, a heavy thump and a groan.

"Step away from him!" The warrior's voice, firm and commanding.

"Acroyear, is that you? It's me. It's Knave."

Footsteps crossing the hangar, boots ringing on the metal floor. "What happened in here?" asks Acroyear. "What happened to Ogwen? He called for help."

"He just went crazy," says Knave. "I was checking over the *Sunrunner*, tuning up the engines; next thing I knew, Ogwen was behind me, screaming at me. He shot at me!"

"Did he hurt you?"

"He's a lousy aim."

"So, you rendered him unconscious."

"He kept yelling at me, telling me to keep away from him. He called me a 'filthy animal.' "

"I believe he mistook you for an Antron." I can only imagine Knave's reaction to that. "You must admit, there is a superficial similarity."

"Yeah, thanks for pointing that out. I tried to stay clear of Ogwen, I hid behind the Rhodium Orbiter—that's when he got to the compad and called you—but he kept firing that blasted pistol. He was shooting at shadows. I was worried he might take a chunk out of our ship. I managed to sneak up behind him. I used a Laen Ka nerve pinch. He'll be out for a minute or two. I was taking his pistol from him when you came in."

"I wonder," muses Acroyear, "what made him see you as one of the enemy?"

"You're asking me? He was drunk, as usual; maybe he was hallucinating. Maybe he finally flipped out altogether. He's always struck me as being a few pegs short of a Karrio."

"There is another possibility," says Acroyear mildly. "Perhaps Ogwen was right."

I frown. Knave, too, is confused; it takes him a moment to work out how to react. "What are you saying?" he asks.

"Perhaps you are working for the enemy."

"Hey, hey, now come off it big guy, this is Knave here—your old pal, Knave."

"I am not your 'pal.' I know almost nothing about you."

"There's nothing *to* know," Knave protests. I can hear movement, and I know that he's backing away from Acroyear, just as surely as I know that Acroyear is following him. "I'm just the typical kid who ran away from the circus to join…okay, maybe not so typical…"

"I have only Archer's word that you can be trusted—and he, too, came into my life without invitation. You are working for Ki, aren't you?"

"Maruunus Ki? The Baron of Micropolis? You told me he was dead!"

"Or maybe that is what you wanted me to think."

"Okay, you're starting to scare me now. What's going on here, Acroyear? Did I just slip into a parallel—Hey!"

"Keep still," growls Acroyear. "Keep still, you infuriating jackrabbit!" More scuffling, punctuated by the whoosh of an energy blade igniting.

Knave mutters something that sounds like, "Not likely." And Unit #30 arrives on the scene to see the Vaerian performing an impressive back flip, bouncing off the hull of Koriah's Orbiter to somersault over Acroyear's head. The warrior swipes at him with his blazing sword. He means business; had he been any slower, Knave would have been decapitated. He lands atop the golden bubble of the *Sunrunner*'s cockpit. Acroyear tries to leap after him, but Knave plants a foot on his armored head to push him away. Then he springs across the ship's gray hull, and up onto a raised wing, where the warrior can't reach him.

"Okay," he says with a dry, humorless laugh, "I get it now. A little slow on the uptake, maybe, but I see what's happening. You're working for him, right?" He stabs a clawed finger in the direction of Unit #30, and I wonder if he's referring to me.

"Unlike you, I work for nobody!" Acroyear clambers up onto the *Sunrunner*'s top, but Knave is a step ahead of him, taking a running leap across the gap to the Orbiter.

"What's up, Shell-Head?" he taunts his pursuer. "The hero gig not paying enough? You had to sell your friends out to a scum-sucking bounty hunter?"

With a furious roar, Acroyear hurls his sword, its blade leaving a trail of fire. Knave's black eyes widen, and he propels himself backwards, losing his footing in the process. Acroyear sees his opportunity and leaps to intercept him. He hits the floor with a reverberating clang, but Knave has flipped himself upright in mid-fall, landed on his feet, and somehow avoids the warrior's flailing hands. He darts into the shadows, and Acroyear retrieves his weapon and casts around for him. He grunts, more with irritation than pain, as two laser bolts stab out from behind the *Sunrunner* and punch into his side. By the time he reaches Knave's hiding place, the Vaerian has moved on, unseen.

"Come out and fight me!" he yells, but the demand is answered only by its own echo. "I know you're watching me," roars Acroyear. "You're always there, always watching!"

A chink of metal on metal: a machine part, kicked or dropped. Or thrown. Acroyear starts toward it, recognizing the diversion too late. I see a blur of purple behind the spherical hulk of my shuttle pod. Acroyear moves to cut off his quarry, but Knave reaches the door before him, bounds through it on all six limbs, and then he is gone.

Pushing Unit #30 aside, Acroyear races after him, but comes to a halt in the wide, empty corridor outside the hangar bay. For a long moment, I hear nothing but the sound of his deep breathing. Then, slowly, he rounds on the watching Biotron, raising his sword, as if blaming him for this setback. "Defend yourself," I instruct the unit. "Employ lethal force if necessary." But the threatened attack never comes. Acroyear remains frozen for a few seconds more, then

he deactivates his weapon and, to my surprise, lets it
fall from his hand.

"Tell your master," he says, "that I know what he
has done to me. I know what he wants, and I refuse
to play his game any longer."

He turns and walks away, leaving his sword behind
him.

Unit #30's audio receptors pick up another sound.
Turning, he sees Ogwen fleeing down the corridor in
the opposite direction.

The main computer chatters away to itself, calculating
the final details of Archer's path through time, align-
ing the Rift to direct him where he needs to go. The
boy left the laboratory without a word to me, just
after Wroje gave us both our sonic bafflers. His work
is done, his fate sealed. Unit #39 finds him wandering
the corridors between the refectory and the bridge,
hollow-eyed, clutching a plastic cup that contains a
hot stimulant drink. I decide not to disturb him. I can
only imagine what he is thinking. He has just under
one hour of life left to him, but I don't doubt that it
will feel like an eternity.

He is about to turn a corner, out of the Biotron's
sight, when he collides with an agitated Wroje. "Oh.
Oh, thank goodness," she trills, "thank goodness I've
found somebody. It's Kellesh—she's taken him!
You've got to help me find him."

Archer blinks, and puts a tentative hand to his head.
"What…what are you…?"

Wroje takes his arms and shakes him urgently.
"Kellesh! When I went to the medical bay, he'd gone.
She's taken him, Archer, I know she's taken him!"

"Who…?" he stammers groggily. "Who do you
think…?"

"Koriah, of course. She hates me! She's doing this to hurt me. She'll murder Kellesh, like she murdered LeHayn, and then I'll be alone again..." She can't say any more. Her words dissolve beneath a deluge of tears.

"Whoa, hold on a minute! Koriah? You think she'd...? No. No, she wouldn't. She just..." Archer has snapped out of his daze; now, he just looks bewildered.

"She's taken him, I tell you!" wails Wroje. "Do you know where she is? You don't, do you? Nobody knows. Nobody's seen Koriah for over an hour, and now Kellesh has gone, too, and...and who else could it be? She's killed before, she can do it again!"

"Look, Wroje, you've got to...I know what happened to LeHayn was terrible, but it was an accident. Koriah explained—"

"She tricked us! She lied to us!"

"If she—if anyone—wanted to kill Kellesh, they'd have done it in the medical bay. Why move him? Maybe he just, I don't know, woke up; maybe he was confused, and..."

"He's dead," moans Wroje. She collapses against the wall, the fight gone out of her. "I can feel it. Kellesh is dead! She killed him, then she hid the body somewhere, so no one would believe me, so no one would stop her. She'll kill Ogwen next, and then Karza, and in the end there'll be only me left, and she'll have won. She'll have won!"

"You're not making sense," says Archer helplessly. He reaches out to comfort her, but Wroje pushes him away with a scream.

"Don't touch me! That's what she wants! That's what she always said to me when I got this mark, that no one would want to touch me now. She told me I was cursed, that I'd taint anyone I came into contact with, and she was right. That's why she's here now, that's why she's tormenting me, because I started to fool myself. I thought I could live a normal life, I thought I didn't have to be lonely any more."

"I don't…Slow down, I don't know what you're trying to…"

"That's why she's killing them—to prove that she was right. She was right about me!"

"Koriah?"

"No!" Wroje's voice has dropped to a whisper. Suddenly, she fixes Archer with a look of unnerving intensity. "My mother! She's back! She's come back to punish me!"

"Come out of there!"

With almost two-thirds of my Biotrons out of action, I feel blind. Events are happening that I can't monitor, can't plan around. I tell myself that it doesn't matter, that the actions of Koriah and the others are of little importance, but it's hard to relinquish that measure of control once you've had it. I have been scanning all radio frequencies inside the station, searching for our missing personnel. That's how I came to pick up an unexpected voice from an unexpected location, out of range of my listening devices.

"I know you're in there. Come out and face me, or I'll shoot!"

The bowels of the Astro Station, where the recycling tanks were once stored—now open to the void. Kellesh must be wearing a spacesuit, broadcasting his warning on its short-wave communicator—to whom, I wonder?

I soon have my answer. "Don't fire! It's me, Kellesh. It's Koriah."

"I know who you are," says Kellesh. "I want to know what you're doing."

"Hey, someone had to keep this station going while you were out cold," says Koriah with forced levity.

Kellesh isn't fooled. "Do you think I don't know what's behind that access panel? You were trying to bypass the command routines for the auto-destruct system."

"This isn't what it looks like."

"No? How did you even know that circuitry was there? You must have seen my schematics of the station. You've been spying on me!"

"Look, Kellesh, I'm glad you're up and around again, but you shouldn't be down here. You need rest. You're confused!"

"How can I rest with those creatures on board?" The Terragonian's voice has risen in pitch. I've rarely heard that happen before; he is usually so even-tempered.

"Creatures?"

"You think I should have stayed where I was, strapped to that table, so those lizards could…could operate on me, slice me open like they did my wife and son!"

"Kellesh," says Koriah quietly, "I want you to lower that pistol."

"You're working for them, aren't you? They found out I'd escaped, and they told you to destroy the station. They don't want me to live!"

"Please, Kellesh, don't make me do anything we'll both regret."

I picture them, dancing around each other in the wreckage. The darkness must be lit only by the chest beam of Kellesh's spacesuit and the energy helmet of Koriah's airtight armor. The absence of gravity must render their movements almost balletic. I picture their gazes, and their pistols, locked in mutual distrust.

"I'm warning you for the last time," says Koriah. "Please, Kellesh, I beg of you, lower that weapon."

"Repto spy!" hisses Kellesh.

I have no way of knowing what happens then. All I can say for is sure is that neither Koriah nor Kellesh have anything more to say to each other.

"They don't understand," I observe. "They don't know what is happening to them."

"Of course they don't. They lack your insight."

"An obvious trick; not up to the Centauri's usual standards at all."

"You should be insulted, that they thought you weak enough to be fooled."

"I could stop this now. It would be easy."

"Indeed."

"A simple cancellation wave," I say, "to blot out their subsonic signal. My people would soon come to their senses, stop seeing things that aren't there."

"But then our enemies would know we're alive, that we are still here."

"Then I shall dispense headphones, and broadcast white noise to them."

"That would work as well. But ask yourself, young Karza: Isn't there a way to turn this situation to your advantage?"

I nod, slowly. "Once they know what I am planning, they will try to stop me."

"Best, then, to keep them at each other's throats. Let the Centauri alter their brain chemistry, fuel their paranoid delusions. They may even do your job for you."

"Even if they don't," I realize, "I could act with impunity."

"Kill him now," urges the velvet voice of the man behind me, the dark presence at my shoulder. "Kill him, and in their misguided compassion, they will absolve you of blame. They will believe that you—even you—could lose your mind. They will seek elsewhere for their righteous vengeance, and you will be free to do what must be done."

"Then...then you agree with me? I've made the right choice?"

"In choosing the possibility, small as it may be, of glory over oblivion? Unquestionably. In choosing order over chaos? You know the answer to that."

He steps from the shadows, then, his black cloak sweeping across the floor. Those red eyes glare out from his black helmet, and a thin-lipped sneer stretches across his cracked chin. But I am no longer afraid of him. I bask in his approval. I don't ask where he came from, for in some sense he has always been with me. It seems fitting that he should show himself now, as I prepare to meet the destiny for which he shaped me.

"I am proud of you, my son," says the Emperor.

CHAPTER
TEN

A volley of laser fire.

Archer dives for shelter, finding it in the refectory doorway. He tries to pull Wroje after him, but she breaks free. For a moment she is lost, throwing up her hands in alarm as another blast sizzles past her ear. Then she turns and, tears streaming down her face, she runs.

Unit #39, in the meantime, bears down on the source of the threat. He finds Ogwen around the nearest corner, his back flattened to the wall. His eyes are wide and crazy, his face shiny with sweat. "Did it work?" he pants. "I don't dare look. Did I hit her?"

"BOTH WROJE AND RYAN ARCHER ARE UNHARMED," says the Biotron. "PLEASE EXPLAIN WHY YOU TRIED TO TERMINATE THEIR FUNCTIONS." The screen that displays his output blinks urgently, a request for instructions. I'm tempted to order Ogwen's execution, but he could be a useful distraction, so I hold my tongue.

"Damn! *Damn!*" Ogwen stares up into the Biotron's eyes. "You're programmed to protect us, aren't you? Well, do something! Get Archer out of there!"

"THE ONLY THREAT TO RYAN ARCHER OF WHICH I AM AWARE IS POSED BY YOU."

"No, no, no. It's that purple-haired bitch, don't you see? She's one of them. A Centaurus! She could change at any time. None of us are safe!"

In the absence of guidance, the Biotron acts on his own initiative. "I BELIEVE YOU ARE MISTAKEN. IN HER ALTERED FORM, WROJE DOES HAVE CERTAIN TRAITS IN COMMON WITH THE CENTAURI. HOWEVER—"

Ogwen backs away suddenly, feeling his way along the wall. "They've got to you, haven't they? They've reprogrammed you! It's Karza. He...he's sold us all out!"

"AGAIN, I MUST CORRECT—"

Ogwen isn't listening. He makes a run for it, and Unit #39 makes to follow him at his own pace. "No," I tell him. "Show me Archer."

I can already hear the boy talking. "I knew it was you," he says. "I knew you were behind this, somehow. You've always been out to get me. Well, congratulations—you've maneuvered me into throwing my life away, and you know what? I don't care. I don't care, because at least I'll be doing something worthwhile. I'll be saving people, not hurting them like you do. And this way, my dad gets to live and the universe gets to be free from you, so I win, right? I win!"

He's alone, of course, sitting in a straight-backed chair in the refectory, forever shifting around as if trying to retain eye contact with somebody who is circling him.

"Yeah. Yeah, I remember you now. You came to me in the other timeline, only you didn't look like you do now. You had the chestplate, that was the same—but your body, it glowed. You were almost transparent, like solid light, except that I could see this freaky circuitry inside you. And you…" He shakes his head, as if hoping to make the memory clearer. "You took me to the past. I should have realized then. I saw your life story; I mean, what was that about? You thought I'd sympathize with you, if I saw what they did to you? You thought I'd see how similar we were, and give in to you? You said you'd come to help me, but all the time you were playing some kind of twisted game, and there I was wondering why your voice sounded so familiar, why the touch of your hand made my skin crawl."

"Who are you talking to, Archer?" I ask.

He starts, as if only now seeing my Biotron at the door. "You don't recognize him without his mask on? Look again, Karza—I *am* talking to Karza, right? Go on, take a good, hard look at the man who's shaped your life and mine, played us like puppets."

"The Time Traveler?" I guess.

"The one and only! The Time Traveler—only now, I can see who he really is."

"The Time Traveler is you, Archer. He always was."

"No, no, no, that's what he wanted us to think. He wanted me to take over from him. That's what he always planned—for me to become him!"

"I don't recognize him," I say quietly. "Who is he?"

The boy's voice has the edge of hysteria. "Don't you see? He's you! He's your future. Your past. The supreme being of the universe: the big, bad Baron Karza!"

And then Archer starts to laugh, rolling about on his chair until he cries.

I can hear Wroje and Knave taking potshots at each other from opposite ends of another corridor. Wroje accuses Knave of working for her mother; Knave, in turn, is convinced that Wroje is somebody called Nova. "You won't take me back to that circus," he swears. "You won't turn me into one of those creatures—I'll die first!"

Elsewhere, Ogwen rounds a corner and almost hurtles into Acroyear. He howls in fright, skids to a halt, turns and flees. The warrior doesn't break his step, doesn't show any sign that he even saw the bureaucrat.

Somehow, Koriah has managed to climb up from the station's bowels, past the wrecked service elevator, with Kellesh over her shoulder. She bundles the unconscious Terragonian into the arms of Unit #35, stressing that he needs to be returned to the medical bay. "I don't think I hurt him too badly," she says, "but he was firing a laser pistol. He could have torn a hole in my suit, or his own. I had to restrain him. What the hell is that noise?"

"I BELIEVE A DUEL IS IN PROGRESS—"

"The Centauri?"

"—BETWEEN WROJE AND THE VISITOR WHO CALLS HIMSELF KNAVE."

"What's happening around here? Has everyone gone insane?"

"I CAN ONLY OBSERVE THAT THE RECENT ACTIONS OF SOME INDIVIDUALS—"

"Why aren't you doing something about this?"

"I HAVE NO INSTRUCTIONS."

"Karza!" The Galactic Defender's helmet flows back from her head, revealing a scowl on her dark-skinned face. "You're doing this, aren't you? What is it—they decided to run out on you? Surrender to your enemies and hope for the best? So, you thought you'd teach them a lesson, like you did the insectoid! I warned you, Karza. I told you I wouldn't let it happen again. I'm coming to see you, Karza. We're going to have this out, once and for all!"

As she stalks away, toward the laboratory and this chamber, I realize that Wroje has stopped firing. Knave follows suit a few seconds later, and I hear his voice, bewildered and apprehensive, "Acroyear?"

He comes into sight of Unit #35, backing nervously away from the armored warrior, who in turn is acting as if he hasn't seen the Vaerian. His head is lowered, his concealed eyes apparently fixed on the ground. He marches past Knave without sparing him a glance.

"He called you 'Baron.' "

"I know."

"He recognizes your potential, as I did those many years ago."

"The confirmation I needed," I mutter. "But how can it be?"

"I expected no less," says the Emperor. "You would have ruled, had it not been for the distraction of the Time Traveler. In another timeline, freed from that distraction, you *did* rule. You saw the figure in Archer's visions, the one whose identity he hoped to conceal—who else could it have been? Who else could have succeeded to my throne?"

My head hurts. I am torn by conflicting emotions. Everything I have always wanted only a twist of time away, and yet..."I saw how that Emperor ruled. I saw what he did to Archer. He murdered his father. He did to him what...what you did to me." I find the strength to look into the Emperor's red eye, expecting him to be angry. He just smiles, indulgently. "I swore it wouldn't be like that. I swore I wouldn't be like you!"

He gives a dismissive snort. "The arrogance of youth! You were always ambitious, Karza. You wanted the power to change the galaxy, but you never learned the price of that power. I would have taught you, had your obsession not turned you from me."

"You...would have brainwashed me," I stammer, confused.

He is leaning over me, a paternal hand on my shoulder, his voice lowered. "Listen to me, Karza. You aren't the same as the others. You are better than the cattle out there. Like me, like my father before me, you were born to the throne. Fate, in the form of Ryan Archer, took it from you. Now, you have the opportunity to reclaim it."

"What...what if I don't want to be Baron Karza?"

"You have always wanted it."

"But on my terms," I cry, "not yours!"

"Do you think so little of yourself? That other Karza was not my puppet; would any Karza have let me break him like that? You know his story, don't you? You know how it must have been. He must have killed me, as you did. He must have replaced me, as you had the chance to do. He made his own choices. Yes, he made compromises—often out of necessity, sometimes out of expediency; he learned that tough decisions had to be confronted. He grew to understand his part in perpetuating a cycle of peace and prosperity, and he became the man you saw in Archer's thoughts: the ruler you were destined to be, the only ruler you could have been. He became Baron Karza!"

"He murdered Archer's father," I repeat stubbornly.

"You, too, have killed."

"That was different! I...I thought I could bring them back." I realize how inadequate my protest sounds, and I cringe as the Emperor responds with a cruel laugh.

"You killed them because they threatened you. You killed them, and you plan to kill again. You do not have to be ashamed, Karza. I would have done the same in your place."

"I am not you!" I howl.

The Emperor stoops until his Sharkos teeth are an inch from my ear, and he whispers, "Are you sure of that?"

I follow his gaze to my monitors. Most of them are dead now, but, on one corner screen, I see Koriah approaching the main lab, her jaw set determinedly. In her delusion, I think she may actually try to kill me. Unit #23 has been feeding information into the main computer for me, his unwieldy hands making the task a slow one. However, his work is done now, so I send him to intercept the Galactic Defender. As these two forces converge, I ask myself what orders I will give to my Biotron. Must the girl die to ensure my safety? Was the Emperor right—is life so cheap to me, so easy to discard when it stands in my way?

Koriah makes to push past the obstruction in her path. "I'll deal with your master," she says curtly. The Biotron's hand snags her, and holds her tight. I see her face in close-up, angry at first, becoming fearful as the pressure around her wrist intensifies.

With a sinking sensation, I remember that the order has already been given. I issued it some minutes ago, without thinking twice. I instructed my Biotron to kill.

My microphones pick up Archer's voice again, providing a welcome distraction. He is in a tiny, and rarely used, auxiliary laboratory just off the port habitation corridor—where, apparently, he has found Acroyear.

"We need you, man," he insists. "Everything's gone crazy! The Time Traveler explained it to me. This whole place, this station, it's a trap. Karza wanted us to come here. He sent Persephone to Micropolis, he planted the clues that brought us to him. Koriah, Wroje, Kellesh, all of them, they're part of it." A short pause. "Are you hearing me? We've got to get off this wreck! As long as we stay here, we're in danger. I don't know where Knave is; he could be dead by now. We have to find him! Acroyear!"

I am beginning to think that Acroyear isn't present, that Archer is imagining him as he imagined the Time Traveler, when he speaks in a baritone rumble. "You can tell me all the stories you like. I will not believe them. I know where I am."

Hesitantly, Archer asks, "Where…where do you think you are?"

"Micropolis."

"No, Acroyear. We left there. In the *Sunrunner*. Remember?"

"I have forgotten nothing. I remember it all now: All the wasted seconds of my life, wired to a terminal, losing my mind in the dreams you made for me."

"The System. Ki used the System to brainwash you, but you're free of it now."

"Am I?"

"We dropped an airship on the computer complex. Don't you remember?"

"The System will never be destroyed. The System takes care of us."

"What is this, Acroyear? I don't understand. Some kind of freaky flashback?"

"The future. The past. All the same—one endless

nightmare. I know where I am now. I'm still lost in the System. Still dreaming your dreams."

"No. Look around you, Acroyear. The Astro Station! You must remember. Knave, Karza, Koriah. Don't you remember me?"

"Ghosts, that is all. Phantoms in my mind. Part of your game. You let me think I was free. You raised my spirit, just to have the pleasure of destroying it again. Well, I won't play anymore." The warrior's voice grows louder. "Do you hear me, Ki? I won't play. I won't believe in your dreams. You can keep up this fantasy for as long as you like; I won't react to it. You might as well kill me, because you've had all the sport you will get from me!"

Koriah puts up a good fight. She isn't as strong as her enemy, but she's much faster and more agile, and she knows how to use this to her advantage. Unit #23's clumsy thrusts can't touch her as she twists and turns, never staying still for an instant. Again and again, her laser pistols flare, the beams concentrated on a vulnerable joint at the Biotron's left hip. At last, with a shower of sparks, his leg buckles beneath him, and the floor rushes up to meet his face.

The floor is all I can see for a moment, until the Biotron is able to turn himself over. He extrudes his radiation blaster, but Koriah is already on top of him, pinning his arm down with her foot, both pistols aimed directly into his eyes. I haven't seen her in combat before, except for when Wroje surprised her. I underestimated her.

A laser beam cuts into the wall beside her, and suddenly she is gone from my screen. All Unit #23 can see now is the dirty white ceiling. He lifts his head in time to catch a fleeting glimpse of a shadow.

Koriah, who has dropped to her haunches beside him, an arm raised to protect her exposed face, fills in the details. "Ogwen!" she yells. "What do you think you're doing?" Our resident bureaucrat, I assume, is still seeing Antrons.

Unit #23 raises his hand and fires. In the instant that his blaster flares green, Koriah seems to sense her peril and turns, lashing out with her foot, kicking the Biotron's arm aside so that he pumps a cloud of radiation into the wall. She hesitates for a moment, as if wondering whether to press her advantage; instead, she chooses to pursue Ogwen.

Much as I hate to admit it, I'm relieved. I don't think Unit #23 could have defeated her. Fortunately, she seems to have forgotten about me. She's moving away from my chamber, following whatever unfounded suspicion the Centauri signal has bred in her confused mind. I pity her prey when she catches him.

"You did not see the Time Traveler's timeline—the real timeline—as it would have been experienced by the vast majority," insists the Emperor. "You saw only one point of view: the skewed worldview of an embittered rebel."

"Maybe," I concede, "but it was a familiar sight. It reminded me of my childhood, of the tyranny against which my father prepared me to fight."

"You cling to an idealized image of your birth father, Karza. The truth is, he, too, was a dissident, kicking blindly against the order I had established. He could not see, or did not care, that my subjects had all they required. He was prepared to take that from them, to plunge their lives into uncertainty, for his own selfish ends."

"I had dreams," I say hesitantly. "I dreamt of a

society working in concert. I dreamt of the technological leaps we could make."

"In the real timeline, those dreams came true."

"But at what cost?"

"You cannot please everybody, Karza. You can feed them, clothe them, shelter and protect them, build machines to ease their lot, and still there will be those, like Archer, who hate you, consumed with jealousy for all you have achieved. You cannot reason with such people. They are malcontents, and their terrorist tactics cannot be tolerated."

"There can be no order," I agree thoughtfully, "without conformity."

"And the seeds of chaos grow fast, and must be weeded out. You have always believed that, Karza. Do not balk now, because of the imagined consequences of such a philosophy. If some people must suffer, then it is only for the greater good."

"I...accept what you're saying, but..."

"You must make up your mind, Karza. Look at your monitors. One of the Battle Cruisers has broken formation. It is heading for the Astro Station."

"I see it." My gaze is riveted to the screen in question, my muscles frozen. Why does my head hurt? Why is it so hard to think?

"The Centauri are preparing to board us!"

A flexible docking tube extends from the Cruiser's side, from between weapons turrets. It flails about for a moment, then finds the station's main airlock and clamps its circular end over it, a powerful magnetic charge holding it in place. The Centauri know that they won't be welcomed into the hangar bay, so they're planning to enter my home by force.

"The cancellation wave. Must send...the countersignal..."

"No, Karza."

"I have to. We can't fight them like this!"

"You will betray our presence, throw away our only advantage."

I shake my head, trying to clear it but only making the pain more intense. "That advantage will be worth nothing if we are too confused to fight. I'll be telling the Centauri nothing they don't already know: Wroje never reached Koriah with a baffler—they can still read her life signs. They know the station is still occupied, but we can surprise them with our numbers."

"If you do this, Karza, I will be forced to leave you."

"You will always be with me. I recognize that now."

"Then why do you hesitate?"

My dry lips twist into a cruel sneer. "The audio feed from the secondary lab...Acroyear has attacked Archer. Just a moment's delay on my part, and he may kill the boy."

The Emperor smiles. "You are your father's son, after all."

"Acroyear!" Archer's voice is strained. I think the warrior has his hands around the boy's throat. "Don't do this to me, Acroyear. It's me—Ryan. Acroyear!"

"If you are indeed real, as you claim," snarls the warrior, "then you are the only part of this scenario that is. That means you must be working for Ki."

"You're...choking me...please..."

A scuffling sound; the tinkling of a metal object being knocked from a lab bench. Archer must have tried to break free, but to no avail.

"It was you who persuaded me to leave my home," snaps Acroyear, "first my apartment, then Micropolis itself. You brought me here. You have been guiding me through the levels of this maze, one by one. You are responsible for everything I have endured—and unless your master shuts down this virtual nightmare now, I will squeeze your neck until it snaps!"

"Go...go on, then. Do it. That's why Karza sent you here, isn't it? That's why you came to Earth. You've already killed my dad. Just...just get it over with, can't you?"

A long silence follows. I can hear somebody breathing heavily, but I can't tell if it is Acroyear or Archer or both. I wonder if the warrior has made good on his threat. I am disappointed, then, to hear Archer's voice again, hoarse and subdued. "What's happening to us, Acroyear? For a moment there, I...I thought you were somebody else. A Harrower...one of Karza's soldiers, from the alternative timeline. The ones who..."

"I was under a similar delusion." The apology emerges grudgingly from Acroyear's throat. "I trust you are not harmed?"

"I'll have your fingerprints on my larynx for a while—but no, no lasting damage."

"The Centauri have done something to us. Even now, my instincts tell me not to trust you, that I must kill you before you kill me. It is all I can do to keep that impulse suppressed."

"Just...just keep trying, yeah? We need to get to the bridge, see if we can work out what..."

"No. The Centauri are my responsibility. You have a more important task to perform."

"You...you're right. Oh, God, you're right. I...I almost forgot..."

"How long do you have?"

"I don't know. I've kind of lost track of time. It can't be long, though."

"You must return to Karza's laboratory. You must become the Time Traveler."

"I know. But...but I can't leave you like—"

"You must. For the sake of the universe, Archer, you must do this. My fate—the fate of all of us here—is unimportant in comparison."

"Maybe I was wrong. Maybe it's not this universe I should be saving."

"We have discussed this. You are doing the right thing."

"At least in the other timeline, you had a fighting chance!"

"Go," says Acroyear, with surprising softness.

A long silence. Then, in a choked voice, Archer says, "It...it's been a privilege to fight alongside you, Acroyear. In whatever reality. You've always been there for me."

"I'm only sorry I cannot stay with you until the end."

"I understand." An attempt at a laugh. "I know you've got other things to do, intergalactic horses to fight."

"You will not be forgotten."

They part, then. Acroyear leaves first, his stride purposeful and uninterrupted. Archer remains in that tiny room for a time; if I listen hard enough, I can hear his breathing, and the occasional nervous clearing of his throat. Then he takes a deep breath, mutters something to himself in a determined tone, and goes to meet his fate.

I can feel my own chest swelling with anticipation, hear liquid gurgling in the nutrient tank behind me. Archer is coming here. I know what I must do when he arrives. It is time. I open my mouth to say something, but realize that I'm alone again.

No. Not alone. Somehow, I can still feel the Emperor's presence, even though I have negated the Centauri's hypnotic signal, even though I know that his physical form was no more than an illusion. I feel him watching over me. I can almost see the smile on his cracked face as I prepare to follow the path he laid out for me, the path he trod before me.

As I approach the destiny for which my father prepared me...

Acroyear is gathering forces on the bridge, under the supervision of Units #30 and #35. Kellesh was the first to respond to his broadcast call to arms, teetering unsteadily from the medical bay to pledge assistance. Koriah was only a short way behind.

It took Wroje a little longer to be convinced; eventually, however, she and Knave negotiated a ceasefire, each realizing that they had no idea why they'd been trying to kill the other. Ogwen, I can't locate. I can only assume that he's in hiding, his natural paranoia taking over where the Centauri signal left off.

Kellesh has taken a seat at the main control panel. It didn't take him long, with a clear mind and the equipment now available to him, to work out what's been happening. An uncomfortable, awkward silence settles over the gathering as recent actions are reexamined in a new, colder light. Koriah and Kellesh avoid each other's eyes, and Wroje attempts a stammered apology to the room in general.

Acroyear, however, pulls them back to the present. "A Battle Cruiser has docked with the Astro Station," he announces grimly. "The Centauri are staging their final attack."

"They're burning through an airlock door," reports Kellesh from his console. "I have the auto-repair working flat out, but it can only gain us a few more seconds, a minute at most."

"Okay, people," says Koriah, "looks like it's the

moment of truth. We're outnumbered and outgunned, but I for one don't intend to be taken without a fight. Are you with me?"

"I'll do whatever I can," says Kellesh.

"What the hell," says Knave. "I had nothing else planned for today."

Wroje just nods, hugging herself tightly.

"THE BIOTRON UNITS WILL ASSIST TO THE FULL EXTENT OF OUR CAPABILITIES."

"They're almost through," reports Kellesh. "This is it!"

"Prepare to receive boarders," intones Acroyear.

Archer has been pacing the corridor outside my laboratory for almost five minutes. His unique senses must be warning him against entering. The tragedy, for him, is that he will pay them no heed. He will mistake his feeling of dread, the voice in his head that tells him to turn and run, for an entirely normal reaction to his situation. He will override it, sure that he is doing what he has to do.

He makes his decision, and acts before fear can stop him. He opens the door.

From the corner of the lab, Unit #23 turns to watch the boy as he steps over the threshold, shaking, his face pale. Half-crippled, the Biotron is of little use to me other than as a pair of eyes. I considered summoning another to my side, but the remaining units are better employed holding off the Centauri. Anyway, I feel I should do this myself.

I'm not sure why that's important to me. Maybe it's a symbolic gesture—after so many years of holding life at arm's length, I want to grab hold of it. After so many disappointments, so many blows to my spirit, I want to feel passionate again. And maybe, just maybe, I want to know that I did this, that I took this opportunity myself. I want to know that I *could* do it.

I want to know that I'm still that man. I need to know that I am Karza.

Archer operates the computer again. A green spark erupts into a flame, which dances within the rigid confines of the containment grid. The call of the Rift seems stronger than ever, as if it can sense somehow that I am almost ready to answer it.

Archer makes his final few checks, then stands and crosses the room. He knocks on my door, and I hesitate for only a moment before allowing him into my chamber. I disable my monitors and listening devices to afford us some privacy.

"I'm ready," he says, numbly, his eyes not quite meeting mine.

"I know," I say.

"I need the suit."

I nod toward the containment suit in its alcove. Archer approaches it, reaches for it, runs the tough but flexible material through his hands. He looks into the empty eyes of the Time Traveler, and I wonder what he is saying to him in his thoughts. With a quick glance back at me, as if ashamed of his show of apprehension, the boy lifts the red and silver suit from its peg. He cradles it in his arms, and a bolt of jealous anger sears through me.

The gun has always been here. It was my last resort. In the event of an enemy bypassing my Biotrons, taking me by surprise, it might have bought me some time; enough to operate the auto-destruct or, if needs be, simply to deny my attackers the satisfaction of killing me themselves. I tease it, now, from its secret pocket beneath the arm of my chair. I conceal it in the palm of my hand, resting my thumb against its trigger device. The miniature pistol is good for one shot only—but one shot is all I will need.

Archer is starting to don the costume of the Time Traveler over his clothes. For all his vaunted intuition, he is oblivious to his danger. He doesn't see the door closing behind him, doesn't hear the soft click of its locking device.

"I can't let you do this," I say.

He freezes, one foot stuck halfway down the containment suit's leg.

"You have stolen my destiny from me once," I remind him, "when you rewrote the past to shunt me into the footnotes of history. Now, I have a chance to reclaim what I have lost. You won't take it from me again!"

"You know," he gasps.

"That I should have been a king? Yes, Archer, I know."

His eyes widen with realization. "I told you, didn't I?"

"Indeed. In your delirium, you betrayed your greatest secret."

"It…it's not what it looks like. In the old timeline, yes, you were a baron, you ruled this galaxy, but you aren't that person now, Karza. You're a better man!"

"A man whom, nevertheless, you didn't trust with the truth. Why is that, Archer? You must have sensed something inside me. You must have recognized my ambition. You must have known that, had I seen a chance for power—true power, the type that changes worlds—I would have done anything, risked anything, to claim it for myself!"

"No," he protests in vain. "I…I…was trying to protect you."

"From what?" I roar scornfully.

He flinches from me and whispers, "You would have become a monster."

"Instead of which, I have achieved nothing. I *am* nothing."

Archer shakes his head. "That's not true. You created the Rift. You built this facility. You...we...between us, we're saving the universe!"

"And what," I ask coldly, "if it is not *this* universe I wish to save?"

"You...you can't..." Archer's voice trails off. He doesn't know what to say.

"You presume to tell me what I can't do?" I snarl. "You were the one who took it upon yourself to decide the fate of two universes. You were the one who chose, on a whim, to compound the mistake made by your alternative self. My sole desire is to put things right, to restore the old timeline—the true timeline! You, on the other hand, would condemn us all to life in this aberrant, abhorrent reality, this shadow of the original."

"I...we...thought it would be better this way."

"And you consider yourself the best judge of that?"

Archer stares at the floor. "I don't know," he mumbles.

I'm almost disappointed. It's proving much easier to shake his confidence, to make him doubt himself, than I expected. Maybe I won't need the gun after all.

"But," he says, "this way, it's easier. I mean, the path I need to take is all programmed. I just have to download it to the Time Traveler's control unit."

"The easy path is not always the right one," I remark.

"I know that. But...but, let's say I did agree with you, let's say I wanted to restore the old timeline...I'm not even sure I could do it. I don't think I know how."

"Yes, Archer, you do. You know it as well as I do. You simply lack the necessary belief in yourself, in your abilities, to accept it." He shuffles awkwardly and waits for me to spell it out to him. "When you guided my probe across the time stream, your instincts didn't lead you toward the past—at least, not to the past that we know. You picked out an impossible path, to a time that should no longer exist, a time to which the strands of cause and effect no longer point. Had it not been for the Centauri's untimely intervention, you would have reached the end of that path. You would have found the Time Traveler."

"I could have stopped him," Archer realizes. "I could have warned him about the dangers of using the Pharoids' machine. History would never have been changed."

"You could set things right."

"But," says Archer, suddenly afraid, "what would happen then? He—I—was trapped on that world, hunted by Azura Nova and her troops. The time machine was our only way out. Without it, we'd have died, and that would have been it for the rebellion. He would have won. He…" He shoots a guilty look at me, as if realizing what he is saying.

"You would have saved the universe," I remind him.

Archer nods, defeated. "You're right. I know you're right—only, it's too late now. The probe was destroyed. We can't retrieve that data."

"The data was not lost."

"But…but it's incomplete!"

"True."

"We'd have to program the rest of the course blindly." Archer thinks for a moment, then shakes his head. "No. No, Karza, if you're thinking of asking me…no, I can't do it. These senses of mine, they don't make me Superman. It's too much."

"I know. However, there is a chance…"

He looks at me in horror. "You can't mean…You really want to take that risk?"

"The reward, I believe, is great enough."

"Let me get this straight, Karza. You're saying you want to throw away our only shot at saving the universe—*this* universe, the one we all know—for the possibility, and not a very good possibility at that, of restoring another one. And why? Because, in this other timeline—the one we've only glimpsed, the one we know almost zip about—you think you might be a little better off?"

I shake my head, sadly. "You don't understand, boy. I was foolish to think you might. I am concerned not with my own comfort, but with the good of everybody. It is my duty, my destiny, to save them from the chaos in which we are forced to wallow like pigs."

He sees the gun too late. He doesn't move; perhaps he is waiting for his senses to tell him what to do, but there is nothing he *can* do. Nowhere to run, no way to fight back, and no time for either, now. The deed is already done, without fanfare, without any sound at all. The mini-pistol doesn't even kick against my palm as it delivers its invisible beam.

Somehow, it all feels anticlimactic. I can almost identify with Archer's nonplussed expression, the disbelief in his eyes, that appear with the perfectly circular hole that smolders in his forehead.

"I will excise the chaos," I vow as his legs realize that his brain is dead, and he falls at last. "Cut it out like a cancer. I will bring order, whatever the cost."

CHAPTER
ELEVEN

I expected the Centauri to hold back, to send only a small boarding party to begin with. I thought my threats of mutual destruction would make them cautious. I was wrong.

They've arrived in force. A hidden Biotron watches them crowding into the airlock corridor, pressed so close together that it's hard to see where one creature ends and the next begins. Still more of them emerge from the Battle Cruiser's docking tube, trotting confidently over the melted slag of the airlock door.

As Koriah predicted, they're taking no chances. Black armor is plated around their chests and their fetlocks, seeming to absorb the artificial light of the station. Their black crossbows are readied, energy bolts loaded.

Each of the Centauri has a pentagonal gem grafted into his or her stomach, at the point where their humanoid torsos merge with their quadrupedal back halves. These gems burn with white energy, which also courses beneath the armor to flare in its eye sockets. The Centauri warriors' long, thin faceplates look like grinning skulls, like harbingers of death.

They divide their forces, pouring down the corridor

in both directions, the larger group separating again at the first junction they reach. A third of them are heading for the bridge; another third are following a Centaurus with a handheld detector who spurs them on with insults, feeding their bloodlust. Their destination, I know, is the port habitation corridor, in which they read the life signs of a single being.

The remaining Centauri are on their way here.

Archer's corpse lies before me, the Time Traveler's costume still tangled around his feet, a surprised expression on his face. Out in the main lab, my computer ticks away, processing the numbers that Unit #23 fed into it earlier. I find it bitterly ironic that, with all the years of my life stretched out behind me, it comes down to this in the end: a race against time.

The invaders are close now. The more ground they gain without being challenged, the more confident they become, the faster their progress across the Astro Station. The empty corridors give them reassurance that their sensors were accurate, that their radiation weapon wiped out all but one of us. This, of course, is what Acroyear wanted them to believe.

He was waiting for them above the ceiling, in the hollow space between the inner and outer skins of the hull. As they pass beneath him, he drops onto them, sword whirling. Before they can even react, the first two Centauri are dead, and Acroyear is using their bodies as a shield, the push of their comrades keeping them upright against him. The Centauri are hampered by their narrow confines, their bulky forms trapped between corridor walls, most of them unable to use their crossbows for fear of striking an ally. Acroyear is able to stride through their ranks, cutting them down one by one. Energy bolts crackle around his head, but only a few find their target, and these he deflects with his arm-mounted shields.

Elsewhere, more Centauri search the living quarters in the port habitation corridor. One of them yanks open the door to Wroje's room, to take a face full of radiation fire from the waiting Unit #30. The creature recoils, clutching at his eyes, his agonized scream alerting his fellow soldiers to his plight. The Biotron, however, has already turned his back as if the invaders' response is of no concern to him. Behind him, there is a hole in the wall the size of his metal fist. Beyond this hole, the outer skin of the hull is visible, already dented.

Centauri troops pour into the room to find the Biotron landing punch after methodical punch on this weak spot, smashing his way out to space. Alarmed, they rush to restrain him, firing energy bolts into his head at point blank range. The unit is staggered—damaged, I fear, beyond repair—but, doggedly, he perseveres with his programmed task.

It only takes a small crack. Air whistles past the invaders, buffeting them, leaving them short of breath. They abandon their attack, and attempt to retreat. Meanwhile, on the bridge, Wroje operates the control that will bring down an airtight bulkhead behind them.

Only a few meters away from Wroje, I hear Koriah and Knave greeting more Centauri with a fusillade of laser fire, using opposite corners of a corridor junction as cover. Their beams aren't powerful enough to penetrate the invaders' black armor, but a few lucky shots keep them at bay, the cramped environment again working to the defenders' advantage.

"They're all inside, Kellesh," Wroje squeals into a communicator. "Do it now!"

Down in the exposed bowels of the Astro Station, a space-suited Kellesh hooks up a canister of poisonous cleaning material to the oxygen recycling system, and twists open its nozzle.

The Centauri are rallying against Acroyear, pushing him back toward me. They let out a collective roar as he turns and withdraws. They surge forward, eagerly—into a wide-angled burst of radiation from the waiting Unit #35.

They keep coming. The first of them almost makes it, but he is already losing blood from a deep sword wound. As his hands reach for the bio-mech, his back legs buckle beneath him and he falls heavily, two more soldiers stumbling over his rump. Suddenly, the Centauri are trapped, arms and legs thrashing uselessly, crossbows firing into the ceiling, only adding to the chaos as wave after wave of green radiation washes over them, draining their strength.

With the Biotron's blaster spent and his foes weakened, Acroyear returns to the fray.

The air in my chamber has taken on a pale yellow tint. Kellesh's poison is being pumped throughout the station. Fortunately, my air tubes guarantee me a fresh supply of oxygen. Koriah is likewise protected by her uniform helmet, and Acroyear claims that his armor too will filter out the worst of the toxins. Wroje and Knave are both wearing oxygen tanks. Knave waits a little too long before he clamps his mask to his face with a spare hand, and I hear him coughing and retching.

My computer continues its work. I need only a few more minutes.

Yellow clouds drift across my screens, and for a time all I know of the continuing battle comes from its sounds: the whines of laser pistols, the explosions of energy bolts, the grunts and cries of anger and pain. Only as the poison clouds begin to clear, dispersed by the recycled air behind them, can I begin to take stock of the situation again—and I find that things aren't going well.

The Centauri don't seem to have been affected by the gas. I can only assume that they anticipated such an attack, and wore filters beneath their faceplates.

They have divided their forces again, sending a number of soldiers around the station to surprise Koriah and Knave from behind. I can't tell how they are faring, but as long as I can hear their laser pistols firing, at least I know their reflexes are keeping them alive. The pair have been driven to their prearranged fallback sition—a storeroom—where they're pinned down. The Centauri, therefore, have free access to the bridge.

They presage their arrival by firing several dozen energy bolts through the doorway. They ricochet from the walls, filling the air with fire. Several instrument panels explode. Wroje shrieks, and dives for cover behind a chair. Unit #39 moves to protect her, meeting the Centauri advance. I realize that I'm holding my breath, praying for Wroje to find the strength she needs to unleash the warrior within her.

There is some good news. Through Unit #30's eyes, I watch the Centauri in the port habitation corridor suffocating and dying, clutching at their throats as they collapse in droves. And Acroyear is standing his ground against overwhelming odds—for the present.

I need to prepare myself.

I start by removing the various plugs and cables from my flux armor, the bonds that confine me to this seat. I hesitate for a moment, then I breathe deeply, stiffen my spine, and clutch at the arms of my chair as if afraid that I'll collapse like a marionette with its strings cut. There is no reason to believe such a thing, of course. The exo-suit is fully charged; I have at least two hours before its power is spent. As always, however, the severance of my connections to the Astro Station leaves me feeling helpless.

I'm no longer in control. I am in the hands of destiny.

It takes a supreme effort to push myself to my feet. I stand, shaking, feeling dizzy as my head adjusts to its new altitude. I curse my frailty, knowing that once again it is the Time Traveler who is responsible for this weakness in me. As the parts of my body failed, I could have replaced them with stronger, bio-mechanical components. I knew how, but he never gave me the time to realize that vision.

The mask of the Time Traveler stares up at me from the floor, and I see my red eyes reflected in his, as if I have ignited some long-buried spark of life within him. I stoop to retrieve the suit, but the effort of untying it from around Archer's ankles is too much. I drop heavily to one knee, black spots swimming before my eyes.

I am disgusted with myself. I am Karza. I will not be disgraced like this.

But, as I gather my resolve, my eyes are drawn back to my monitors, and I witness another defeat playing itself out. Unit #39 has been overcome, his radiation blaster destroyed. The Centauri sweep across the bridge, and Wroje falls backs before them, mustering no more than a defiant whimper and a few ineffectual bursts of laser fire.

Two soldiers pin her arms, while another takes Wroje's chin in her gauntleted hands, her death mask appearing to leer at the frightened woman. Wroje is in tears, her jaw working as she attempts to stammer a voiceless plea. For a moment, I think the Centauri will break her neck, but she contents herself with constricting her captive's windpipe until she passes out. Wroje folds, but her soldier escorts keep her from falling. The female, apparently their leader, gestures to them to remove the prisoner from her sight.

Then she steps onto the main platform, nodding with approval as a seat swivels to greet her. She lowers her haunches onto it, straddling it awkwardly, and runs her hands almost lovingly over the instruments in front of her, a territorial gesture.

And that is the last I see of that scene before a concentration of energy bolts takes the Biotron's sight from him forever.

"Knave?" Koriah's voice, picked up by a microphone outside the storeroom, faint but discernible over the continuing gunfire. "I want you to do something for me."

"I'll try my best," grunts the Vaerian. "Thing is, I'm a bit..." He squeezes off four more shots down the corridor. "...tied down at the moment."

"I want you to get out of here."

Knave laughs hollowly. "First chance we get, I promise."

"No. I want *you* to get out of here. You see that grille up there?"

"Air ducts. Don't think I hadn't thought about it—but we'd never make it before..." A short pause. "No!"

"It's the only way, Knave. These pistols don't have unlimited power. Even if they did, we couldn't hold off the Centauri forever."

"I made a vow to myself, a long time ago. I said I'd never turn my back on a friend. I have to keep that promise, Koriah. It's what separates me from the rest of my people. I have to believe I'm not like that!"

"There's no point in us both staying to die!"

"Then you should go. You're smaller than me, anyway. It'll be easier for you."

"With your gymnastic background? You can get into those pipes, and through them, faster than I ever could. Let me have this one, Knave. You talked about the vow you made—what about me? When I entered the service, I promised to defend the innocent. I haven't had too much success at that, recently."

Knave doesn't answer—at least not that I can hear—but his expression must say it all, because, in between shots, Koriah continues, "I'm not leaving here, Knave. Whatever you do, you won't budge me from this doorway. So, it's up to you: You can die with me, or you can try to save yourself. Find Kellesh, see if he has any more bright ideas. But make up your mind quickly, because I can't keep you covered for much longer."

There are no more words after that.

A few seconds short of a minute later, even the gunfire stops.

I tear the containment suit from Archer, and stand. Now comes the difficult part. The suit won't fit over my white armor. For the first time in over six decades, I will have to remove it. I will have to expose my wasted body to the elements. I was always aware of this, of course. I told myself that, when the time came, when I no longer had the exo-suit to bolster my resources, sheer willpower would lend me the strength to keep on living. I knew that I *couldn't* die, so close to achieving my goals. I wish I could be so sure now.

I close my eyes, set my jaw, concentrate on keeping

my muscles rigid, and operate the laser key in my glove. With the sound of a cracking Lobros shell, the panels of my armor pop from their sockets—and suddenly, everything feels different. The air is like pins on my arms, my chest, my back, pricking sweat from my pores. My brain feels numb. I am still wearing my helmet, but a dozen needles have just retracted themselves from inside my skull—I had grown accustomed to the pain they caused, and it makes itself felt now by its absence.

I take a great, shuddering breath. I open my eyes, half expecting to find that I have fallen without my senses registering it, but still I stand, albeit feeling more vulnerable than I have since childhood. My exo-suit, my armor, is piled around my feet, so many lumps of useless metal. The circuitry on its inner surfaces has corroded, and I wonder that it could still function. My body bears the dry holes made by its neural connectors. My skin is pockmarked with sores, patterned with purple bruises, the pain of which the suit blocked from me. They are beginning to tingle now, as if slowly reawakening.

I am horribly aware, for the first time, of the fragility of my Astro Station, now that the thin walls of this battered container are all that protect me from the freezing void.

I could almost laugh at this latest cruel irony; that, ultimately, I should be so helpless. But there is no turning back. I raise my hands, fighting to keep them still. I take the helmet between them, and I lift it. I work its air tubes out of my mouth with my tongue, and take my first tentative breath of the station's stale, recycled air.

A lingering trace of Kellesh's poison scratches my throat and I cough up acidic bile, each spasm of my lungs sending a lance of pain through me.

At last, I compose myself to lift my head, to stare into the reflective blankness of one of my defunct screens, to face myself—my real self—again, at long last.

For seconds uncounted, I stare into my own eyes. No longer do I see the armored monster that reminded me so much of the Emperor—but neither do I see any trace of the man I was before, the young firebrand whose image never quite faded in my mind's eye. Somehow, impossibly, I think I expected to find that man again in these final moments. Instead, I am confronted by a pale, emaciated wreck of a creature whom I don't recognize at all.

I avert my gaze, feeling something like a tear well onto my cheek. I brush it away with a finger, which comes away stained red. Blood. An after-effect of the removal of my helmet.

I mustn't dwell on this. I mustn't doubt myself. If anything, this reminder of the pathetic shell I have become should spur me on. My life *has* meant nothing, but I have the chance to change that now. I can make myself over, reinvent myself again.

I place my first foot into the containment suit. I can't keep my balance, and have to rest a hand on the back of my chair to steady myself. But I try again, and roll the golden fabric up over my left leg. The effort leaves me short of breath, and I have to sit down.

But already I can feel a sense of excitement rising in my stomach, chasing away my foreboding. This is it: The moment to which my entire life has been leading.

I am about to become the Time Traveler.

On the bridge, a Centaurus throws aside the lid to

the disused cryo-crypt, to find Ogwen inside. He's clutching an empty bottle of methohol to his chest, so drunk that his only reaction to being dragged from his hiding place is to lapse into a giggling fit. He is taken to the refectory, where Wroje is already secured.

Unit #30 limps into the storeroom corridor, his circuits sparking, his display flickering and strobing, in time to see Koriah being likewise dragged from her bolt hole, held almost aloft by baying Centauri. She has been divested of her helmet and pistols, still struggling and kicking to no avail. The Biotron lurches to a clumsy halt as the invaders spot him, as they turn on him. He can't use his blaster without harming the Galactic Defender. His processors whir sluggishly into action, a request for instructions forming on his monitor.

He's still waiting for a response when Knave bounds onto the scene, leaping over his head, guns blazing from all four arms. He lands in the Centauri's midst, his lithe purple body twisting and coiling like that of a snake, never still, never remaining in the same place for even half a second. The creatures fire upon him, but only succeed in pumping crossbow bolts into each other. Even from my vantage point, I can hardly keep track of the Vaerian. He disappears into the throng for seconds at a time, making me think he has been felled, until he pops up elsewhere to wreak more havoc.

There's a method to his apparently random actions. He's working his way toward Koriah, distracting the Centauri who hold her, giving her the opportunity to break free. Already she has dropped to her feet, although she is still held from both sides. Knave wouldn't turn his back on a friend, after all. Wrong choice.

He can't have seen, as I see, the blood on Koriah's

head, a glistening black trail against her dark skin. In restraining her, the Centauri have reopened the wound inflicted by Wroje. Spirited as she remains, the girl's strength is fading—and although she manages to pull free from one of her captors, the other retains a steadfast grip on her shoulder, her face twisting in pain as she attempts to break it.

Even now, Knave could abandon her and escape. His persistence proves to be his downfall. The Centauri have abandoned their weapons, striking at him with fists and hooves. They close ranks so that, even with his astonishing agility, the Vaerian soon has nowhere to go in the enclosed space. It isn't long before he disappears between them and doesn't surface again.

Belatedly, I answer Unit #30's request. I tell him that both Koriah and Knave are useless to me now, that their presence should not keep him from discharging his duty. He steps forward, raises his hand, and perishes in a brief but furious volley of energy bolts.

I tell myself that it doesn't matter. I need only be concerned with Acroyear's progress. I am pleased to see that he has made great inroads, his blade scything through enemy armor. Even the normally fearless Centauri are beginning to shy away from physical confrontation. They're trying to pull back, to use their crossbows from afar, but Acroyear keeps bearing down on them, denying them the respite they need.

In the end, the creatures' leader has to sacrifice three more of his troops to give the rest a chance to withdraw to a more strategic position. They form up farther down the corridor, managing to squeeze three abreast between the walls, the front rank squatting on their haunches. As the last sacrifice falls, Acroyear is suddenly, briefly, surrounded by space, and the bolts come thick and fast, spattering against him, making him stagger.

He drops his head, clenches his fists and marches onward through the barrage. Holes are being blasted in his armor, he must be in agony, but he doesn't let it stop him. The Centauri are scattered like tenpins as he closes with them again.

He can't win.

Fresh from their victory over Koriah and Knave, Centauri reinforcements are coming up behind the warrior. Unit #35 can delay them, but not for very long, and then my final defender will be surrounded. This cold fact spurs me onward, although I know that haste will not serve me. I am still at the mercy of the main computer.

I wrestle my shoulders into the containment suit, plunge my hands into its armholes. The silver control unit, with its triangular panel, has become partially detached, and I fumble to reconnect it. The Time Traveler embraces me, his skin becoming my own. Gold fabric knits itself together up my back, and I start to feel safe again.

Unit #35 has been felled. His internal camera is still broadcasting, although most of his other systems have ceased and his artificial heart has stopped pumping. I watch from his frozen worm's eye point of view as Centauri soldiers gallop up behind Acroyear. The warrior sees them coming and swings his sword to discourage them, but their energy bolts are already smacking into him. Forced to half-turn, he presents an opportunity to another of the creatures, which rears up and strikes him with its front hooves. The force of the blow is enough to dislodge his helmet, knocking it askew.

All he can do now is flatten his back to the wall, cutting down the angles from which his foes can come at him. He strikes out to his left and his right in turn, varying the pattern and direction of his thrusts, but the Centauri can afford to keep their distance. They know that the battle is over; they're just waiting for the inevitable opening. Acroyear's attention is divided. He is forced to use his sword to block their incoming energy bolts, and even he can't look both ways at once.

Finally, when there is nothing else he can do, he lets out a blood-curdling war cry and launches himself into the ranks of the Centauri that first engaged him. He disappears beneath them, visible only by the tumult that his unexpected, suicidal charge has caused. The Centauri's animal howls, and the sprays of blood in the air, tell me that Acroyear is still fighting, still determined to take as many of the creatures as he can down with him.

And now they have him pinned to the floor among them, striking down viciously and repeatedly. I know that it's all over.

A hoof slams heavily into Unit #35's head—another Centaurus, galloping to join her comrades—and his picture fizzles and is lost. Only one Biotron is still broadcasting to me: The damaged Unit #23, out in the main laboratory. Through his eyes, I can see the Rift, and its green light still calls to me. My defenders have failed me—flesh and blood always will—but *I* will not fail.

Cradling the protective mask under my arm, I haul myself from my seat again. I half-walk, half-stumble to the chamber door. I lean on it for a moment, its cold metal soothing my fevered forehead. I think I could stay like this forever. I have to force my free arm to move, my hand to feel along the wall for the opening mechanism.

The door slides aside, and I have to support myself again. I am given encouragement, however, by the sight of the Rift directly in front of me. It has been many years since I last saw it with my own eyes, and even then it was tinted red by the lenses in my helmet. Even with the technology I've created, a mere electronic image could never do justice to this phenomenon. I had forgotten how deep, how bright, the Rift's light was, how vibrant its color. I had forgotten how it seemed to draw everything into itself, including a part of me.

I had forgotten how strong its call could be.

Soon, I promise it, *very soon. I am almost ready. After all this time...*

The computer pings softly to inform me that it has finished its work. The path for my momentous journey has been calculated. I operate the unit on my chest, forming an infrared connection to the mainframe. A light blinks in the center of the triangular control panel, indicating that data is being received. *Soon, very soon.*

"Unit #23," I instruct, "stand guard outside this room. Do not allow anybody to enter. Kill anybody who tries." The hapless Biotron moves to obey, dragging his injured leg behind him. I hardly spare him a glance as he passes me, except to note that, in his current condition, he will cause the Centauri minimal delay. I only hope it will be enough.

And then he pauses in the doorway, turns back to me, and says, "ON BEHALF OF ALL OF US, LORD KARZA, I WOULD LIKE TO SAY THAT IT HAS BEEN AN HONOR TO SERVE YOU. I ONLY HOPE THAT YOU WILL ACHIEVE EVERYTHING YOU HAVE WISHED FOR."

He is gone before I know how to respond to him. Suddenly, I have a vivid image of myself at the control platform on the bridge the first day I arrived on the Astro Station; of a Biotron—the same unit—enquiring after my state of mind. Perhaps his circuits were damaged, too, when Koriah attacked him; perhaps that's why he has disregarded his subsequent programming. I programmed the Biotrons to overcome such sentiment, to resist forming attachments. Just as I programmed myself. And suddenly I'm a young man again, confronted with the twisted, crumbling wreck of a loyal friend whom I sent to his death.

I want to call him back. I want to thank him. But I don't.

The door closes behind Unit #23 with a final click. I hear hoof beats approaching.

Gunfire: The staccato sounds of energy bolts, the answering crackles of a radiation blaster. The belligerent yells of the invaders. More hoof beats, closer.

I'm waiting impatiently for the chest unit to tell me that my course is programmed in. I wish I'd devoted some time to increasing its processing speed, but I never thought it would be an issue. Each second seems to trickle by, bringing with it fresh disappointment.

The Centauri are hammering on the door. It bulges and buckles under the onslaught of their hooves. I pray for a few more seconds.

But, too soon, the final barrier falls, and the enemy are upon me.

I scream: A lifetime's worth of frustration channeled into a single "No!" burning my throat.

I expected them to shoot me. Instead, they canter confidently, arrogantly, into the room. I have always thought of this laboratory, as much as the chamber beyond it, as my inner sanctuary. These monsters defile it with their presence.

They surround me, their crossbows raised. One of them asks, "Is this him, Leader?" And I become aware of a darker presence among them. A creature who, despite her metal mask of war, I recognize from our many long-distance conversations.

She struts up to me and takes my chin in her hand, her eyes glistening as they stare appraisingly into mine. "Could it be?" she sneers. "But no—tell me it is not possible. The great and powerful Karza, the mighty warrior who thought he could resist our superior race—an old and feeble biped, after all." She casts a glance back at the Rift, and spits derisively, "Reduced to this pathetic attempt to escape our vengeance!"

She tosses back her mane and lets out an unpleasant, snorting laugh. Obsequiously, her troops follow suit.

"Computer," I say quietly, "operate protocol Karza 7434-5840."

The Centauri leader's eyes widen, and she delivers a backhanded slap to my exposed cheek. I gasp and, to my disgust, my legs fold beneath me. The Time Traveler's mask falls out of my grasp, and under a lab bench.

»AUTO-DESTRUCT SEQUENCE INITIATED,« reports a tinny voice, which I know is being broadcast throughout the station. »PLEASE EVACUATE. THIS FACILITY WILL BE DESTROYED IN...« A pause, as the computer checks its database for the information. The default timing for the auto-destruct countdown is one hour. I changed it. »...TEN SECONDS.«

Just long enough for the Centauri to contemplate their fate, to appreciate what I've done to them. Not long enough, by any means, for them to avoid it. I may be on my knees, but I'm laughing, laughing until my chest aches. It's either that, I think, or cry. If there was time, I'd probably do both.

The Centauri leader stoops, having to fold her front legs awkwardly. She grips my shoulders, pulls me to my feet and slams me brutally into the bench, bearing me down until I'm bent backwards across it. "Stop the countdown!" she demands. "Stop the countdown, or I will inflict excruciating pain upon you!"

»AUTO-DESTRUCT IN FIVE SECONDS.«

"Do your worst," I taunt. "While you can."

»FOUR.«

"I warned you, Centaurus. You should have listened to me."

"I'll share the time technology with you!"

"It is not yours to share!" I hiss.

»THREE.«

The Centaurus rounds on her troops. "Destroy that computer!" she instructs in an insane screech, pointing with a trembling finger. The creatures oblige. I flinch as the room is filled with light, my ears assailed by the cacophony of a hundred explosions.

The computer's voice is stilled, slurring into silence. The noise continues for at least ten seconds beyond that—or so it seems to me, although I know this to be impossible. When finally it stops, the silence itself is deafening, making my ears ring.

The silence stretches on, long enough for me to know that something is wrong.

Smoke drifts in front of my eyes. I can hear a small fire crackling.

The Centauri couldn't have halted the countdown. They couldn't! The auto-destruct circuitry is buried too deeply within the station. And yet, somehow, it *has* been halted.

The female looms over me and, although her mask conceals her expression, I can see the smugness in her eyes. The control unit on my chest lets out three short beeps, signaling that the course coordinates for its journey through the time stream have been received and processed. Slowly, the cold reality of my defeat sinks in. Even this, my final gesture of defiance, has been denied to me.

I push myself up from the bench. The Centauri press in around me. I struggle. I didn't think I had the strength, but I find it. I ignore their glancing hoof blows. I think their leader gives them an order not to kill me, but I hear it distantly, as if through a long tube. All I can see is a shifting kaleidoscope of dark shapes. I feel dizzy, nauseous, and I press my eyes shut. I'm relying on sheer instinct now—instinct and adrenaline. I should have fallen long ago. I will, soon. I am battered, spun around, but I never lose my orientation. I know where the Rift is. I can hear it calling.

And I know, somehow, I just know, when my path to it is clear.

I take my opportunity: my leap for freedom, for the Rift. And I know it will destroy me, because I'm not wearing the mask, I'm not protected. But my heart sings, and I force my eyes open because I want to drink in that green light one last time.

Only the green light isn't there. The siren call was an illusion. I'm looking at the pale, blank wall of the laboratory through the black containment frame. The abused computer must have lost control of the energy grid; emergency systems have shut down the Rift.

The Centauri hold me again, and I can't escape this time. I have no strength left. If they let me go, I would only fall. Their leader squares up to me, her face an inch from my own.

"Well, well," she says in a mocking tone, "there is some spirit in you yet. But where do you think you can run to, little man? This station is ours. Your project is ours. And so, now, are you!"

CHAPTER
TWELVE

I'm paraded through the corridors of what was once my home, my tiny kingdom. Two Centauri soldiers march ahead of me, two more behind, one to each side—this latter pair holding my shoulders so that my unresponsive feet drag on the floor. Six guards; I ought to be flattered, given my current condition.

Two more stand outside the refectory. One operates the door control—no doubt the corresponding panel inside the room has been disabled—and I'm bundled through the aperture and left to stand unaided. For an instant, watched by so many waiting eyes, I think I can do it. I fall on my face, of course, humiliated.

As the door is closed and locked, my fellow prisoners gather about, concerned.

"Are you okay?" fusses Wroje. "Are you hurt? What did they do to you?"

"And, while you're considering those questions," puts in Knave, "here's another one for you: Who are you?"

"The Time Traveler?" asks Koriah.

"Archer?" guesses Acroyear, peering at my age-worn face. Under other circumstances, I could laugh.

Somebody *is* laughing: Ogwen, heaped in a corner,

on the verge of hysteria. "Don't you recognize him? Don't you recognize our lord and master? It's Karza, you fools, Karza!"

They're beginning to see it. Wroje gasps, putting a hand to her mouth. Koriah raises an eyebrow. Acroyear says, "You're wearing the Time Traveler's containment suit."

"Well observed," I say dryly.

"Then, what became of Ryan Archer?"

"He's dead." I wait a moment for that to sink in. "I planned to enter the Rift in his place. I wasn't quick enough. The Centauri found me."

"Then…then you didn't make the repairs," stammers Wroje. "The time stream…it's still unraveling!"

"One in the eye for the Centauri," giggles Ogwen, "when they find out."

"You must tell them!" cries Wroje. "If they knew how important it was, if they knew that the whole universe was in danger, they'd let you—"

"I will tell the Centauri nothing!" I snap. "They are animals. They won't understand!"

Acroyear leaps to his feet and begins to pace like a caged beast, showing no sign of the injuries he must have sustained. The Centauri took his sword, but they couldn't remove his armor without killing him; he still looks like a formidable foe. My best hope, such as it is. "If only there was some way out of this room…" he growls. He halts, his eyes alighting upon the grille to the oxygen ducts, high up on the wall opposite the door.

"Been there, done that," says Knave. "They'll be wise to that trick now. They'll have guards watching the ducting."

"All I need," I say, lifting myself into a sitting position with some difficulty, "is access to the Rift, just for a second. The course is still programmed into my chest unit."

"Why don't you accept it?" groans Ogwen. "The Centauri have won. We can't fight them—look what happened when we tried! Archer's dead, and the rest of us are lucky not to have joined him. They've beaten us!"

"Not all of us!" cries Wroje suddenly.

"Wroje…"

Fired with enthusiasm, she ignores my warning growl. "No, don't you see, they haven't got Kellesh! He was underneath the station, out in space. They might not think to look there, and…and he's still wearing a baffler, so they can't detect him. He's free! He'll think of something. He'll lash together some gadget, and he'll come rescue us."

"Maybe," I say tartly, "if you haven't just betrayed his presence."

Wroje looks horrified, her jaw trembling as she tries to work out what she's done wrong.

Koriah frowns. "What are you telling us, Karza?"

"He's saying that the room's bugged," offers Ogwen. "All the rooms are bugged. I'll bet he has cameras, too, in the walls. I always knew he was watching us, always watching."

"Karza?"

I shrug. "One microphone, located half a meter below the oxygen duct—buried, as Ogwen correctly surmises, in the wall. Its output is encoded, and can only be unscrambled by the receiver in my chamber. With luck, the Centauri won't have activated it yet. I would advise, however, saying nothing aloud that you would not wish to be overheard."

"You were spying on us?" bleats Wroje. "All this time…?"

"Of course he was," laughs Ogwen. "What else did you expect?"

"But...but not all the time? I mean, not when we were in our quarters?"

I don't say anything; I don't have to. Anyway, it is taking more and more effort to think through my dizziness, to block out the pain that is growing to encompass my body. I didn't count on spending this long without my exo-suit. My years are catching up on me.

Koriah rounds on me, always eager to side with a lost cause. "That's out of order, Karza! Bad enough you had the Biotrons marching around like your personal watchmen; at least they stayed out of our rooms. We're entitled to some privacy!"

"And I'm entitled," I respond hotly, "to know what's happening aboard my own station."

"But...but sometimes," stammers Wroje, "when LeHayn and I were alone—when I *thought* we were alone—I...I talked to her about things. Personal things."

"I have no interest in your dreary life," I snap. "All I was concerned with was the project, and anything that might jeopardize it."

"Such as?" Koriah challenges.

"Such as Veelum encouraging the insectoid to abandon me. Such as Ogwen planning to betray me to the Centauri to save his own skin."

"You can't control everything that happens around you, Karza!"

"Can't I?"

Koriah scowls. "Oh, sure, you'd like to. That's one thing I've realized about you, Karza. You want power, and you don't care what you have to do to get it. All this talk of saving the universe—I know you mean it,

I know you genuinely want to repair the timelines, that's why I haven't tried to stop you. But why, Karza? I don't believe it's out of altruism. I don't think you even care what happens to the rest of us after you've gone. It's a means to an end for you, isn't it? The Galactic Defenders were right. You want to be able to travel in time, to change your life. You want to rewrite history, to put yourself in control."

"And would that be so bad? Or would you prefer this chaos?"

"I prefer to be responsible for my own actions!" storms Koriah.

"Such as disabling the auto-destruct system?"

"I...I..." I've thrown her off-balance, but not for long. "Yes. Yes, I did that. It was one of the first things I did after I arrived here. I went down into the bowels of the station and I disconnected the bomb that you'd so considerately placed under us all. I tried to reconnect it when Acroyear's plan hinged on us being able to use it, but the Centauri broadcast their hypnotic signal, Kellesh attacked me, and there just wasn't time."

"That bomb was our last hope."

"*Your* last hope, Karza. No one else could activate it—and I didn't trust you not to misuse it. I wasn't sure you wouldn't sacrifice us, each and every one of us, for a final grand gesture!"

"Then it's thanks to you," I snarl, "that the Centauri have the time travel machinery. You've caused exactly what you came here to prevent. I hope you're proud!"

"Hey," pipes up Knave, before the argument can escalate further. "The universe is still doomed, right? How much worse could the Centauri make things?"

"When you have suffered a lifetime as their slave," I say through clenched teeth, "always assuming that they let your miserable species evolve at all, and given the infinitesimal chance that we will remember this conversation or anything about our current existence, then I swear I will find you and remind you of that inane contribution, Vaerian."

Knave shrugs. "It was a rhetorical question. The point is—"

"The point is," interrupts Acroyear, "that, whatever the reason, we are alive. It's futile to debate how we came to be here; recriminations will not aid our escape."

An awkward, reflective silence follows. Then Wroje asks hesitantly, "Why *haven't* the Centauri killed us? What do they want from us?"

"The same thing they have always wanted," I say. "My project."

"They have that already," says Knave.

"Perhaps they don't. I could have deleted vital files from my computer's drives—files that, intellectual dwarves as they are, they could never reconstruct."

"And did you?"

"No, but, ironically, the Centauri caused a great deal of damage themselves, whilst trying to abort the auto-destruct countdown. It will take them some time to repair the computer. Until they do, they can't know for sure that they have all the data they need—or, equally importantly, that their scientists can interpret that data. They may need me, after all."

"And the rest of us?" asks Acroyear.

"They will probably threaten your lives to gain my cooperation."

Koriah laughs hollowly. "Then they don't know you very well."

"Indeed."

I am thinking back to the offer the female Centaurus

made, when she thought I had power over her. She was lying, of course. She had no more intention of sharing my project than do I. As soon as I had stopped the countdown, the power would have been hers again, and she would not have relinquished any fraction of it.

Now, however, the situation is different. I may have a bargaining tool. I can make a deal: I can help my foes to reopen the Rift; I can plant the idea in their minds that I may have created a death trap, for anyone who steps into it; I can let them send me in first. A long shot, but it could happen. And once it has, this aberrant timeline would be extinguished in a heartbeat. Nobody would be able to follow me.

"What happened to Archer?" asks Acroyear.

I shrug. "Does it matter?"

"To me, yes. You say the Centauri soldiers were instructed to keep us alive. Why, then, did they kill him?"

It would be easy to lie, but I am weary of all that. "I did not say the Centauri killed him, only that the boy was dead. Yes, Koriah, there's no need to look so scandalized. It was me. I murdered Archer. He would have destroyed everything."

The next thing I know, Acroyear is on top of me, hands around my throat, squeezing the life out of me, and everybody else is shouting. I can't make out their words, only the muted rhythms of their voices crashing in my ears like waves breaking against a cliff side. I can only hear Acroyear:

"I should have done this days ago—Archer warned me that you were a monster!" The image of his helmeted head fades from my sight, as if I'm being pulled away down a long, dark tunnel.

I'm lying on my side, floundering as if half-drowned. My heart pounds so hard that I fear it will give out. The act of breathing is like scouring my lungs with sandpaper, but my chest aches for air and so breathe I must. My vision is hazy with tears. I try to blink them away, try to focus on the muffled sounds around me.

"—don't like it either," Koriah is saying, "but if he's telling the truth, if Archer didn't make it into the Rift, then we need him. He may be the only person who can repair time."

"The girl is right," I say. The words come with difficulty, my lungs protesting at this extra demand upon them. I give myself a few more seconds, during which I see Acroyear's fists clenching. Koriah places a steadying hand on the warrior's shoulder. "We seem to have become distracted again. As Acroyear said, we should be planning our escape."

"Why, Karza?" the warrior growls. "Why did you do it?"

"Was it the hypnotic signal, affecting your mind?" Wroje asks, hopefully.

I sigh. "Don't be obtuse! The signal could only heighten existing anxieties. Ogwen, for example, wouldn't have been so terrified of Knave had a part of him not already believed he might devolve into Antron form. Your attack upon Koriah was born from the very real fear that our Galactic Defender might turn on you at any moment, as she did on LeHayn."

Koriah gasps. "Wroje, I never...I wouldn't..."

"Of course you would," I say scornfully, "if you had to. And why not? What good is she to you? To anybody? It is only through LeHayn that she had a place here at all."

"That's enough, Karza," growls Acroyear.

I continue. "For me, the experience was illuminating. The Centauri unlocked a part of my psyche that

I'd refused to acknowledge. No, their signal did not compel me to shoot Archer."

I drag myself to the edge of the room, so that I can prop my head against the wall and face my accusers. In the silence that accompanies my slow, painful crawl, Knave turns to Ogwen and says bitterly, "So, it's guilty until proven innocent with you, huh? All Vaerians tarred with the same brush. Shoot first and ask questions later."

"Well, I don't know what causes the change, do I?" Ogwen defends himself. "For all I know, you could turn into one of those…those animals at any moment. Like she does!" he adds, nodding toward Wroje. Already tearful, she swallows her pain at this further insult.

"Perhaps it's skipped your attention," says Knave angrily, "but Wroje and I fought to save this station, to save your butt, twice—while you were doing what, exactly?"

"Comrades in arms now, is it?" snorts Ogwen. "The way I heard it, you two were taking potshots at each other just an hour or two ago."

"That was different!"

"Yeah? How?"

"You're wrong about me, Ogwen," snarls Knave. "You want proof? The proof is that I haven't torn out your throat by now!"

Acroyear is still glaring at me; I can tell by the tilt of his head, although his eyes are hidden. "You claimed that Archer would have 'destroyed everything,' " he muses.

"That is correct."

"And yet you would have us believe that you plan to enter the Rift, to sacrifice your life, in his stead—to do what he would have done. It does not make sense. Unless…"

I don't say anything. I let him work it out for himself.

"Archer planned to save this timeline. We talked about it. Perhaps you murdered him because you disagreed with that choice."

"Archer would have shorn up the time stream," I confess, "at the expense of all future travel into it. He would have ensured that this miserable reality endured forever, could never be usurped." I look to the others for support. "Is that you want? Any of you? I promised LeHayn that I would change your past, Wroje. I promised Kellesh that I would save his family. Most of all, I promised myself that all those who have given their lives for my project—the insectoid, LeHayn, Veelum, even Archer—would have a second chance."

"B-but…" stammers Ogwen, straining to think through his intoxication, "what would that mean for us? The people we are? We…we wouldn't exist…would we?"

"On the contrary, our lives would be improved. We are, all of us, a product of our experiences. Imagine, Ogwen, if you had not come to this station. Ima gine if you had been protected your whole life, if there had been nothing to fear. With your intellect, you could have been a builder, a leader, instead of the cringing wretch you have become! And you, Acroyear—how different would your life have been had Maruunus Ki not defeated and enslaved you? How many years did you waste in his mines? Can you hear the ticking of the clock yet, the whisper in your ear that tells you that time is racing onward? Do you even know how long you have before that armored suit of yours consumes you?"

"Presumably," Koriah points out, "your argument didn't convince Archer."

"He wouldn't see," I snort dismissively. "He didn't

understand. But you understand, don't you? All of you—with the possible exception of Koriah—wish your lives could have been different. Well, I can make it so. I challenge any of you to look me in the eye and tell me that that isn't your fondest desire!"

"You make a persuasive case," concedes Acroyear.

"Yeah," adds Knave, "but nobody's life is perfect, is it? I mean, sure, I'd give anything to reverse what happened to my people, for my circus not to have fallen into Ordaal's hands, but how do I know those things didn't happen anyway in the original timeline?"

"And there's one part of this little fairytale you haven't mentioned yet," Koriah points out. "You've talked about how the rest of us might fare in this other reality—but you, I suspect, would gain a lot more than most."

"All I would gain," I say cautiously, "is the chance to improve the lot of billions."

"Your precious order," says Koriah, "at all costs."

I have no wish to get into this argument again. My head aches. It's an effort to keep my eyes open. "Whatever your opinion of me, Koriah," I say, "the situation is this: Archer is gone, and only I can replace him. My path is programmed into the Time Traveler's chest unit. It is unlikely enough that I will ever get to follow it. Certainly, I foresee no possible future in which I have a chance to reprogram that path, even should I wish to."

"So, it comes down to a choice," says Acroyear. "Either we allow you to rule the galaxy, or it will be destroyed."

"A fair summation." I try to smile, but my muscles protest at even this small effort.

Another long silence, ended again by Wroje. "I think we have to do it," she says. "It's like Knave said: That other timeline, it's the original one. It doesn't matter if we like it or not, it's the way things should have been. We're the ones who oughtn't to be here."

"For once, Wroje has the right idea," I prompt, since nobody else seems to want to respond to that. "In the end, all I'm proposing is that we put things right. If we can."

I'm still waiting for somebody to speak when a high-pitched whistle whines around the refectory. Instantly, Acroyear, Koriah and Knave are on their feet, looking for the source of the sound. I make a token effort to raise myself a little, to shake the shadows from my eyes and get a better view across the room, but I soon give up and sink back down. Ogwen takes a swig from his bottle, squints down its neck distastefully when he realizes that it's empty, burps and mutters an embarrassed apology.

The sound comes again, like a sonic drill boring into my eardrums. I wince. There is no other indication that anything is amiss, however—no sign of an attack. The refectory door remains closed, and I detect no alteration to my brain chemistry this time. My cellmates see this, too, and allow themselves to relax a little.

Knave is the first to find the source of the disturbance. He homes in on the grille to the oxygen ducts, and then to an area of the wall beneath it. "Sounds like feedback from that bug of yours," he says.

"Does...does that mean the Centauri...Are they listening?" asks Wroje, trembling.

The sound has softened, become less distinct. It is like the wind now, rustling through leaves—and I start as the wind whispers my name.

I must have imagined it, my mind constructing patterns where there are none. But I hear it again: "Ka...za...kar...zaa..." And then, unmistakably: "Ac...royear..."

Koriah springs across the room and speaks urgently into the wall. "Kellesh?"

"Koriah…" breathes the whistling wind. "Koriah…that you?"

"Kellesh," warns Acroyear, "the Centauri may be monitoring this frequency."

"…can't…isolated the circuits…can't eavesdrop…"

"Where are you?"

"Still…exposed part of the station…below…"

"We can't hear you," says Acroyear. "You're breaking up."

"Best I can…modulating the feedback from the…hear you fine, but…"

"Listen, Kellesh," says Acroyear brusquely. "We need you to get us out of this room. There are two guards outside. Can you deal with them?"

"…might be able to rig up…diversion…some time, though."

"No hurry," says Knave. "We aren't about to starve with the food machines in here."

"No," I interrupt forcefully. "A simple diversion is not good enough this time, Kellesh. We need those Centauri dead, and we need you to open this door from the outside. And we don't have as much time as our Vaerian colleague suggests: My strength is fading."

A short pause. Then Kellesh responds, "…see what I can do…need…help, though. Give me…then make…much noise as you…distract the guards, and…"

"Say again," urges Acroyear. "How long, Kellesh? How long do you need?"

The answer comes through a static storm. "Ten minutes."

"Bring weapons," I say. "As many as you can."

"Do you think he can do it?" Knave asks, after a

long enough pause to be sure that the Terragonian is no longer listening. "I know he's resourceful—he just doesn't strike me as the kind of guy who has the killer instinct."

"He fared adequately against the Antrons," says Acroyear.

"Until they overpowered him," Knave points out.

"An entirely different circumstance," I say. "No doubt it was easy for Kellesh to think of the Antrons as subhuman, and to treat them as such." I cast a sly glance at Knave, whose mouth tightens into a straight line. "The Centauri have the power of speech, and a certain level of intellect; he will find it harder to resist anthropomorphizing them. Nevertheless, they too are monsters. After what happened to Kellesh's family—knowing that the Centauri might do the same to us—I believe he will accept that."

"So, you think he'll come through," says Koriah. "Why didn't you just say that?"

"We don't have long," says Acroyear. "We must be ready when Kellesh makes his move."

"Am I to assume, then," I ask, "that you have decided to assist me?"

"Do we have a choice?" Knave grumbles.

Acroyear walks up to me, looms over me. "Whatever I may think of you," he says, "your argument has logic. For the sake of the universe itself, we must do as you say. We must do all we can to get you to the Rift, and allow you to make your journey."

He turns back to the others, as if expecting an argument. Nobody speaks up. I wonder how they would react if I told them all that my plan has a far lower chance of success than did Archer's. I have burdened them with enough knowledge, however. All they need to know is that my way is the only way. It offers the only prize worth the struggle.

Even Ogwen seems to accept this, lapsing into sober contemplation. When Koriah offers a stimulant from one of the food machines, to chase the methohol from the bureaucrat's system, he assures her in a clear tone that this will not be necessary. I had wondered to what extent his habitual drunkenness was a front, a means of keeping a frightening world at bay; I always knew we didn't have *that* much methohol on the station.

I clear my throat. "I, on the other hand…" I say self-consciously.

Koriah looks at me as if I'm beneath contempt, as if to assist me in any way would be to sully her soul. I can do nothing but return her gaze, blankly, straining to keep a plea from my eyes. I won't be that weak.

I can't feel my legs.

The girl's expression softens, and this is worse. I don't want her pity. I may have fallen far, but I will rise again. She leans over me and empties a syringe into a vein on my neck. I convulse as its effervescent payload sparks in my chest. My nerves twitch.

I feel hardly any stronger—what extra reserves the injection has given me have been diverted straight to my system's war against total collapse. My hand darts out, catching Koriah's wrist as she withdraws. "More…" I croak. She looks as if she's about to argue, but then she performs a facial shrug—of what concern is my health to her, anyway?—and returns to the machine.

The second injection restores some measure of control to me. While I still have it, while I can force my muscles to take my weight, I lever myself to my feet. I'm forced to use the wall as a crutch—nobody offers me a hand, nor do I ask for one. The stimulant has bought me a little more time, but not much. My brain feels swollen, too big for my head. I concentrate through the muzziness and the flashes of pain.

"This is what we must do," I say. "When—if—Kellesh frees us, we must separate. I need all of you to make as much trouble in as many different areas of the Astro Station as you can. Koriah, I want you to target the bridge. Knave, you are to go with Kellesh, protect him while he destroys the life support systems. If this plan doesn't work," I add quickly, forestalling Ogwen's objection, "we're dead anyway. If it does, it will not matter."

I turn back to the Vaerian. "When you've completed that task—assuming you survive that long—you should join Koriah. As for you, Ogwen, you are to do what comes naturally: run. Take a ship from the hangar bay—the Centauri Battle Cruiser, if you're able. You may even get lucky: You may escape. The important thing is that the Centauri respond to what appears to be a full-scale breakout."

"No matter how we divide their attention," says Acroyear, "they will not leave the laboratory unguarded."

"Indeed. That is why I need you with me. Your task is the most important of all, Acroyear. You are to get me to the Rift."

"What about me?" asks Wroje plaintively.

I pretend not to hear her. I say to Acroyear, "I trust you are as useful with a laser pistol as you are with an energy sword? You will need to be."

"What should I do?"

I turn to Wroje slowly, eyeing her with disdain. "Do as you wish. I don't imagine there's anything you *could* do that would make the slightest difference."

The young woman's face crumples as, predictably, Koriah's righteous anger flares. "You're some piece of work, you know that, Karza? You brought Wroje into this—she's been loyal to you, she's helped you, spoke up for you—and in return, you treat her like dirt! I'd hoped that staring death in the face might have given you a little perspective."

"On the contrary," I contest, "it has done just that. It has focused my mind on what is important—and I can see, if you cannot, that Wroje has no practical use to us. To delude her, and ourselves, into believing otherwise would be a monumental waste of time."

"In some ways," says Koriah defensively, "she's the strongest of us all!"

I let out a scornful laugh. "You mistake potential for actuality, dear girl. What use all of Wroje's strength if she is too weak, too afraid, to release it? Even now she relies on you to argue her case. She lacks the courage even to speak for herself!"

"I *can* help," insists Wroje, sullenly. "I can...I can..." She fumbles for an idea. "I can analyze the Centauri's subsonic signal. I can duplicate it. They won't be expecting that. Their brain chemistry isn't too dissimilar to ours. The signal should play with their minds, as it did with ours. They won't be able to tell friend from foe."

"And how exactly do you plan to accomplish this?" I scoff, puncturing her building optimism. "Do you think the occupiers of this station will let you just stroll up to a computer terminal and leave you to work?"

"It's an idea, Karza," says Koriah pointedly. "We could at least discuss it."

"You see?" I snap. "Wasting time! You want to 'discuss' this foolhardy notion, squander the few minutes we have left to plan, for no better reason than to spare her feelings. This woman, whose own mother hated her so much that she kept her locked in a room for half her childhood. This…this miserable half-breed; this product of one of the most vile acts of betrayal imaginable!"

"Karza…" warns Koriah.

"Stop it!" wails Wroje. "Stop…stop saying those things! Stop telling those lies!"

"Lies? Is that what you tell yourself, Wroje? Perhaps you've said it enough times that you've even begun to believe it. You've rewritten your own past already. Perhaps you believe that those people—those men your mother let take you—inserted the monster within you somehow. But that isn't true, Wroje. You know it isn't true. They only branded you, marked you so that ordinary, decent people wouldn't be taken in by your outward appearance."

"No!" Wroje turns away, her hands pressed over her ears as if my words cause her physical pain. Koriah is torn between comforting her and yelling at me.

Acroyear has sidled over to me without my realizing it. "You're playing a dangerous game, Karza," he mutters in my ear—but he makes no move to stop me. Knave is looking from one of us to the other, not sure what's going on.

"Why do you think your mother despised you, Wroje?" I snarl. "Why do you think she couldn't bear to look at you? *You* are the monster. It's a part of you—the most important part—and it always has been, ever since your mother was assaulted by your Centaurus father!"

Wroje's heartfelt cry of misery is punctuated by three small explosions from outside the room. I grit my teeth. I had hoped Kellesh could be a little more subtle. He'll put our foes on alert, bring reinforcements running from all over the Astro Station.

Acroyear and Knave hurry over to the door. At least one of the Centauri guards is still standing, and returning fire. I don't have long.

"What are you doing here, Wroje?" I snap. "You aren't one of us. Your people, the Centauri, are out there! They're massacring and looting and bullying the rest of the galaxy into submission, but at least they have the courage to be true to themselves."

"It's not true!" she screams. "I'm not like that, I'm not!"

"You don't expect me to believe that? I've seen you, Wroje; I've seen the real you, the monster! Do you really think you can fool me—fool anyone, anymore—with this pathetic, simpering, whining shell you've built for yourself?"

There is silence outside. Kellesh has triumphed, or more likely failed. Either way, it's over.

"LeHayn said—"

"LeHayn pitied you. That's what she told me." It isn't true, but that doesn't matter now. I bear down on Wroje, taking her by the arms, shaking her. Trying to shake the creature out of her. "How do you think I know so much about you, Wroje? Your friend confided in me, many times. She asked me—no, begged me—to go back in time, to destroy the Centauri before they could spawn you. She wanted to snuff out your miserable hybrid existence before it began. She knew you'd be better off dead; that the universe would be a better place without you. And she knew it was the only way she'd ever be rid of your clinging—"

Koriah is between us, her expression thunderous, her fist drawn back.

Her punch seems to land in slow motion, still too fast for me to react in time. My jaw explodes into a ball of pain. My muscles lose their artificial strength in one frenetic burst, snapping like over-tensed elastic bands, and I'm falling. I can't help myself. I hit the floor face-first, boiling with frustration. Stupid girl! Can't she see what I'm trying to do?

And suddenly, everything is happening at once. The door is opening, and Wroje is leaping at me, transforming in midair. I find the strength to twist, to roll out from beneath her striking hooves, because I know the only other option is to die.

I catch a brief glimpse of Kellesh's face, his expression confused. Then Wroje rears up to attack me again, Equestron nostrils flaring above snarling white teeth, and I know I can't avoid her next blow. My heart feels heavy in my chest, pinning me to the spot. I can't even raise my hands to protect my head. I try to cry out, but can muster only a pitiful squeal.

An energy bolt glances off my attacker's head, a corona of fire fizzing around her ears. With a furious whinny, Wroje abandons me for this new threat. She tears into the Centauri guards that have just dragged Kellesh in here, the force of her anger taking them by surprise. My eyelids flutter shut, and I draw a deep, wracking breath. I am soaked through with sweat. Part of me is scornful at myself, that I doubted my own judgment. I took a calculated risk, and it paid off; my timing was perfect. But another, larger part of me is still stuck in that moment of absolute terror.

I hear the sounds of battle: the cries of comrades, and the screams of our Centauri guards as they are beaten to death. I hear the hoof beats of arriving reinforcements. But all those sounds seem so distant. I can't open my eyes.

My mind is wrapped in shadows. There is only the darkness, and I am helpless to resist as it pulls me down into its depths.

CHAPTER
THIRTEEN

Smoke. Heat. Pain. If I didn't know better—if I wasn't clinging, with the last shreds of my will, to my rationalism—I might think I'd come to some mythical Hell. Giddily, my mind runs away with that idea, painting fire and bones and leering demons around me. My demons have been waiting a long time to claim me.

Instinctively, I cower from them. I try to run, but my legs won't hold me. I'm caught—a strong arm around my waist—and I scream, and try to fight it. My captor is a shadow against the flames. Dark red eyes, staring into my mind. A specter of times gone by, and of those that will never come. The sight of him freezes my heart.

I realize that my eyes are closed. I pry them open, gasping with the cold shock of reality. Acroyear. The shadow demon was Acroyear, holding me, keeping me standing, protecting me. The fire and the pain...they were all too real. I've been hit—a Centauri energy bolt, between the ribs of my left side. A patch of the Time Traveler's containment suit has melted and congealed over the wound. It won't hold: When

I step into the time stream, that part of me will be torn open.

I don't have time to take in what's happening, can't discern any pattern in the barrage of movement and noise, before Acroyear manhandles me into a cool, dark space and lets me go, lets me spin into a corner. As a door closes behind us, the sounds of battle are cut off, all but drowned out by the sound of my own ragged breathing.

"What...what's happening?"

"Shh!" says Acroyear, sharply. Hoof beats clatter by outside. I think my heart will explode with impatience. At last, the warrior turns to me. He whispers, "The others are doing their best. Wroje finished off the guards; we got back the weapons they'd taken from Kellesh." He brandishes his arm, on which is perched a laser pistol; he takes the opportunity to tighten its straps. "Just in time. The Centauri attacked. Fortunately for us, they weren't prepared for Wroje's transformation. I was able to carry you out of there."

"Where are we?"

"A storeroom." My eyes are adjusting to the gloom—to seeing at all—and I make out empty, dusty shelves. We haven't come far. "Another minute," says Acroyear, "to be sure we're behind Centauri lines, and then we'll make our move. Are you ready?"

"I can't move," I say. My voice sounds more plaintive than I thought it would.

Acroyear slaps me. He doesn't hold back. My neck cracks like a whip; I knock my head on a shelf. His metal knuckles have drawn blood from my cheek. I start to slide to the floor, but the warrior hoists me up by my chest unit. The blow has served to sharpen my mind, to focus my eyes upon my sallow reflection in his red faceplate, but such clarity is an elusive commodity, already beginning to slip through my fingers.

"I won't let you give up now, Karza!" Acroyear snarls. "You're going through that Rift if I have to carry you to the laboratory and hurl your dead body into it!"

"W-wouldn't do you much good." I'm laughing. I am actually laughing. A wave of adrenaline has broken inside me—but instead of bolstering me, it threatens to tip me into delirium. I can't stand this. If I can't even control myself, then what hope have I?

"Archer said—"

"—that only the costume was important. But we aren't following Archer's plan now."

"What haven't you told me, Karza?"

"Need...need to reach someone. Across the time stream. I need to warn him..."

What hope have I? No hope at all.

"You aren't making sense!" says Acroyear urgently, raising his voice as high as he dares.

"Doesn't matter now." I'm a rag doll, limp in his grasp. "Can't...anyway. Knew it was too late...knew I couldn't keep on...should have accepted...it's over."

With that, I let my heavy eyelids fall again. I seek out the darkness, realizing with sudden clarity that it doesn't *matter* that I've lost. Time will endure without me, unchanged by my brief passage through it—but that thought causes me no anguish, no regret. I feel only contentment, and relief at relinquishing a long-held burden.

And armored hands, shaking me, holding me here. I let out a moan, and plead with Acroyear to leave me alone. He refuses. "People are fighting for you, Karza."

"Then…then their cause is lost."

"They're dying, to give you a chance that you've done little to deserve. They're counting on you to put things right!"

"A chance? No chance at all. The odds…too great…Look at me, Acroyear!"

"They're doing as you told them. They're separating, making for the bridge, the hangar bay, the life support systems. Wroje is wreaking havoc. The Centauri won't know which way to turn. With luck, it will be some time before they even miss us."

"*Look at me!* What use am I to anybody? I just want to die. Let me die!"

He lets go of me. For a moment, I think he might grant me my wish. Instead he sighs, and addresses me in a softer voice. "Ryan Archer told me about the other timeline," he says, "what little he saw of it. He told me of a galaxy over which one man had absolute control. He was afraid to come here, to this station, although he knew he had to—afraid to face the all-powerful figure he had seen in his nightmares. And he spoke of technology beyond anything we know now: of giant mechs and rocket tubes, and genetic monstrosities bred in vaults."

I sneer. "Don't tell me you approve."

"Archer also described the fate of Knave's race."

"Oh?"

"The Vaerians were massacred, as in the history we know—sacrificed for their genetic potential. The difference is that, in the other reality, it was *you* who ordered your biosmiths to create the Antrons, *you* who committed that atrocity."

"I assume your friend Jafain is unaware of this fact?"

"If he knew—if he were here now instead of me—I'm sure he would accede to your request. He would let you die! Koriah, I suspect, would do the same, were she to learn that, in the timeline you wish to restore, she is fated to become the last of her proud organization."

"And you? What about you, Acroyear?"

A drawn-out pause, before the warrior answers. "This I swear, Karza: Should we succeed here, we will meet again in another life. I will oppose you, then, with every fiber of my being. I won't rest until I have brought your empire crashing down around your ears."

I grin, holding onto the vestige of hope that, somehow, he has managed to dredge from me. "I look forward to the battle."

And that's when the lights go out.

I don't quite know what has happened at first. This storeroom is dark anyway, so the shift in visibility isn't too noticeable; I fear my sight might be failing, that this is yet another symptom of my inexorable decay. It is Acroyear who reminds me of Kellesh and Knave's mission, which has evidently met with success. He asks me how long we can survive without life support.

"Given the number of Centauri aboard, and the fact that our oxygen reserves were already depleted by the damage done to the station, I would estimate no longer than about twenty minutes." I don't add that, with the respiratory problems I already have, I will probably collapse in half that time, as soon as the air grows thin. The important thing is that the Centauri will have to evacuate—unlikely, given the situation—or divert vital resources toward repairing Kellesh's sabotage. The gloom of the emergency lighting—a faint green glow now seeps under the door—will also aid our cause.

Acroyear is holding something up to my eyes. It

takes me a moment to discern the shape as that of another laser pistol. "Can you use this?" he asks. I nod. Still, he is forced to strap the weapon to my arm himself, as I lean against the shelving. "We can't win this war by stealth alone," he says. "Sooner or later, we are going to have to fight."

"I won't let you down," I promise.

Acroyear nods grimly, seeming to accept that. He opens the door and peers out into the corridor beyond. When he's satisfied that it is clear, he turns and extends a hand toward me. For all of two faltering steps, I am determined not to take it.

We stumble out of the storeroom together. Acroyear's right arm is around my waist, his left hand raised as he sights along his laser pistol.

We are spotted within seconds. My unlikely ally fires, almost before I see the first Centaurus rounding the corner ahead of us. The shot flies true, striking her in the face, making her recoil; however, Acroyear's pistol is not as effective as his energy sword was. Protected by her faceplate but blinded by the flash of the attack, the Centaurus gallops forward, screaming for reinforcements. I couldn't get out of her way even if I had somewhere to go.

Remembering, belatedly, that I, too, am armed, I get off a shot. It goes wild. Beside me, to my gratitude, Acroyear stands his ground, firing a second, a third, a fourth time. The Centaurus has almost reached us—she's rearing up, ready to crack my head open with a double-hoofed blow—when the cumulative effect of her punishment takes hold, and she topples backwards.

Before she even hits the ground, Acroyear is running, pulling me along. He leaps over our fallen foe, and I stumble in his wake. I think it's only momentum that keeps me on my feet. The warrior bundles me around a corner and presses me to the wall, clamping a hand over my mouth to stifle the sound of my panting. Four Centauri rush past in response to their comrade's call, passing within a few meters of our hiding place.

I feel as if a buzz saw has been let loose in my chest cavity, as if my lungs will collapse in on themselves. Does Acroyear know that he's killing me? Bile rises in my throat, and I find the strength to tear his hand away, to gasp for sweet air. My eyes are misted with tears.

And then he's propelling me onward again, and I have to suffer the ignominy of being so utterly dependent on one who should have been a sworn adversary. I am more determined than ever, now, to reach the Rift, to alter my history, because only this will erase my shame. That I, Karza, should have begged this savage for the release of death...It is a moment in time that, for the sake of my legacy, I will see obliterated.

The next few minutes dissolve into a red haze. It has always been difficult for me, a man of intellect, to surrender to my base instincts, but that is what I do. It is only through disengaging my brain that I can keep my pain, and my sense of hopelessness, at bay. I must not pause to dwell upon my situation, lest my mind be forced to accept it.

I am afraid of the future, so I live in the moment. As more Centauri come at us, I embrace my hatred for them until there is nothing else. My reactions become quicker, my aim more precise. Acroyear is still claiming the majority of the kills, but I make a contribution. The air around me is thick with the answering fire of crossbows, but I hardly care. Let them strike me—if that is to be my fate, then I can do nothing to avert it.

I think of the scientists' rebellion, of Fzzzpa's blood draining into the ground. I think of Wroje, and the beast inside her. I disdained her, because she couldn't control it; I taunted her into releasing it, because I needed its chaos. I never once considered my own inner beast, so long imprisoned, so long denied. I told myself, for so many years, that I could control it. I *can't* control it. I could only keep it subjugated. For the first time, as a bloodthirsty scream is ripped from my throat, I appreciate that distinction.

I think I fell, once. I think I was separated from Acroyear. He couldn't reach me.

I have a memory of lying on my back, twisting and writhing to avoid being trampled, staring up at the stomach of a Centauri soldier—but it seems to belong to a distant time, or perhaps to an old nightmare, and I can't be certain that it happened at all.

I think I found a patch of exposed flesh between the armor plates strapped to my attacker's underside. I think I fired into it. I think the Centaurus reared up in animal pain, and I targeted his weak spot a second time before rolling out from beneath him. I think I did all those things, but I don't know how I *could* have done them. Did I really find the strength to leap to my feet unaided? To rush the Centaurus before he could recover his wits? To knock the crossbow from his hand, pressing so close to him that he couldn't raise his hooves to strike at me? To fire repeatedly into the eyeholes of his faceplate?

The more I think about it, the more I doubt myself. It's as if, all of a sudden, I can see what I'm doing, and it terrifies me because I know I *can't* do it. I keep seeing myself lying on the floor as hooves crash around my head, and I think the reason that the image has a dreamlike quality is that I didn't let myself think about my situation at the time.

I mustn't think about it now. I mustn't pierce the protective misty bubble in which I've wrapped the memory; I would release enough fear and self-doubt to incapacitate myself.

I must keep going. Stop analyzing. Suppress the dreams that have kept me alive this long. Don't think about my ambitions. Forget the future.

I don't stop—can't stop—even after the last foe has fallen. I'm fighting empty air, looking for somebody to vent my fury upon. There is only Acroyear, shouting something I can't hear. I try to keep hold of the moment, afraid to let it go, but my hatred dissipates in the absence of an outlet for it. The thoughts I've been keeping at arm's length overwhelm me, memories striking me like fresh revelations. I feel as if I were temporarily possessed by the soul of another man, another Karza; that it was him, not me, who fought his way to here.

The main lab. I didn't recognize it before, hardly glanced at my surroundings. I do have a vague recollection of passing through a doorway. I don't think it was guarded, but there were several creatures inside the room, working at the computer. Technicians—but, being Centauri, they were bred to fight anyway. Not well enough.

"—done my part. It's your turn, Karza. Open the Rift. Don't let all this be for nothing!"

"How...how long...?" I feel as if I were fighting forever, but the fact that I'm still breathing, albeit in labored gasps, proves otherwise.

"As long as it takes the Centauri to shoot their way

in here," says Acroyear. The next wave is already approaching. Stationing himself beside the open door, the warrior leans out into the corridor and lets off a volley of laser fire. "I'll give you as long as I can."

I nod and, with trembling hands, work the straps of my own pistol free from around my arm, then toss it to him. I'm beginning to suffer the aftereffects of my exertion; my body feels like an eggshell, about to collapse in on itself. I try not to think about it, but it's harder to focus past that sort of pain now. My beast has gone, my chaotic side reined in once more. It is the ordered, analytical side of my nature that I need now—the true Karza, I once thought.

I sag into the chair before the computer's main console. The lab, like the rest of the station, is cast in a dull, emergency lighting glow, but the computer has its own power source. It is unaffected by Kellesh's sabotage. The question is, how much damage have the Centauri wrought? And how much were they able to repair?

A voice bleeds through the rushing sound in my ears: the Centauri representative, her hateful tone distorted by electronics. "A spirited attempt, Karza—I'll confess, we didn't expect the Panzerite—but you can't hope to defeat us. We have the bridge, and we have your friends, the Galactic Defender and the Vaerian; the others are dead. If you care anything for them, you will surrender and leave the time travel machinery intact. Cooperate, and I will petition the Centauri council to grant you a stay of execution."

"A less than generous offer," I respond tersely, "under the circumstances." I launch a diagnostic program, rigid with anxiety as I await the results, wishing I could speed up the process. I try to ignore the continuing sounds of battle behind me, try not to think about what will happen should Acroyear fall.

The next voice I hear belongs to Koriah. "They want me to plead with you. They say they'll torture me if you don't give yourself up, but you know—" The speech turns into a gargling groan as she bites back a scream. Involuntarily, I say her name. "Don't...don't weaken on me now," she gasps. This time, I hear the whine of whatever device it is they're using to burn her. The girl's voice cracks with pain as she forces out the words, "You know what you have to do, Karza. This is no time to give up being a heartless bastard!"

She screams then, and I find myself wincing, caring more than I thought I could. I have come to realize how strong she is; she must be in agony, to lose control like this. I raise my hands to my ears, knowing the futility of the gesture but just wanting the awful sound to stop. And then, mercifully, it *does* stop, with an electric fizzle and an odor of burning, and I see that Acroyear has half-turned to fire his pistol at the compad on the wall.

"The Rift, Karza," he says gruffly, as he turns back to the door. "Open the Rift!"

"You can't control them," says a voice at my shoulder. *"You see that now, don't you?"*

"Now is not the time for this conversation," I say through gritted teeth.

"Can't think of a better one."

He steps into my field of vision. Incongruously, his forehead still bears the entry wound of my killing shot. He is dressed, as am I, in the costume of the Time Traveler, minus its mask. *"You can conquer them, Karza,"* says Archer. *"You can take their freedom, but they'll despise you for it. As soon as they see an opening, they'll turn on you. As soon as you turn your back, they will betray you."*

"Get out of my mind, Archer!"

"Can't do that either, I'm afraid."

"I know you aren't real. You are a figment of my imagination, a delusion caused by..." By what? The Centauri again? No. I hadn't realized how hot, how stuffy, it was in here. My skin prickles. Sweat pours down my face. My suit sticks to me. My lungs are a pair of blast furnaces. "By the first stage of oxygen starvation."

"You think I'm your conscience?" the ghost says with a smirk.

"Whatever you are, you won't dissuade me from this course. As I told the others, my path is already programmed. I couldn't vary it if...if..." I stop myself, realizing the foolishness of speaking out loud. I need to conserve what breath I have left.

"We both know you won't reach the end of that path alive," says the image of Archer. *"The best you can hope for is to touch the thoughts of your counterpart in the alternative reality. You hope to send him a warning—but against what?"*

The computer delivers the results of its scan. The damage isn't extensive—but it's bad enough. I stare at the cold, angular numbers on the screen, unable to take them in. It seems so cruel, so unfair, that I have come this far, clawed my way back from abject despair, only to have fate deal me this final shattering blow.

"You make your own fate, Karza. Didn't I teach you that?"

My ghost's voice has grown deeper, scratchier. I don't have to look up to know that its shape and its colors have changed too, its golds darkening to black and its reds deepening and shrinking to a single fiery pool in its head.

Under the Emperor's monocular gaze, I feel shamed into renewing my efforts. I can't fix the physical damage—though the Centauri have left their tools scattered about, I have neither the time nor the strength to wield them—but maybe I can find a software workaround. I focus on the keyboard and the monitor, trying to fill my mind with equations and data strings, trying to find my way back to the state of distraction I achieved in the heat of combat.

But what, I keep asking myself, if my dreams are unattainable?

"Don't give up on me now, son. I didn't raise you to be weak!"

What if Archer was right? What if I can never control them? What use my vaunted order, if it is built on unsound foundations?

"You'll be making their lives better." The voice has changed again. This time I do look. The figure beside me is still dressed in black, but its red eye has split into a pair of triangular points. Its helmet has grown to encase the figure's chin, its splayed fins narrowing and dividing into a crown of horns. *"Only as Baron Karza can you save them. Only as Baron Karza can you elevate them from the mire of superstition, give them knowledge. Yes, they will kick against you—they are cattle; it is in their nature to fear the new, the unfamiliar—but, in time, they will see the benefit of your vision, and grow to share it. They will understand that progress—true progress—can only be achieved through perfect order."*

"Yes," I mutter to myself. "Yes..."

My fingers are a blur on the keypad, the accumulated knowledge of my life flowing from my brain. I can do this. I don't have to reconstruct every one of the corrupted files: It doesn't matter if the Rift I form is ultimately unstable, so long as it endures for the seconds I need.

"Don't do this, Karza."

I stiffen. Is my own subconscious determined to torture me? The lines of the phantom have softened, its colors brightening, as if light has chased away the darkness. I'm faced with the image of an attractive young woman, blonde hair flowing onto her shoulders. Her expression—the purse of her lips, the arch of her eyebrows—makes her face look hard. Persephone was like me in so many ways—committed, pragmatic, strong—and yet she could also be optimistic and compassionate. I admired her. I sent her to her death.

"I thought you, of all people, would understand." I forget my resolution not to speak. The sight of her has destroyed that.

She leans over me, and I imagine I can detect the sweet fragrance of her soft skin. *"I love you like a father,"* she says, *"but I can't condone what you're doing."*

"The universe needs order," I say. "Isn't that what you believe?"

"Once, maybe—but I won't be a party to tyranny, Karza. In time, I will see that your order is not worth the price. You will turn me against you."

"Never. I would never drive you away. I couldn't do anything to hurt you."

"It is already written, Karza. There is only one way to stop it: Turn from this course."

"I...I must enter the Rift. The universe...everything...I have no choice."

"I know that. But, when you contact your alternative self—when your mind touches his—what will you tell him?" That question again. I thought I knew the

answer, but now I am confused. It's the lack of air, I tell myself. I can't trust my own mind, in this condition. I have to block out my ghosts, concentrate on the task before me. This is everything I have ever wanted; should I doubt myself now, the hesitation would prove fatal.

"You're dead," I say, in a final attempt to drive the ghost away. "You're dead, and I swore I would do all I can to bring you back—even if it means I must lose you."

I am almost there. Just a few more computations. But, with each second, it becomes harder to draw breath. My chest groans. I feel as if somebody is holding a pillow over my nose and mouth. My vision blurs, the symbols on the screen swimming and dividing.

I ignore Acroyear, at first, when he appears at my side. I think he is another illusion.

"The Centauri have withdrawn," he reports. "It is my guess that they have decided to evacuate the Astro Station."

"Contact Kellesh," I instruct tersely. "Tell him to restore life support, if he's able."

"I have already tried. I can't rise anybody."

It was too much to hope that the Centaurus was lying, that any of them would have survived. I remind myself that they suffered, gave their lives, in a good cause. The best cause. They have bought me this chance.

"Then bring me an air tank. The Centauri will return soon, with spacesuits—but until they do, I have a little more time...if only I could *breathe*!"

Acroyear shakes his head. "Our foes have sustained heavy losses. They have seen their prize damaged, and apparently they believe that you intend to destroy it. If I were the Centauri leader, I would not waste further resources. I would turn my guns on the Astro Station itself as soon as my Battle Cruiser was clear."

I shoot the warrior a withering glare. It comes automatically. I want—I need—to argue with him, to dispute his assumptions. I can't. He's right.

One way or another, this ends now. I save the file I'm working on and hope that I have done enough. The computer's voice receptor is down, so I manually enter the command to open the Rift. The keyboard seems sluggish, unresponsive. Or is it my fingers that are moving clumsily, slowed by my fear of an uncertain fate? I have lost so many chances already. I have given up more than once, only to find that, by accepting the help of those I considered my inferiors, I could still find hope. But is it rational to hope at all—to imagine that, after a lifetime of thwarted ambitions, I can achieve everything in these last seconds? Am I fooling myself?

"Help me," I request, holding out a hand to Acroyear. He takes it and lifts me from my chair. I'm still trying to straighten my legs when I see the Time Traveler's mask, discarded on the floor, its golden eyes staring out from beneath a bench. I stoop and reach for it, closing my fingers around it and clasping it to my heart like a treasured trophy.

Then, I stand at last, and face the black containment grid. Something is happening, but I'm not sure what. The air inside the grid is sparking green, but the flames don't seem able to take hold. The grid itself is buzzing, crackling, and I fear it may overload. *It doesn't matter if the Rift is unstable...I need only a few seconds...*

I realize that I've crossed my fingers. Once, I would have been angry with myself that one of my final acts

in this world should be one of superstition. Now, I
don't care. I will say anything, do anything, pray to
a thousand gods in whom I don't believe if there is
the slightest chance that fate can be persuaded to make
this happen for me, to make the Rift form.

And finally, after the most interminable wait, it
does.

It happens suddenly, in the end. A spark ignites and
I'm blinded, almost physically driven back, by the
flaring light. This close to the Rift, I can feel it pulling
at me. I want to resist it, want to just stand here and
drink in the glory of this moment of fulfillment, but
Acroyear is yelling at me: "Go, Karza! Go! Go! *Go!*"

I fumble with the mask, pulling it down over my
head. This makes it harder than ever to breathe, of
course—but I'm holding my breath, anyway.

I can hardly believe that this is happening at long
last. It doesn't seem real. I'm terrified that it might
be another trick of my mind, that I'll blink and it will
all be gone.

*"Oh no, no, no, this is certainly real. Most cer-
tainly—and a remarkable achievement it is, too. Hmm."*
One final ghost: my old colleague, Fzzzpa. The Rift's
light seems to bounce off the professor's bald head,
although he must be insubstantial. He stands, deep
in thought, his eyebrows beetled, his lower lip drawn
up over the top one to suck at his moustache.

I greet him with a sense of resignation. "I thought
you might come."

*"Yes, yes, you've never quite forgotten me, have you,
my friend? Never forgotten what you did to me."*

"I did what I had to do. That is all I have ever
done."

"And the fruits of your labor—they speak for them-

selves, don't they?" Fzzzpa squints into the green light, then casts a critical eye over the black framework around it. *"Yes, yes, a remarkable achievement. You have a brilliant mind, Karza, I have always said so. A brilliant mind. If there were any justice, then history would give you the recognition you desire."* He glares at me, his watery eyes suddenly piercing. *"Ironic, then, is it not, that your efforts will* rewrite *history? Nobody will know what you did here—perhaps not even you. They won't see the scientist, the savior of the universe; they will know only the tyrant, the monster."*

I open my mouth, but Fzzzpa interrupts me with a dismissive sweep of his hand. *"Oh, I know, you're doing what you have to do—for the sake of your order, am I right?—but what happens in the next reality, Karza? There'll be no threat to the universe, then; no convenient promise of a reset button to excuse your atrocities. Will you kill me again? What happens in the end, when you have the power you have always coveted? Will you accept the cost of your victory? Or will you give it all up, to go back to the start again?"*

"I don't know," I murmur under my breath. Then—because, insanely, I feel that the phantom has not heard me—I lift my head and shout at him, *"I don't know!"*

I start forward, almost involuntarily—and suddenly, the pull of the Rift takes me over. I can't stop myself—I know that I shouldn't try—so, instead, I give in. I don't know if I jump, or if I'm snatched off the floor by gravity gone wild; all I know is that I am hurtling into the mouth of the tunnel, and the green light enfolds me in a welcoming embrace...

But Fzzzpa's last words to me ring in my ears; the same impossible question that the ghost asked me, as had Ryan Archer and Persephone.

"What will you tell him, Karza?"

FOURTEEN

I first saw the Time Traveler on the darkest day of my life.

I have never liked dreams. In dreams, the mind is given over to chaos. It spins its narrative with scant regard for the rule of order, of cause and effect. It confuses reality, clouds clear thinking. I have trained my mind to resist such weakness. I have augmented my body until it no longer needs sleep.

And yet, sometimes, a dream sneaks up on me, catches me unaware and pulls me into its thrall. This was one of those times.

My position within the dream varied, as is often the case. I was on the outside, watching as the Time Traveler glided on the currents of the time stream. I admired his elegance, envied him his freedom. But I was also *inside* his golden containment suit, feeling his elation as I soared through infinity. I felt I was achieving everything I had ever wanted.

Then, the dream turned sour.

Time turned against me, like the sea turning on a lone ship. It tossed me, buffeted me, dragged me from my goal. Its currents pulled me in all directions at once, tearing me apart. I felt a terrible stab of fear, and knew that I was dying. I accepted this—I had expected it—but far more than my own life was at stake.

I had a vital task to perform. A message. I couldn't let go until I'd delivered it.

When I emerged from the dream, I was sweating despite the coolant system in my armor. My heart was beating faster, despite the regulation of my pacemakers. I could still feel the desperation of my dream self, the overwhelming belief that there was something I had to do, only I didn't know what. There was a gnawing discontent in my stomach, which I couldn't dismiss. For the first time I could remember, I couldn't make my emotions bend to the logic of my mind.

Most dreams dissipate with the light of waking, leaving only a secret shame that I succumbed to their seductive fantasies. This dream was different. It was more lucid, more detailed, than any I had had before. This dream felt like reality.

I still suffered the pain of disintegration, could feel it jangling my every nerve. Perhaps, I thought, my dreams had been made stronger by my efforts to suppress them.

Or perhaps this dream had not been a dream at all, but a telepathic contact. A warning, delivered in images rather than words. Perhaps the Time Traveler was real.

It was not inconceivable. I had heard tell of such beings before: Enigmatic figures who phased in and out of this universe, whom popular rumor held to be from the far future—or from the distant past, no one was sure. I'd even tried to capture one of these phantoms, without success. They had always seemed content to observe events, not to interfere. Maybe that was all they were able to do. Still, I couldn't ignore the potential threat they posed. I knew that, one day, I would have to learn their secrets.

At this point, though, so many years ago, it didn't seem important. Other matters took precedence. I had all the time I needed already.

If I close my eyes, I can see my throne room again, can almost feel the press of my seat as it molds itself to the contours of my back. And Mechopolis, of course; I can see my city, the world I created, laid out beneath me on the other side of a vast portal. A permanent symbol of everything I had achieved.

Sometimes, in those days, I allowed myself a rare thrill of pride. I thought about the lowly circumstances of my birth, the impoverished upbringing that seemed so far behind me—and I thought about how I had raised myself to this, how I'd realized my vision, reshaped an entire galaxy. How I had established order. I was still a man, then—barely, beneath all my augmentations—and still capable of such sentiment.

I had power. The masses looked to me for guidance. They feared and respected me. I was the most important man in their lives—and that was how it should have been, because without me they *had* no lives. I was their Emperor. I was Baron Karza.

At other times, none of this meant anything. It had come too easily. I had been taught to fight, first by the Pharoids and then by my predecessor to the throne. I feared that, without an enemy to practice those skills against, a part of me would atrophy. And what purpose all my power, anyway, if I had nobody against whom to pit it?

I had lived for a long time, even then—and I was becoming bored.

I remember how I felt after the dream, as I looked

out across Mechopolis and saw nothing different, but knew that everything had changed. An electric mixture of fear—because something was happening that was out of my control and I'd almost forgotten what that was like—and anticipation, because at last I had a challenge.

When the first explosion came, I think I may actually have smiled.

Memories. Dreams of the past. Though I have replaced the last organic part of my brain with circuitry, still they won't let me go. And yet, as I stand here on the threshold of the end and the beginning of my long life, it seems only apt that I should look back on the path that brought me to this place.

I remember the day that fire rained down upon my world. I remember kneeling by the corpse of my birth father, the burning red eye of the Emperor. I remember how much I hated him as he dragged me from my home. I remember my grief and my anger, but with a sense of detachment, as if the feelings belonged to somebody else. Now, of course, I recognize my rite of passage, and I'm grateful to my dark guardian for all he taught me.

I remember my first sighting of Throne-World, through the glass bottom of the Emperor's zeppelin: the towers, the chimneys, the factories, the airships; the crimson fog that closed in around us like a funeral shroud, blotting out the sky. I remember, my eyes pulled down toward this horror by the weight of my slave collar and by my fear of the black-clad figure beside me. There was no hope here.

And yet, somehow, in the years to come, I found hope—fuelled at first by my desire for revenge, then later by the ideas that filled my head, the future I planned to build.

The Emperor kept his people in line through his church. He maintained order, but in so doing, he held them back, keeping them mired in superstition. He feared technological development because he didn't have the intelligence to understand—and, through understanding, to control—the new ideas of the heretic scientists.

I killed Professor Fzzzpa and put down his technocrats' rebellion because I had to, because it threatened the established order. But I knew that, under my rule, the order would change.

Throne-World was mine long before I actually took its throne, before I drove my sword through the Emperor's heart. I remade it, transforming its dark towers into gleaming spires. I laid the foundations for Mechopolis, and I did so with the Emperor's approval, because he believed that, through me, he could maintain his control over this new world.

He was wrong. I had given his people an appetite for change.

They came out in their millions, filling the main stadium and the streets for blocks around to witness my investiture. They applauded my speech, in which I renamed their world and promised it would live up to that name, that I would continue to improve their lives. And they cheered as—ironically—a Pharoid priest lowered my black helmet, my crown, over my head.

But I felt no pride, then, no achievement. My work was just beginning.

For days, the image of the Time Traveler haunted me. I told myself I had imagined him, but I didn't believe it. I told myself that I knew nothing about him, but this, too, was a lie. I simply couldn't bring myself to put my logic to one side, to accept that something was true just because I could feel that it was.

I *felt* that the Time Traveler had come from the future, although I wasn't sure if it was *my* future. I knew in my heart that he had risked all to contact me. I was sure that something had gone wrong in his life, something with immense and disastrous consequences, and I knew that he wanted to put it right. The Traveler wished to change his own past, to correct one terrible mistake. And I think I knew, deep down, who the Traveler was, and why he had chosen me as the agent of his change, the recipient of his fateful message.

As soon as the explosion sounded, before its echoes had died down, I summoned my closest advisers, among them Generals Azura Nova and Maruunus Ki. They were already en route to my throne room; had they not been, I'd have wanted to know why.

By the time they arrived, they were in receipt of the latest reports from Mechopolis's sentries, its Harrowers and its Harriers. The explosion had been a diversion, covering the escape of prisoners on the opposite side of the city. I knew immediately that one of those prisoners was the Earthman, Ryan Archer. It was only later that I learned he'd been taken from his iso-pen by a force led by a Galactic Defender, apparently the last of her kind. And it was only later that I learned that the rebels had allies within my own forces, allies who had also freed the warrior Acroyear and a Vaerian by the name of Jafain.

I called for Biotron, but he didn't respond. The Biosmith informed me that he was offline. A few hours later he would betray me, leading my enemies to safety. They would take my adoptive daughter, Persephone, with them, poison her mind against me.

I remember standing on the tarmac outside the bio-vaults, flanked by my guards. Acroyear had his sword to my daughter's throat. *"We're leaving. And you will allow us safe passage, or I will take your daughter's head without a thought!"*

I asked myself, then, how so much could have gone wrong so quickly, how a challenge could have turned into a threat. Chaos had taken root on my world without my knowing it. And I wondered if this was what the Time Traveler had been trying to warn me about.

I was determined to retake control, had to destroy this cancer before it could spread, even if it meant cutting out a part of my own heart. I knew I had to sacrifice Persephone, but I didn't know if I could give the order that would doom her.

I was fortunate, in a way. The decision was taken from me.

Archer saw it coming. He cried out a warning. I remember marveling, even in that desperate moment, at his unique insight. Even then, as the rebels' bombs exploded, as my bio-vaults were blown apart and I was washed with fire—even then, I was still thinking of the boy as a valuable tool, the means to my ascendance. I don't think it occurred to me until much later—until Earth—that Archer could be a formidable foe, that by bringing him here to my kingdom, I might have engineered my own downfall.

I was used to getting what I wanted, to bending even fate to my indomitable will. The very concept of defeat was alien to me. Perhaps that's why I didn't realize straight away. Perhaps that's why it took me so long to see how firmly the cancer had already taken hold.

"Give me this chance, Lord Karza. I won't let you down."

Azura Nova stood flanked by Harrowers, her wrists shackled before her. She understood the magnitude of her situation—she had administered enough punishments herself to know the likely fate of one who had incurred my wrath. Still, she did not plead, she didn't promise. She didn't abase herself. Her words were a cold statement of fact, her expression as rigid as her stance. I remember thinking that she could have been attractive, had there been any softness in her. Cast in the harsh white light of my courtroom—the light of truth, as I'd been known to call it—her elfin features seemed sharper, more starkly defined, than ever.

I frowned down at her from my lofty seat of judgment, flanked by General Ki and Commander Lear Sethis—the leader of the Harriers in Nova's absence. "You have done that already, General. I trust the new arm the Biosmith gave you functions to your satisfaction?"

Nova chewed on her lip, biting back an instinctual response.

"I saw such potential in you," I continued, my anger tempered with sadness. "You are dedicated, passionate, proud—and, although you are still young, you seemed to recognize the need to control those qualities, to direct them into the proper channels. I even made allowances for your brashness, your overconfidence—but this latest error, I cannot forgive."

"With respect, sir, I couldn't have anticipated Biotron's—"

"Enough!" I roared. "I will not listen to excuses, Nova. I entrusted Persephone to your charge. All you had to do was train her in self-defense; instead, you allowed her to fall into the hands of a ragtag band of malcontents."

"Yes, sir."

"What's more, you allowed those same malcontents to mutilate you. You are the head of my airborne forces, General. That you could be so easily defeated by an Acroyear is not only a personal humiliation, but a blow to the very heart of my order. The consequences of your failure will reverberate throughout the Empire. They will foment chaos, sewing the seeds of futile bravado in those who wish they had the will to oppose me."

"Then I suggest we stamp out those seeds!" Nova's top lip curled into a snarl. "We should pursue the escapees and crush them—destroy them so utterly, so painfully, that the merest whisper of their fate will keep the populace in line for the next century!"

"You know as well as I do, General, that my resources are committed to the invasion. The planet Earth, the Macroverse itself, is within my grasp at long last, and nothing—not even my daughter—will keep it from me."

"A Harrier squadron and six ships," said Nova. "I'll have a result for you within four days."

"What makes you think you can find these rebels, let alone recapture them? There have been reports of sightings from eight different worlds, light years apart."

"Deliberate diversions. The escapees have divided their forces—but Persephone, Acroyear and the Earthman, Ryan Archer, are still together."

"You are rather well informed," I remarked, "considering you have spent the past two days confined to quarters."

"I wasn't aware I was denied outside contact," said Nova, a little stiffly.

I was more concerned with the fact that somebody had risked my displeasure by communicating with her. A small matter, I knew—almost insignificant—but enough small cracks can shatter the sturdiest edifice, and this was not the first. How far had the cancer spread, I wondered, while I had allowed myself to become preoccupied? Was this to be my lot now? Had my Empire grown to the point when it would take all my time, all my attention, to maintain it? Could I never again strive for more than I had?

I refused to accept that. Not when I was about to seize the greatest prize of all.

"What else do you know?" I rumbled.

"I know Acroyear," said Nova. "I know how he thinks. I know which of the reports to believe. He and his cohorts have seized Ordaal's ship, the *Sunreaver*. They're allied with a Galactic Defender by the name of Koriah. She is not with them at present; she is working contacts, trying to learn more about your plans. She thinks she can do so whilst remaining undetected. Unfortunately for her, I have contacts, too."

I narrowed my eyes behind my mask. "You believe you can find this Koriah?"

"She will rendezvous with the others, eventually. She can lead us to them."

"And you need six ships to bring down one?"

"The *Sunreaver* is fast. Given Ordaal's line of business, it had to be. I intend to herd the escapees into an ambush. Once they have taken the bait, it will take only one ship to spring the trap. *My* ship. I can do this, sir."

She had put her case well. If Nova could repair the damage she had done, I'd be free to attend to more important concerns. It wasn't a matter of giving her a second chance—I would decide her fate after she had brought my daughter and the Earthman back to me.

"Very well, General," I said, "you may have your ships, and your personnel."

"Thank you, Lord Karza." She allowed the merest hint of a smile to tug at her lips.

It faded as I continued. "However, this tribunal is not concluded, merely adjourned. You are still to consider yourself in military custody." At my right shoulder, Ki's features twisted into a sadistic grin. The winged figure of Lear Sethis stood opposite, stoic and proud in the distinctive scarlet breastplate and plumage that, along with his aggressive but precise style of combat, had earned him the nickname Red Falcon. "Commander Sethis will accompany you on your mission in a supervisory capacity. Should you succeed, I may be minded to exercise a degree of leniency in this case." I leaned forward in my seat. "Conversely, General, I am sure I need not remind you of the consequences of failing me again."

Nova said nothing. At my signal, her escorts removed her bonds. She acknowledged my decree with a slight nod, before turning and leaving the court, stiff-backed.

No. That's not how it happened at all.

The ground crunches beneath my feet as I tread the wreckage of my kingdom. The final irony: My detractors claimed that I'd built Mechopolis on the bones of my enemies; now, it has been reduced to just that. Its once-proud spires are skeletons, too—those few that still stand. There has been no industry here for decades, but the sky has not lightened; it hangs above me, still heavy with the pollution of the previous regime, the color of blood.

I remember the day that my palace came crashing down, the fire and the fury. The cancer had begun with Ryan Archer, but by the end, it seemed that all my subjects were only too willing to take arms against me. How soon they forgot all I had done for them. How blind they were, how stupid, to disregard the inevitable outcome of their actions.

I remember, as the bloodlust faded from my eyes, how I sheathed my sword and watched the last flames burning themselves out. A single object called to me, mocking me. It sat incongruously amid the debris: my throne, fashioned from an indestructible alloy. Slowly, numbly, I lowered myself onto it, planted my feet on the ground before it, rested my hands on its arms. I had won. I had held onto this, at least. I was still the Emperor.

But I was the Emperor of nothing, of nobody.

Even the throne corroded, in time. I look down at it now, and my memories seem to drain away, receding until they're no more real to me than the echoes of a story of another man, told long ago. I reach after them, fearing that without them I have nothing. I call to mind the courtroom again, General Nova standing before me looking so young, but I can longer be sure what is real and what is not about those days.

"General Azura Nova, you have been summoned here today to receive judgment."

Footsteps behind me. I don't turn. I have received only one visitor, here in my wasteland.

"I have had time to consider fully the causes, consequences and ramifications of your actions, and you have been found sorely lacking."

"I knew," I say. "I always knew. The problem was, I was too proud to accept it, too arrogant and afraid to admit to myself that history was malleable, that my order could be so easily unraveled. I deluded myself into believing I ruled a galaxy, when in fact I controlled only one possibility among many billions."

"You are hereby stripped of your rank as Commander of the Harriers."

"Looking back, I see that this was Ryan Archer's advantage over me: that he could see those possibilities, albeit subconsciously; that he could embrace them. Tell me, my friend, do you consider me naïve, that I have taken so long to come to this understanding?"

I face him now, my only companion of these recent years. He is as inscrutable as always. He could almost be a hologram, an intangible construct of light. His body gives off a soft yellow glow, and red lines of circuitry shift, making new connections, beneath its surface. The only part of him that seems solid, real, is the control unit on his chest. It is like the one in my dreams—a triangle mounted upon a rectangle—but red in color.

"Every Karza comes to understand, in time," says the Traveler.

"You, Azura Nova, are consigned to the care of my evaluators, who will advise me, upon my return, as to whether or not you can be salvaged..."

"Who was he?" I ask.

The Time Traveler says nothing, although I'm sure he understands the question.

"What could have happened in his past, that he sacrificed everything to reach me?"

"As you said," replies the Time Traveler, "the possibilities are many."

"Often—as my campaign on Earth fell apart, and during my ensuing exile—I asked myself how things might have been different. Nova was a good soldier. I believe she could have done as she claimed; at least, that she could have hunted down Archer's band—his 'Micronauts,' as he called them—and exterminated them before they could do more harm. And yes, the girl was ruthless—she would have done whatever it took, not caring if my daughter was caught in the crossfire—but then this, too, would have made me stronger."

"You regretted your decision?"

"Many times. I cursed the weakness that caused me to heed a phantasm over my own logic. And yet I knew—can still remember—the all-consuming dread that rose within me when Nova begged for her second chance. In that moment, I could see the possibilities for the first time, stretching ahead of me—and I could see that they all led to desolation."

I remember, as Nova was taken away, the contempt in her eyes. She was disgusted that I, of all people, should have opted for pointless revenge over practical expediency. Or perhaps I was just projecting my own inner conflict upon her?

"You found the time machine," the Traveler reminds me.

"Indeed—many years later, on an abandoned Pharoid world close to one of the reported sightings of the *Sunreaver*. I analyzed it, learned its flaws. That was when I began to see the chaos I had averted. Even so, it is difficult to imagine: my whole life, rewritten."

I hesitate for a moment before asking, "Is this always to be the fate of Karza, Traveler? To live his life only to negate it; to pass the sum of his experience onto another man in the hope of writing a better obituary?"

"Once you have seen the possibilities," says the Time Traveler sagely, "it can be difficult to settle for what you have."

"But there is hope," I say, "that some day, in some reality, I will find what I am looking for. I will have my perfect order."

"I think it is time," says the Traveler.

I look down at the clothes I'm wearing: The golden containment suit, which looks and feels so strange after so many lifetimes in another guise. As if it belongs to somebody else, somebody I once knew. "I'm ready," I say.

The Time Traveler nods, without emotion. He operates the controls on his chest unit, and a tiny point of green light forms at its heart. The light streams outward, and coalesces into an upright disc, which hangs suspended in midair. It is perfectly flat and yet, when I look into it, it seems to stretch forever. The light shines bright—almost too bright for me to face it—but it casts no shadow.

My own chest unit beeps three times, drawing my attention to it. "Your course is programmed," says the Time Traveler. "The Rift awaits."

"Time to begin again," I say.

I saw a billion worlds.

They flickered before me, each image lasting a microsecond, crashing into each other. I saw the rise and fall of empires, wars played out in an instant, champions rising against the shadows and always, always, towering above all, I saw myself.

I saw an unfeeling machine, alone at the end of time. A black-clad despot with an army of Acroyears at his command. A tyrant, slain by his foes but taking a world with him. A scientist in a white containment suit, contemplating the destruction of everything. I even saw a reality in which I became a Panzerite, fusing myself to an Equestron body. The myriad ghosts of other Karzas shared my journey, and I wondered if I was seeing the echoes of times long gone, or the promise of possibilities yet to be grasped.

As I sailed the time stream, wrapping myself in its fabric, I felt that I could bring any of those possibilities to me. A tug on the right strand. I only had to reach out, and it would be mine. I would do it, one day. I would have a control panel like the Time Traveler's, one that allowed me to open my own Rift and steer myself through it rather than trusting to a pre-programmed course. Next time, maybe.

I can't feel the ash beneath my feet, or the heat in the air, although I remember both well. I am still out of phase with this time, invisible to all who dwell within it, until I operate the final control and become solid. I wonder how many other Time Travelers, from how many more futures, are here to witness this event: the destruction of all I knew.

The cryo-crypts are burning. The sand is black with the shapes of the Emperor's soldiers, the sky alight with the guns of his ships. The Pharoids are falling, ill-prepared for this battle they were born to wage. And, in the midst of it all, a young boy's face is filled with fear as he huddles to the side of his gray-bearded father—a father prepared to break his neck rather than allow him to be captured. "Shut your eyes, my son. Sleep is coming."

The last words he spoke to me—how could I have forgotten?

I am filled with a sudden horror. I want to leap forward, to stop what is to happen, but it is not yet time. Still, I avert my gaze as the old man is gunned down. I don't want to see the tears, the bewilderment, in my young self's eyes as he kneels over his father's steaming corpse. I don't want to watch as he is surrounded by the enemy, helpless, cringing with the expectation of a similar brutal death.

A thought shifts in the back of my mind. For an instant, I feel I'm missing something. Something else that the Time Traveler tried to tell me in my dream, only I couldn't hear him. I try to catch hold of the memory, but it slips away, leaving me with a sense of foreboding.

"What about you, little one?" The Emperor's words pull me back to the present, still sending a chill down my mechanical spine after all this time. "Are you a threat to me?"

"Oh, yes," I snarl, in a voice he cannot hear. "Oh, yes, I am a threat to you."

The boy feels pain now, but already in that pain he is finding strength. That is what the Emperor saw in me. It is what I see now. And, in the years to come, Karza will grow stronger. He will build a future for himself, and I will guide him in that task. He will realize all his dreams. Or he will find himself here, at the end, ready to choose another road, almost dizzy with the possibilities before him.

I will have my perfect order one day. It is only a matter of time.

I first saw the Time Traveler in a dream.
  And some dreams won't die.